SEAL

INTESTINE

RAINCOAT

rosie chard

SEAL

INTESTINE

RAINCOAT

NeWest Press

Library and Archives Canada Cataloguing in Publication
Chard, Rosie, 1959–
         Seal intestine raincoat / Rosie Chard.
(Nunatak first fiction ; 28)
ISBN 978-1-897126-44-8
I. Title. II. Series: Nunatak first fiction ; 28

PS8605.H3667S42 2009   C813'.6   C2009-902342-3

Editor for the Board: Douglas Barbour
Cover and interior design: Natalie Olsen
Cover illustration: Natalie Olsen
Author photo: Nat Chard
Text Editor: Tiffany Foster

This book is a work of fiction. Any similarities to places, people, and events are purely coincidental.

NeWest Press acknowledges the support of the Canada Council for the Arts, the Alberta Foundation for the Arts, and the Edmonton Arts Council for our publishing program. We also acknowledge the financial support of the Government of Canada through the Book Publishing Industry Development Program (BPIDP).

201, 8540–109 Street
Edmonton, Alberta T6G 1E6
780.432.9427
NeWest Press newestpress.com

No bison were harmed in the making of this book.
We are committed to protecting the environment and to the responsible use of natural resources. This book was printed on 100% post-consumer recycled paper.

1 2 3 4 5 12 11 10 09
printed and bound in Canada

for Ollie

PART ONE

Three years from now

CHAPTER

I

Fred Forester was sitting on a public toilet four thousand miles from home when the lights first went out. No warning, no announcement, not so much as a cautionary flicker from the fluorescent lights lining the ceiling. Everything just went black. Ink black.

The seat had been lower than he expected and, although he convinced himself otherwise, still warm when he sat down. Under normal circumstances, he would have whiled away the time tracing cracks in the floor with his toe or staring at the wall, wondering if Ivan really did love Cynthia forever. But a high gap between the stall's metal partition and the floor drew his attention to his fellow restroom mates. Convention dictated that he not look too closely, but the remarkable nature of their footwear aroused a voyeuristic curiosity that he couldn't suppress. To his left sat two enormous, thick-soled boots laced up like ice skates and spattered with lumps of melting ice. To his right stood legs in running shoes encased in thick socks and trailing sodden laces onto the floor. A tiny pair of rubber boots swung down in between, kicking the bowl.

Now thrown into darkness, he flinched as the owners of the feet on either side began to shout.

"Christ almighty, not again!"

"Dad!"

"Johnny, don't move."

"Where's the goddamn handle?"

"Ouch, John, you're standing on my foot."

"Darnit!"

"Hold my hand, buddy."

"Dad!"

Fred sat silent, unwillingly squeezed inside the conversations, yet at the same time outside of them. He straightened his back and took a deep breath, smelling a noseful of foreign disinfectant that settled menthol onto his tongue. He stood up and began to feel, feel for the waistband of his jeans, feel for the cold steel of his zipper, feel for the door handle. Dead space met his fingers as he passed through the doorway, shuffling forward with outstretched arms, weight shifting from foot to foot. Enamel banged painfully into his hip and he stopped to explore the sink, running his fingertips into the bowl, retracting from the dampness of the drain, and lingering over the slimy mouth of the soap dispenser.

Then, with dark-sharpened senses, he grew busy: discovering the inside of the faucet, listening to the quiver of a little boy's voice, and smelling the rotten fruitiness of freshly applied aftershave. So busy that he was unprepared when the ceiling lights flicked back on.

A boyish face blinked back at him from the mirror, its skin blanched by jet lag, the chin still raw from its first shave. He flinched, balking at his bloodshot eyes, then prodded the bags hanging beneath them, checking if they were as big as they looked. Beside him stood a man, blinking as well. Fred could not help but gawp at the adjacent figure, huge and bear-like and encased in a massive winter parka. Wet beads clung to the top of his eyebrows and drips of sweat ran down his cheeks before trickling through the fur of his collar, leaving dark blots across the front of his coat.

"Idiots," said the man.

"Pardon?" replied Fred.

"The Hydro."

"Who?"

"He means the power company." A third face had appeared in the mirror. Tired eyes matched a tired mouth.

"Second time this month," growled the bear man.

"It's only temporary," replied the tired man. "They'll sort it out."

"Bloody better," said Bear. "Anyways, I'm out of here."

The tired man smiled, then turned his attention to a small boy who was stretching up to reach into the sink. Reminded of his thirst, Fred turned on the tap, rinsed his hands, and leaned forward, cupping a mouthful of water in his palm.

"Ugh!" he said, spitting into the sink.

"You okay?" asked the tired man.

"Yes, thanks. The water was a bit of shock. It tastes as if it comes from a farm or something."

Fred stopped. He had spoken his first sentence. His first conversation with a citizen of his new country was happening in a washroom, and he had been rude already. "Sorry, that's not what I meant. It just tastes different."

The man laughed. "You're not from round here, are you?"

"How do you know?"

The man laughed again. "The accent's a giveaway. Where are you from?"

"England. I just got here. Thirty seconds ago."

"Awesome."

"I come fr — "

But the sentence was never finished. Their conversation

came to an abrupt end as the little boy's cuffs dipped perilously close to the taps, distracting the tired man.

Fred gazed back at his reflection, silently inserting the stopper into the story of his old life, which he had hoped to uncork. He washed his hands, noticing the tap was threaded the opposite way, jogging his memory about the teasing he had received back home. "The water goes round the other way over there," his mates had decreed. But it was not so easy chasing a swirl of water with a tired pair of eyes, so he turned his attention to the soap dispenser. Its workings were obscure, but a little experimentation roused some invisible mechanism and he felt warm satisfaction when a huge ball of foam ballooned onto his palm as if controlled by some mischievous imp hidden in the plumbing. Drying his hands was less successful, and he spent a humiliating few seconds pressing plastic handles, trying to drag paper from the reluctant clutches of the holder. Several attempts later, he abandoned the array of levers and resorted to drying his hands on shreds of paper. While dabbing and rubbing, he turned back to the tired man, who was ripping out paper towels with an expert flick of his wrist.

"Do the lights often go out here?" Fred asked.

"Now and then. It's just a glitch in the system. Anyways, I must go and find Johnny's mom. She'll be crawling up the walls if we're not back soon. See you and, yeah, welcome to Canada."

"Oh ..." said Fred. "Thanks."

Left alone in the room, Fred glanced at his watch and sighed. Nine in the evening meant the middle of the night in his time — in real time. Everyone at home in London would be asleep by now, their bedside clocks ticking loudly, marking the seconds with a rhythm that he was no longer part of. With the spin of the earth, he had fallen behind. His old life would always be ahead of him, his friends packing up the parcel of their day just as he was opening his. He would never catch up.

He picked up his rucksack and left the room, heading towards the pack of luggage hunters swarming round the conveyor belt. Celebratory hand signals from the tallest person in the throng reassured him that his parents were near.

"Fred, we've got them," came a shout from his father across the arrivals hall.

As he walked towards them, he looked up. A large sign swung on invisible threads, high up on the ceiling. WELCOME TO WINNIPEG.

He wanted to go home.

CHAPTER

2

Two weeks later, a bell was ringing. Flashing lights signalled the approach of the train, and the barrier lowered to its horizontal, keep-out position. Tutting to herself, Poppy Forester shifted the car into park and leaned back in her seat. She rubbed her eyes, blocking out the sunshine that blazed through her window, and tried to focus on the listless lineup of morning traffic ahead. The cars and trucks were steaming. December roads had layered them with grimy ice, and only fragments of people could be glimpsed through the portholes rubbed into the windows. "Clean me," begged the window of a nearby Volkswagen, its glass smeared with fingerprints. She switched off her engine, took off her gloves, and sat back in her seat, ready to be bored.

To kill time she studied the occupants of the surrounding vehicles. Each contained a private world, and she could inspect her fellow drivers without being inspected herself. The usual range of characters was on display: the elderly gent unfurling the lid of his coffee cup with his teeth; the woman dabbing mascara on her eyelashes; and the young boy squashing his face against a window, his mouth opening up an eel-like hole, flattening and bulging with every turn of his head.

During her second scan, she spotted a man sitting beside a yellow dog. He was frowning, pressing his map over the steering wheel, moulding contours into a flat city. Shoving a wet nose off his lap, he turned to face her and opened his window, indicating that she should do the same with a peculiar double shake of his fingers. She wound down her window, just a couple of inches, reluctant to let in the cold air or burst her bubble of privacy.

"Hey, ma'am," he said. "Do you know the way to Alberto's Market? Geez, I've never seen a place with so many train tracks." The last words were hard to catch. The dog had jumped onto his lap, flicking a tail into the man's mouth, giving the fleeting impression that it was in control of the vehicle.

"I'm sorry. I have no idea where that is," she called back.

"All right, see you."

His window was almost up when a couple of extra words squeezed through the crack. "Nice hair."

Nice hair. She felt a girlish glow inside. Forty-two years old, mother of a fifteen-year-old boy, and a stranger in a truck said she had nice hair. Pulling down the visor, she flipped up the tiny mirror inside. She had forgotten to brush it that morning but yes, it looked all right, thick as a squirrel's tail and even holding its natural colour. Maybe slightly thin around the parting, but only she noticed that.

Not daring to look directly at the yellow dog man, Poppy felt flattered that he was watching her as she gazed down the track looking for the train. A double flash of light on metal signalled its arrival, emerging from behind a low, cardboard-coloured building flanking the railway. It crept forward, dragging a mile of steel containers behind it. Giant labels plastered the walls and she caught herself mouthing the words as CHINA SHIPPING followed CHINA SHIPPING, again and again and again.

She stretched her neck to catch sight of the end of the train. But it had no end. It stretched away along the track, through the edge of the city, disappearing into the blue haze of the prairie.

She pulled out her notebook, small and black with a trailing ribbon — her usual remedy against the tedium of the crossing wait. Feeling the pencil for sharpness, she began to sketch. The outline of the train took shape, box after box piling onto the page, pressed beneath the weight of an immense blue sky. She slowed the pace to write the words, curling the Cs of China into perfect semi-circles and bending the Ss into a snake-twisted typeface. Finally she traced a line of cars crammed together and driven by dogs: a poodle in the first, a clever Labrador in the second, and, in the third, a hapless dachshund, hardly able to reach the wheel. Pausing, she stared down the track, hoping to catch sight of that last container, always rushing to keep up, always late. It was then that she noticed a flicker of red on the second to last one. It jarred, breaking the monotony of the line, disturbing the sequence of brown ochres and hammer greys trundling across the horizon. She stared. A mere spot in the distance at first, it sharpened to a human form as it moved closer, its shoulders tucked tight against steel corners. Seconds passed — the figure grew bigger, the image sharpened. She adjusted her glasses on her nose and stared.

It was a man. A man in red clung to the train. Red coat, red hood, and a black hat. His boots were half hidden but rigid knees stuck out sideways, jolting with the rhythm. Not struck so much by the oddness of the scene but more by the fortitude of the unorthodox traveller, Poppy could think of nothing but numb fingertips and frozen toes, both of which hardly squared with the demeanour of the figure passing her eyes.

With his head thrown back, he laughed, he admired the sky, he whooped in delight. Then he jumped. In front of her eyes he actually jumped, gyrating round and up like a discarded sycamore seed. The train rolled on, uncaring, as she leaned forward to catch sight of him. He re-emerged suddenly, pulling himself out of a bush and brushing snow off his jacket with unbroken arms. Then he strode away in the direction of what looked like, from her perspective anyway, nothing.

The train had passed. Only her breathing disturbed the calm of her rapidly cooling car. She opened her purse and, with half an eye on the cars revving up their impatience, rummaged through her pencils. Vermillion red. Perfect. She drew quickly and a moment later a band of colour streaked off the back of the train and skidded into the margin.

⌒

The bell rang — same tone, new message. The barrier rose, drawing the traffic into a slow sequence of stop and start. Then the work of getting going began in earnest, and clouds of exhaust, made viscous by cold, popped into the air. She drove across the once dangerous, but now domesticated track, and the railway disappeared from sight.

Strip malls soon replaced the wild swathes of land surrounding the track, each gigantic box store pleading its individuality with neon enticements, their tubes daringly suffused with colour. A cubic church loomed ahead, its shape revealing no clue to its purpose. She saw no spire, no windows stained with colour, only billboard messages calling out to the faithful. "Mud thrown is ground lost" remained in her thoughts as she drove across the river. It looked magical at that moment. Ice-bound oxbows carved a wide and sinuous white road through the centre of the city. She glimpsed clusters of skaters down on the ice, some skimming at high speed, others staggering on stiff legs.

The city felt bigger today, and calmer. The multitude of leafless elms suggested a transparency that she had failed to notice when they had arrived two weeks earlier. Hundreds of trees framed her view up the long road ahead. She loved those trees. She loved their deliciously splayed canopies arching across every street, wooden fingertips touching in the middle. She had never lived in a city with so many trees and could only imagine the green blanket that would be thrown down following the spring thaw. And she had never lived in a city that steamed so. Steaming cars, steaming manholes, steaming houses.

She drove the long way home, weaving through a laborious sequence of stop signs, slowing to admire a shoulder of snow cantilevered from the edge of a roof. She even stopped to buy a loaf of bread she did not need. But she could not postpone the moment indefinitely, that part of the day she dreaded, and she could not help crossing her fingers on the steering wheel as she approached the gas station, chanting in her thoughts. *Three dollars, three dollars, three dollars ...*

A new ritual had marked their arrival in the city and life had changed, not just for her small family, but for everyone. Gas prices were rising. Not just a bit, a few cents here, a quarter there, but in great, unforgiving leaps that scared the life out of her and caused a brick of tension to form right in the centre of her shoulders. Every single day she passed the gas station and checked the length of the lineup. Every single day she looked up at the prices high on the steel pole and every single day she jotted a larger number down in her notebook. No amount of hoping could restrain the black numbers that hovered above the street. She could see them now.

Three and a half dollars for a litre of gas.

⁓

Fifteen minutes later, Poppy pulled into her driveway. She removed her glasses and pushed their spidery and unwilling arms into their case. It snapped shut. A hunt to find keys followed, then she entered the house, slinging her coat on the nearest hook.

"Charlie, are you back?" she called.

A voice whistling through crumbs replied. Her husband was eating as he walked around the kitchen; the strong smell of oranges hung in the air.

Charlie Forester enjoyed grazing, often rummaging through the fridge and hunting down ingredients for new combinations with a passion. Fish fingers dipped in peanut butter were his latest experiment, and memories of chocolate-sprinkled salmon were fresh in Poppy's mind. He was wearing his customary "after work" clothes as he came towards her — the much-loved fleece, washed almost to death, and baggy trousers held up by a pair of braces, salvaged from a student jumble sale and still comical after twenty years. The fact that they fit him at all was a testament to his enduring fitness. He moved through space in a different way when clothed in this loose-fitting outfit. The slippered shuffle was slower than his natural rate of movement, and the failure to notice food particles seeding the front of his fleece during grazing sessions would have rendered him unrecognizable to his work colleagues should they have visited the house unexpectedly. This split of work and home personae extended to his hair, pressed down with an invisible slick of something in the mornings then revved up again in the evenings, giving the impression of a man who had just escaped the fingers of a ruthless head masseur.

"Are you all right, Poppy? You look tired." The smell of oranges grew stronger.

"I'm all right but I need to talk to you. Let's go to my study. Is Fred home?"

"Pretending to do his homework," he said, following her upstairs.

The study was her sanctuary, the burrow that held her things. She adored it here. Sketches of clouds covered an entire wall. Dotting the drawings were tiny pins, tucking in corners and stretching out creases. The prairie sky had become her obsession, its breathtaking scale and swatches of colour defying her attempts to capture it as she drew it again and again, without coming close. Here is where she would continue her business — if the commissions came in. "Illustrator to the Gentry," Charlie had called her as he flicked through her drawings, published in Lady Faulkner's *Flora and Fauna of Whistable Bay* two days before they left London. Now she must start again. Dragging her hard-earned reputation four thousand miles, she could only hope it would stand up to scrutiny beneath the intense Winnipeg light. But the signs were good. "Can you draw snow?" she'd already been asked. "And hummingbirds?"

She pushed a pile of papers off the sofa onto the floor. They sat down. For some reason she did not tell Charlie about the man jumping off the train.

But she told him about the new price of gas.

CHAPTER

3

Fred heard voices. As usual in brand-new houses, the walls were as thin as stretched canvas, but it was the subtlety rather than the volume that made him take notice. He was trying to do his homework, but the murmuring from the next room kept butting into his thoughts. Why were they whispering? It was not like them. His was a family that talked to each other. He put down his pencil and marked his place with a six-inch ruler, pleased to have found a distraction from the quadratic equations lining the page. He stood up, banging his knees on

SEAL
INTESTINE
RAINCOAT

the underside of the desk, and left the room. He walked along the landing to the study and, squeezing himself between his father and the arm of the sofa, forced his feet beneath the coffee table. His father hugged him; he had taken to doing that a lot lately.

"So what's happening in the big, bad world?" Fred said, thumping Charlie's knee.

His parents looked at each other. He could see his mother twisting her wedding ring around her finger.

"Well ..." His father hesitated. He often did that, starting a sentence before drifting into another thought. Fred liked to count the intervening seconds in his head — seventeen was the record. Politeness usually held him in a fixed position, but sometimes he got the chance to start a bona fide alternative activity, chewing on a straw or snapping back the end of his pen, both great void fillers.

"Looks like you'll be walking to school soon, Fred. Petrol's going up again."

His father made a half-smile, his lips stretching outwards before dropping back down again before the gesture was fully formed. Fred had read about those in a book once. It meant someone was covering something up, a bit like nose touching when lying but not quite so bad. When he tried it in the mirror he just looked stupid, not at all deceitful or conspiratorial. Then it sank in.

"Walk!?"

Forget half smiling. This was something serious. "Dad, you do realize it's almost two miles."

The wedding ring kept turning.

"I know, but petrol's gone over three dollars a litre. We have to cut down. You understand that, don't you, Fred?"

He thought for a moment. No one walked to school in this city. No one even walked to the store. Too cold, wasn't it? Not even Simon Stokes from his class, who lived three minutes from the school, walked.

Charlie shrugged. "I'm sorry, Fred, but we can't afford it at the moment. And the exercise will do you good."

"Oh, yes. At minus forty, that's really going to be fun."

Fred had been practising sarcasm. His father hated it — a cheapskate's way out of a decent answer, he'd said, but Fred liked to test it out. Even his teacher had changed his tone a little when he had tried it out at school.

"I know it's tough, but you just need to layer up," Charlie said. "You'll be all right."

"You're serious, aren't you?"

"Yes."

"Couldn't I get a lift with someone from your office? Mr. O'Neill lives close by, doesn't he?"

"He does. It's just that we're all going on this trip, all five of us. Don't you remember? The big cheese in London wants the whole team there to discuss a new strategy."

Fred sighed. Since moving to Canada, the climate had regulated their lives. Minus forty had sounded exciting from the warmth of his London living room. He had been thrilled at the thought of ice moustaches and shoes made of tennis racquets, and even though he was fifteen, he could imagine the local kids might need help with the odd snowman or two. He didn't realize back then that extreme cold was dangerous; how it could trick you, welding glasses to faces and thickening engine oil to a standstill. Who back home would believe it was colder in his garden than in his kitchen freezer? And as it turned out, there were no little kids on his street. Home was now a house in a half-built subdivision. He was not really sure what that meant, but he did know that something had been divided up and he was living in it.

Not one of his mates back home could place the city that

was now the centre of his world. He had checked on the internet when his father had got the job that dragged them across an ocean as chief designer at Lombard Instruments.

Where is Winnipeg?
Winnipeg is located smack dab in the middle of Canada.
Is Winnipeg the coldest city on earth?
The lowest recorded temperature is minus forty-five degrees Celsius.
Is Winnipeg the friendliest place on earth?
A city so inviting that they stamp the word "friendly" on their licence plates.

So it was cold and friendly and in the middle of Canada, but the internet had not told him that gas prices would start rising as soon as he got there. It had not told him that the heart of his new city was kept pumping by gas, controlled by people in distant places who, if asked, would be unable to locate this city on a map. And it had not told him that foresight had yet to replace hindsight as the preferred mode of operation in the overheated corridors of City Hall. Within a short space of time he was watching a change and he was worried, worried that things were about to get worse.

What could be worse than walking to school?

CHAPTER

4

Poppy loved the smell of ironing; nothing could beat the comfort of that gently baked aroma. She hummed a tune as the iron swivelled back and forth across the arm of an outstretched shirt. Then a competing tune came into her head, and she reached across the ironing board to turn up the radio as the news started. Pressing down hard on an awkward armpit, she was concentrating on a particularly stubborn crease when a change in pitch interrupted the monotony of the reporter's voice. She stopped to listen.

"Gas prices across Canada look set to break the four dollars per litre mark in the next few days ..."

Steam hissed up from underneath the iron. She released a hot sleeve and re-arranged the shirt, stretching its back across the end of the board, and tuned her ears back to the news.

"...been seen in many countries after the cost of crude oil on global markets rose to its highest level on record. Gulf Coast crude rose to three hundred dollars per barrel yesterday, up more than five dollars on the day and ten dollars more than last month's all-time record of two hundred and ninety dollars."

A hint of smoke dragged her attention back to the board, and she flapped a hand across the smarting shirt before inspecting a hot triangle of glazed threads. The tone of the radio voice went up a notch, pulling her attention back.

"...been compounded as unforeseen and serious start-up difficulties are coming to light at the new refinery at St. François. And technical problems continue to plague the main regional refinery at North Walton. The provincial government is holding an emergency meeting tomorrow to discuss the situation, and they are confident that the crisis will soon be under control. However, sources close to the premier have revealed that the possibility of rationing has not been ruled out...."

A shout from another room cut into the stream of words.

"Poppy, dinner's ready."

"I'll be there in a minute."

She picked up the shirt, sniffed its shoulders, and laid it on the back of a chair. Then she bent over behind the ironing board and pulled out the plug.

CHAPTER

5

The temperature dropped fifteen degrees during the night. The cold crawled over Fred's skin as he left the house and jogged down the road, half-digested breakfast sluicing the insides of his stomach. Even a bowl of hot porridge had not tempered his irritable mood, and his thoughts kept returning to the conversation at supper the evening before. His mother had rushed to the table with mouthfuls of calamitous warnings, gas prices, share prices, prices, prices, prices. A fresh feeling of unease lingered at the back of his mind when he woke up that morning.

The street was empty. "Just needs a bit of finishing off," the realtor had reassured them when they had bought the house long distance. His father had retained absolute faith in the man's words, cajoling enthusiasm back into his dubious family, but even Charlie's smile had drooped a little as they turned into their new neighbourhood on that first day in the country.

Some houses were mere skeletons, their wooden bones braced against the wind that teased bolts from young holes. Others were more complete, with finished walls and weatherproof roofs, yet they were forced into anonymity with thick coverings of plywood revealing no clue to their interiors. Red striped paper wrapped the final category of house, and he could almost sense a shiver in their frames as they awaited their final skin. The word *pioneer* had taken on fresh meaning as they crossed the threshold and stared at the collection of half-finished houses through the kitchen window.

The problem was that, during his first few days in the neighbourhood, he had been unable to suppress the urge to compare — with home, that is. At first he had marvelled at the length and straightness of the roads, scrunching up his eyes in an attempt to see the end where street melted into sky. But soon the impact of the city grid on his movements began to annoy him. He walked west to east or north to south, itching for the pleasures of a diagonal or a teasing bend leading who knows where. What he would not give for a spontaneous shortcut, a hole in the fence inviting a scrambled diversion or a gap in the railings, pulled apart by ill-gotten muscle.

The sky disturbed him, too. Here, the sky was everywhere. It stretched above him, behind him, in front of him, all of the time. The clouds were not like the ones he knew. French loaves were the most common: thousands of them, lining up, moving silently into the distance. He saw them now as he squinted skyward, dotted with what looked like black spiders.

He had never noticed the sky back home in London. The buildings crowded together there, blocking out views and throwing black shadows over the streets. In fact, back home, he had hardly ever looked up at all, his attention always focused at ground level as he elbowed his way through the congested streets, bumping shoulders with strangers, shimmying between strollers and weaving his way through straggly bus queues that spread across the pavements, thwarting all attempts to board the bus. Geography field trips were the only times he ever looked properly up, managing to distinguish stratus from nimbus but never realizing that skies were special to the place they sat above. The grey sky of home, patterned with mackerel and cauliflowers, had been replaced by something much bigger and bluer, and full of loaves.

Something else unsettled him: everything in his neighbourhood was new. Even old things seemed new. Every house was neat and perfectly looked after. And no one let things go. His street in London had been full of people who let things go. Overgrown hedges forced passersby into the road; moss lined the dark sides of garden walls and the end brick was always, always missing. Paint peeled, too. No one ever got around to all that sanding down and smoothing on layers of primer and undercoat, so the window frames split and corners buckled, letting in shots of damp air that sent even the hardiest members of his family scurrying to the radiator, stroking hot metal like it was the perfect pet. But there were no more draughts in his life now; his home was new and sealed like a tin of sardines.

A couple of other houses in his new neighbourhood were already occupied, but he never saw anyone. He never caught a glimpse of who pulled those curtains every night, who dug neat paths in the snow, or who collected letters from those mailboxes. Yet the precision-packed dustbins appearing mysteriously once a week told him a story of lives happening — juice being drunk, coffee filtered, bananas peeled, and letters written. But he never witnessed any of it, not even a glimpse out of the corner of his eye. No litter blew around the gardens, no windscreens smashed, and no broken fridges dumped in the street. No unfathomable shouts in the middle of the night. The constant slam of doors was just a distant memory from his London street.

Except for the old lady, that is. "Grandma Knuckles," he called her in his head. She lived on the corner of his block, always sitting at the window, always resting her chin on her knuckles, eyes always glazed. Sometimes she wore a red blouse, sometimes a blue, and often a hat, but her position never changed. Retrieving forgotten sandwiches was the cause of their single encounter. He had stopped on his way to school and turned to find her eyes on him. A clumsy exchange followed: a smile from him, a step back from her, and the knit-covered head disappeared from view.

Approaching his school neighbourhood, Fred noticed the houses jogging up and down in his sightline. Normally oblivious to architecture, he suddenly became aware of something different about the buildings lining the street — not only the swirls of stucco decorating the walls, but the perplexing absence of a front door. He stood still, looking from house to house, searching for familiar textures and shapes, but as he struggled to locate himself in an alien world he imagined he could hear nothing but threats coming from the black mouths of the double garages that straddled the face of every home.

Spots of orange in the distance caught his eye, and he knew he was nearing the school. Children from the safety patrol, steeped in the pleasure of rarely held responsibility, were organizing the traffic with an air of earnest determination. Walking closer, he watched a young girl finish her routine with a twirl and a flourish of precision choreography.

"Hey." She smiled at him, her face flushed pink.

"Hello."

He walked on, backwards, bumping his shoulder into a SIDEWALK ENDS sign, then stood to watch as renegade newbies gathered behind the girl. Discovering the joys of mock sword fighting, they flashed and flicked with their pointed flags, distracting passing drivers. He felt an urge to join in, flip the flag over in a circle, even throw it across the road like a javelin. But he didn't. He merely gazed at a lone boy at the back, chipping at the edge of a snowbank with his toe.

The city felt smaller today. Overnight snow had changed the

feel of it, houses an inch taller, the footpath an inch narrower, and every tree was marooned in mounds of snow pressed aside by the convoys of snowploughs that surged through the streets. Snow in November. How could that possibly be? He'd only had a white Christmas once in his life. A sheen of snow stretched across the garden like a cheap sheet. Gone by lunchtime.

There were fewer cars in the parking lot when he arrived at school. Normally chock-a-block with bored parents, their motors turning over, today it was half full. Fred went inside.

Being the new boy at school is always difficult, especially when you have crossed an ocean to get there. The teachers insist on creating a great hullabaloo, forcing you to stand at the front, reciting your name and describing your hobbies; if you had any, that is. If you didn't, you had to quickly cobble together an enthralling and worthy life from scraps of passive activity. Channel surfing, internet browsing, and twenty-four-hour gaming could be morphed into digital research or development of hand-eye coordination by the more alert fresher. After this ordeal would come placement next to a student whom the teacher had decided might like you. That is how he had met Johno back home. That teacher had been right. Johno liked him and he liked Johno. "Peas in a pod," his grandmother had said. But then she never was one for original turns of phrase.

Kyle had been chatty on that first day, almost too chatty, happily explaining the rules of hockey. But soon the conversation drifted into "playoffs" and "pucks" and he lost the thread. What a horrible feeling to realize he had no idea what his new companion was talking about. He was used to hockey being played on frosty grass on winter mornings with everyone hurtling up and down the field, boots growing heavier with cakes of mud. He had never worn a pair of ice skates in his life. How was it possible to keep your balance and hit something with a stick at the same time? It sounded vicious, too. "Best part," Kyle said, describing the fights, how he shoved Big Larry into the side and got away with it, and how the cut on Joshua Cox's ear would not stop bleeding.

To add to the confusion of that first day, someone called a counsellor arrived. Expecting a man with a pipe and white hair, like the one he had seen at the city hall near his father's office in London, it was a surprise when a young man confronted him. His counsellor smiled a lot and had the air of an older brother, but he kept using strange words not normally heard coming from the mouths of male siblings. He liked his "counsellor" a lot but could not imagine ever fancying a "discussion" or "needing support."

The Queen had unnerved him, too. While waiting in the school office later on that first day, he was startled by a large portrait of Elizabeth II looking down at him. Everything about her seemed familiar: the regal smile, the trademark perm styled to perfection, the string of pearls. But what was she doing in Winnipeg? For a second he thought his teacher had put her there especially for him, a personal welcome from Her Majesty. Then he remembered: Queen of Britain, Queen of Canada, the long-distance monarch.

His growing sense of disorientation had peaked with an unexpected ritual, which began without warning. Just as his counsellor had started deciphering the forest of acronyms littering his timetable, the national anthem burst out of the school loudspeaker, stopping the world in mid sentence while a loud and distorted *Oh, Canada* shot forth. Everyone in the room froze, some eyeing their abandoned work longingly while others mouthed the overfamiliar stanzas without realizing they were doing it. The power of the song had intrigued him, but he did not know the words and could not recognize the tune.

Today he was late, having underestimated the time it takes to walk two miles. Frozen toes made walking awkward, and after sitting down beside Kyle, he started work on his hamstrings, rubbing and squeezing the life back into them.

"It's bloody freezing out there. I had to walk," he said.

"My dad's been threatening, but he's forgotten about it," replied Kyle.

"Don't remind him. I think I'm going to lose a toe or something." He wrenched off his boot and started massaging his feet. "Do you believe in all that stuff?"

"What stuff?"

"You know, all that global warming stuff, the funny weather and weird gas prices and all that."

"Well, yeah. Don't you?"

"Yes."

They both laughed.

"I heard they had monster hailstones down in Minneapolis last week," Kyle said.

"They did? What are you supposed to do?"

"Run!"

They laughed again, but not so loud.

CHAPTER

6

Poppy sat in the gas station lineup. She could not find the end at first, and only by circling around could she secure a spot. Subzero boredom had fixed the drivers into set positions, and she noticed a pattern of resigned body language repeated down the line: shoulders pulled up, elbows drawn in, alert pairs of eyes watching for signs of movement. Most cars had only one driver. They were mostly men, sitting still, waiting.

There is something about a lineup. It has a magnetic quality that can draw you in, hold you without your realizing it. A lineup means there is something worth having, something worth waiting for. But this line of cars was different. A suspicious mood was palpable in the faces that turned towards her as she tucked in behind a filthy Jeep. Cars were bumper to bumper, and with engines turned off, the place felt eerily quiet. Every drop of gas was precious these days. No more idling for ten minutes to keep the engine warm. No more idling just to keep toes from freezing. And certainly no more chatting to the motorist at the next pump. "Friendly Manitoba," the phrase so familiar on every licence plate, was obscured by the tight line of cars.

She would not have noticed the man walking by had it not been for all his shopping. Four plastic bags strained against their handles, dragging down his shoulders. She noted a red gas can suspended from a spare finger. The eyes of the line followed the weary figure as he swayed towards the gas pump. Poppy watched him too, then glanced at her gas gauge whose arrow had been pointing at empty for the last few miles.

A bang made her jump and she looked up again, surveying the new scene that had unfolded ahead: the swaying man lay sprawled on the ground, oranges dotted the snow, and a trucker stood over him, shouting. A trail of insults spewed from his mouth. "Wait your goddamn turn!" and "Fucking moron!" rolled up inside balls of frozen breath.

She slipped her hands between her knees. Something made her feel nervous around men in big trucks. Something about the size of everything felt intimidating — the colossal wheels, the monumental wing mirrors, the bucket-sized cup holders. She lowered her head but still watched.

People react to violence in different ways. Some are terrified and feel physically sick, unable to move or run, while others are experts at making an assessment, followed by a speedy course of action. A person such as the latter was now making his way down the line of cars. A bouncing walk gave the impression of youth, but the ancient trilby and tweed coat creased at the elbows suggested otherwise. But his walk distinguished him for another reason — the usual clutched-in posture of a very cold person was absent. He could have been strolling through a field of prairie grass on a summer's day, his arms swinging, his shoulders relaxed. Poppy watched. Then she opened her window a fraction, and a shot of freezing air and voices forced their way through the crack.

"Hey, man, you've hurt him," the trilby wearer said.

"He cut in. I swear to God, I was here first."

"Well, you went too far. He's hurt."

The trilby wearer bent towards the man on the ground. Catching hold of his hat, he ducked down further and heaved him to his feet, ignoring the truck driver who was now displaying an odd mixture of bravado and reluctant guilt for all to see. They turned towards her end of the line. Poppy felt nervous as they approached her car, then relieved as they passed. They got into the car behind her and she followed their movements in her mirror. They sat staring straight ahead at first, then, in an unlikely moment of intimacy, the young man pulled a chamois leather out from somewhere and dabbed at the injured man's forehead. Two other drivers appeared at their car door, mouthing offers of help. Poppy sank back into her seat, glad there was no reason for her to get involved.

The car in front had moved forward a couple of inches. She nudged in behind, infected by the new spirit of self-preservation, and pulled out her sketchbook, glancing up occasionally to check for movement ahead. A shaky figure appeared on the page. He wore a trilby hat. He was holding an orange.

The numbers on the pump dial just kept on turning. Poppy stood shivering at the back of her car willing them to stop. She swapped hands, plunging frozen fingers into her left pocket before bringing out freshly warmed ones from the right. At last the dial slowed and she dashed into the pay booth.

"Oh, it's perishing out there!"

"Cold enough to freeze the balls off the Golden Boy," replied the clerk without looking up. "Oh, sorry. I meant ..."

She smiled. "It can't get colder than this, can it?"

"There's a lot worse coming our way. Didn't you see the paper?"

"No, why?"

He pointed to a stack of newspapers piled on the counter.

"'Farmers demand new canola market'?" she said, glancing at the front page.

"No," he said, smiling. "Lower down."

She scanned the page, her eyes lingering on an advertisement for furnace repairs before halting at a small column in the right hand corner.

SASKATCHEWAN STORM HEADS EAST.

She looked up. "Are storms common at this time of year?"

"Well, you never know what's going to happen round here in winter," replied the clerk. "The last couple of years we had a heat wave in April and a blizzard in May."

"That's incredible. Oh, I should pay for my petrol. How much do I owe you?"

"A hundred and sixty dollars."

"What!"

"A hundred and sixty dollars."

"Wait, that can't be right!"

"See for yourself."

She leaned over the counter and peered at the screen. "I can't believe it. The price can't go up any more, can it?"

"Nothing to stop it, eh?"

"That fight out there — has something like that ever happened before?"

"Two bloody noses on Friday, a smashed windshield last Tuesday," he replied. He looked wistful. "Things are changing round here, y'know. People get mean when gas gets a bit scarce."

She turned to see a fridge-sized man heading towards the counter and stuffed her wallet into her bag. She managed a cheery smile as they brushed shoulders in the doorway. The fridge smiled back.

CHAPTER

7

Fred had worked it out. Drifting around a warm place filled with stores was the way to explore a cold city. After wandering about, browsing through a rack of CDs then buying a box of screen wipes for his computer, he sat down on a bench and observed the knee-level world of plastic bags and wet boots that was streaming by.

Slurping on a soda, he felt sweat gathering beneath his armpits, but pure laziness prevented him from taking off his coat. Coats were important in his new city. Back home, coats were optional, an irritated mother and the threat of catching cold being the worst that could happen. But in this city, you could die if you forgot your coat. Kyle said so. You could die if your car broke down beyond the city limits and no one knew you were there.

He looked around, spotting snippets of activity. A sales clerk was tidying her counter, shifting piles of receipts from one side to another and exhausting herself with endless small acts of trying to look busy. She threw on a smile as a young woman stepped into the store, only to lose it amongst her papers when she drifted out again. Back on it went as another woman crossed the threshold, seriously browsing, and the clerk sprang into action and headed onto the main floor.

Three boys dawdled by. Two held cartons of fries, and both wiped greasy hands on their jeans between mouthfuls. A smell of fat trailed in their wake. Fred hated fast food. He hated the smell of fast food. They had visited a food court when they first arrived in the city. Choosing what to buy had been difficult, but as they scanned the wall of glistening photographs, he settled on a bowl of noodles with fried chicken. Smelling the bright orange sauce set his stomach juices pumping, but the taste of warm, second-hand fat and synthetic meat revolted him, sending him running to the trash and spitting out the whole lot in a slimy ball. He had never been back.

A different sort of sour smell now hit his nostrils. Someone had sat down beside him. He glanced sideways but could not form a clear picture beyond discovering that it was a man. It was rude to stare, so Fred looked down at his feet, keeping his head rigid while sliding his eyes to the right. Shoes tell you a lot about a person, and the ones on the floor beside him were special. Grubby laces went through the top two holes, leaving the lower eyelets empty. Both shoes curled upwards at the toes, but there the similarity ended. One was black and speckled with purple paint while the other was longer and brown. The socks were surprisingly white.

Fred turned to look at the man. The man was looking at him. Smiling. Not in the pre-prepared, store clerk way, but in the way his mother smiled at him when he arrived home from school: pleased to see him, wanting to hear what he had to say. Fred felt a line of sweat run down his ribs. "Hot in here, isn't it?" he said. It was one of those useless things people come out with when they are stuck for something to say. No reply required, but if offered, it would be simple and could easily finish off the whole conversation.

"Too hot," the man replied. "The geese told us it is too hot. The geese."

It was not the answer he had expected. It required another question. "Oh, how do you know that?"

The man stared at him. Fred was taken aback to see how ancient he looked. Old skin, the colour of a brown paper bag, was the main impression. Not wrinkly so much, but stretched over his cheekbones like the worn-out arm of a sofa, with the occasional patch of purple. A huge gap lay between his eyes and eyebrows, the skin in between wrinkled up like a drawstring bag. Long black hair without the slightest shred of grey was tied into a black ponytail, so black it was as if he had been picked up, turned upside down, and dipped in a bottle of ink.

"Geese," repeated the man.

Fred got a good look at his mouth this time. Teeth can tell you a lot about a person, too. But there were no teeth, not one — just a black hole surrounded by thin lips. A line drawn on with pencil came to mind, with tiny red cracks marking the corners. Fred knew about those cracks; they were painful and had been forming at the sides of his own mouth ever since he arrived in the city. Only rubbing on regular dollops of moisturizer made them bearable, and smiling hurt.

"What do you mean?" he said.

The old man stared again, then launched into an unexpected speech. All about geese — geese and weather. The explanation was hesitant and repetitive, chopped into random sentences but punctuated with key words that seemed to explain the whole thing. The word *geese* really was the answer and only a few helping phrases were needed to make the whole story clear. Fred had seen the geese in the early winter sky. He had laughed when he saw that they really did fly in symmetrical arrow formations. But now he was hearing a new story. About geese.

As he listened, he noticed the shopping cart stationed by the man's knee: a regular supermarket cart filled to the brim with bags. At first glance it seemed a successful week's grocery shop, but the bags were not fresh and white; they were sepia brown and covered with creases. Mysterious contents bulged outwards, sharp corners breaking through the plastic. Then he saw knots. They sealed the ends of each bag, stretching out the necks. They had been tied in an elaborate way, running in parallel lines, twisting over, vanishing inside themselves, then reappearing unexpectedly further down the line. Fred sneaked another look at the man beside him as he continued to talk. About geese.

No one joined them. A man holding a small boy almost sat down, but froze in mid sit, lurching up again before moving off without looking back. Fred looked again at the man. He was *still* talking about geese, demonstrating something with his hands and waving long, black fingernails. Fred examined his own nails; they were short and pale with white half moons.

Suddenly the talking stopped. The story was over. Fred could think of nothing to say. The old man stood up and began to rearrange the contents of his cart. Some bags looked light while others strained their knotted necks as he moved them from one side to the other. At last everything deemed to be in order and, with no words marking his departure, the old man rolled off down the corridor, his legs bowed into a distinct oval. Fred watched him go, noticing the way his trousers were tucked into the back of his shoes before he disappeared behind a display of socks on sale.

A woman appeared then, holding a damp cloth in her hand. Without a word, she wiped it over the plastic bench, brushing the side of his jeans. "Oops, sorry," she said.

Then she was gone.

CHAPTER
8

"Hi, Freddie. I'm back."

Fred's coat was hanging on a peg when Poppy came in through the front door later that day, his scarf twisted over it in a figure eight. Gloves stuck out from each pocket, their fingers pointing to the ceiling, and a pair of boots blotted damp shapes on newspaper laid out on the floor.

"Hi, Mum," came a faint voice from above.

"What's that funny smell?" she called.

"Dunno."

After hanging her coat on the next peg, straightening out the arms as an afterthought, she went upstairs. She tapped on the door but forgot to wait for an answer. Her son sat at his computer, typing. The desk was arranged in the way Fred liked it — a jar of sharpened pencils lay beside an eraser, still in its wrapping, and a small box of paperclips sat perfectly parallel to the edge of the desk. Beside the monitor lay a pile of books, squared off at the corners, with a copy of *Migrating Birds* lying on the top.

"Are you busy?" she asked.

"Sort of."

"What are you doing?"

"Just looking something up," he said, pushing a handful

of hair off his face and clicking the minimize button on the monitor.

Fred was always looking something up. His obsession with the internet had replaced his boyhood love of encyclopedias and he riffled through it daily, thrilled by the obscurity of digital cross-referencing and inspired by the black hole of knowledge in which he happily drifted.

"What's that? A cat's cradle?" she said, pointing at a small mound of string tied into knots.

"No, I was trying something out. Experimenting. I wanted to see how many knots I could get out of a twelve-inch piece of string."

"How many did you get?"

"More than you'd expect."

The vagueness of the answer caught her attention. Her son had a methodical mind and she had come to expect precision in his replies. She sat down on the bed; he glanced at her. She was on Fred's turf now. She had to obey his rules. Touching his things without permission was not allowed, and logging onto his computer, with its trail of evidence locked into search engine lists and history drop-down menus, all disclosing his recent preoccupations, utterly forbidden. And any temptation to tidy was out of the question. No need. The room was impeccably clean, spotless to an extreme that never failed to amaze her. He went against the grain of teenage expectations, creating a regime of order in his bedroom normally only seen in military academies. He made his bed every single morning before emerging, and it was a paper-smooth duvet that inaugurated his day, not the expected piles of damp towels or heaps of stinking socks.

Her son had certainly not inherited his tidy genes from his parents. Charlie originated from a family of incurable slobs. Generations of Foresters had failed to notice inch-high dust rising on their mantelpieces, were unable to appreciate the significance of blue patterns appearing on their cheese, and spent countless hours each week searching for missing items hidden in the folds of disarray. Her family were no better, renowned for their vast collections of dusty magazines, stacks of unsorted paperwork, and shelves packed with cans of food that were years past their expiry date. During the early days of her and Charlie's relationship, she had remained undaunted by the disorder following in Charlie's wake, a mess that might have scared off a more domestically sensitive girl. But after eighteen years of marriage, they had achieved a happy balance between keeping the most noxious of germs at bay while leaving time to do more satisfying things with their lives, unencumbered by the relentless rigor of high standards of cleanliness. Fred had reacted to the general shambles early in his life, developing an obsession with towels, folding them precisely and arranging them in complementary colour schemes on the bathroom rail. He had even insisted on arranging the family coats in descending order of waterproof-ness during one particularly stressful phase. Surprisingly, his inclination towards order had accompanied him into puberty, and the creases she made on the bedsheet as she sat down were the only dissenters to harmony in the entire room.

"More experiments?" she said, nodding at the string that had been wound around the leg of the bed. He smiled but said nothing.

"I have to take Dad to the airport tonight. Are you coming?" she said.

"Not walking, are we?"

"No, we are *not* walking, but I would like the company. Will you come?"

"Sure."

CHAPTER
9

"When are you coming back, Dad?"

Charlie reached forward and turned down the car radio. "You what?"

"When are you coming back?" repeated Fred.

"Two weeks," replied Charlie. "That's if the ticket price hasn't doubled." Eyes shaped by a grin were reflected in the front mirror.

"You shouldn't joke about it, Charlie," Poppy said.

"Oh, they'll sort it out. Got to, or we won't vote them back in again, will we?"

"Dad, we don't even have the vote here."

"It's not only that," said his mother. "You heard about the storm, Charlie?"

"What storm?"

"Coming from Sas ... Saska ..."

"Saskatchewan?"

"That's it. Coming this way."

"Poppy. There are storms round here every winter. The airports are geared up for it. Brian at work told me. This isn't London; the whole transport system doesn't seize up the moment someone spots a snowflake. Don't worry."

Fred observed Charlie's neck through the hole in the headrest. His father was an eternal optimist. He retained a blind faith in a positive outcome to any sort of dilemma — "It would all turn out all right in the end" was his general philosophy. It got a bit wearing sometimes. Poppy was the opposite — an expert at spotting accidents waiting to happen and endlessly worrying about the rising gas prices. She had even taken to postponing trips to the grocery store until the fridge was empty and they were reduced to scratching around at the back of cupboards for a packet of soup or dipping licked fingers into vintage tubs of sprinkles. Nevertheless, a drive to the airport was an unavoidable necessity that even she accepted. After all, his father was going to England for two weeks and that meant luggage, lots of it.

Charlie was one of life's great packers. Even for short weekend trips he ironed at least seven shirts, trying to relive the pristine pleasure of factory-folded clothes before pressing out his efforts in the bottom of an overstuffed suitcase. He travelled a lot. "Purveyors of fine instruments" he liked to call Lombard's. He designed pacemakers. Someone had to do it. Someone had to look right inside a heart and know which valve goes where. Fred felt queasy just thinking about it, connecting all those cold wires to a beating muscle. And the ticking, wouldn't that drive you mad? But there was no ticking, his father said. Just an elegant little battery that settled people's rhythms so they could get on with their lives without worrying. Charlie had been promoted to top dog and people everywhere wanted his knowledge, his expert opinion on why their batteries were running down and their lives beating out of sync.

His father loved to stock up on shoes, too, a Saturday afternoon shopping trip incomplete without a spare pair in the back. Fred felt confident that nestling behind him in the trunk would be a whole suitcase dedicated to a full range of footwear, one pair for every eventuality.

Charlie liked to drive fast as well. A rapid succession of shoulder checks disturbed Fred's view of the road ahead, switching from left to right as they sped up the highway, but he could still read the giant signs that lined the route: "Immediate Cremation $800" swept by, replaced a second later by "Now Wash Your Hands" flashing in spangle yellow. Then, "Two Fat Boys $6" whipped past his window. They slowed down, juddering below the speed limit as their tires lost traction and they slithered towards the back of a snowplough, missing the warning sign welded to its rear, "Keep back fifteen metres," by a sixteenth of an inch.

"Charlie!"

"Wasn't that fun?" Even from the back seat Fred could detect sheepishness in his father's voice.

"Charlie, slow down, please."

They cruised past a church. Fred glimpsed a cross in the doorway, six feet high and cast from solid ice. He was not religious, but sometimes wished he was. "Atheist" best described his religious status, coming as he did from a long line of atheists. Anything to do with Sunday morning church services left him feeling uncomfortable. He imagined believing in a god should involve extreme levels of feeling, waking up in the morning, doing something wonderful for someone else, or a large crowd of people shouting at the tops of their voices. In his mind, the cluster of people in their best clothes, trickling through the church door, did not quite fit into his idea of belief.

You could not miss the sign they all dreaded: the one at the gas station. Four dollars came into view as they stopped at the junction. His mother let out a little gasp, touching her throat with her hand. Fred could see the man climbing down the billboard ladder, the black numbers of yesterday's price clutched beneath his arm.

"They've got to be joking," Charlie said.

"Some joke," Fred murmured to himself.

"Charlie, shouldn't you postpone the trip?" said Poppy.

He watched his father's forearm through the gap in the front seats, rubbing his mother's knee.

"It will be all right. They're not going to stop flights, are they?"

"But the petrol prices are going up so fast."

"Don't worry, Poppy. Everything will be fine."

They watched the flight leave from the viewing gallery, trying to guess which plane Charlie was on. Fred leaned his forehead against the glass, becoming aware of that feeling in the bottom of his stomach, the one that wouldn't go away. Charlie was going home. They were staying behind.

In just a few hours, his father would be obeying British airport signs, shoving British coins into the telephone box, and cursing British traffic with a healthy dose of British expletives. Most of the time Fred managed to keep the feeling hidden, buried deep down amongst the others he did not want on display, but it would surface when he least expected it. A glimpse of a film set in north London, an east-end accent popping out of the radio, or the taste of an English biscuit, lovingly packed and sent across the ocean by his grandmother, were enough to peel back the layers of contentment that he had been slowly constructing. Only the day before, his counsellor had looked him in the face and stated without warning, "You miss home, don't you?" and the institutionalized support he had so derided was the only thing that kept him from walking home in tears.

Looking up at the sky beyond the flight path, he could see a wide arrow of geese, high up and evenly spaced. Heading towards the warmth of the south.

Geese — they told you a lot.

CHAPTER
10

Christmas was coming. Abandoned merchandise was being wheel-barrowed back into the limelight and topped with a sprig of tinsel, rebranded as stocking fillers. People were spending money they did not have, and above the din of arguments about bouncing cheques and overstretched credit cards came the sounds of Christmas music. Only heard for a few days each year, its sickly drone permeated the folds of every shopping bag, soaked into the doughnut dough, and leached into the tired subconscious of the mall's irritable customers, who were humming along without even knowing it.

Crowds were building and Fred could smell stress in the air as he elbowed and apologized his way through. He had been back twice since meeting the old man but had never encountered him again. Today was different. A sudden unpleasant smell in the air told him he was somewhere near. He spotted a familiar back, bending over a garbage can. The man did not notice him at first. He was rummaging, selecting pieces of rubbish with a bamboo cane. He poked it down to the bottom again and again, stirring up the contents and forcing an assortment of garbage to the surface as the stick turned around. A system was soon apparent. Interesting items sifted out, reclassified as useful, then stored. Rejects were cast to the back for further stirring. Occasionally an aluminium can rode to the top and he would sniff it, swig out any remaining drops, then slide it under his heel, crushing it flat before placing it into the waiting shopping cart. Particular attention was paid to food. Broken cookies, bitten burgers wrapped in ketchup-soaked tissue, and cold noodles were all sniffed and inspected before being placed in a special brown bag hanging off the handle.

"You look busy," said Fred.

The man jumped, then smiled in recognition. "There is enough. There are people," he said.

Fred frowned. In his imagination, the old man lived a solitary existence in the garbage chute of some apartment block, rolled into a blanket of newspapers at night and conducting lonely, unrequited conversations with himself. Now it turned out he was feeding his whole family on the proceeds of one bin.

"I hope you don't think I'm being nosy, but are these things for your family?"

The man turned towards him, scrunched up his nose, and carried on stirring as if no one had spoken. It was time for a formal introduction. "I'm Fred," he said.

The old man stared at him. "Ataninnuaq. Ataninnuaq means a man who has lived." He looked expectantly at Fred. "And knows things."

Fred thought for a moment. "Fred is short for Frederick." This seemed satisfactory. "Can I call you Ata?"

The old man raised his eyebrows but said nothing. They moved towards the bench and sat down.

"I have something for you," said Fred, pulling a small tube of moisturizer out of his pocket and laying it on his companion's lap. "It's for your mouth. Stops those cracks from hurting all the time."

Ata unscrewed the lid, stood up, and pulled an old fork from a bag near the bottom of his cart. A blob of cream squirted onto the back of his hand as he stabbed the seal. After rubbing the tiniest morsel into the corners of his lips, he wiped the rest on his cheeks, leaving behind a glaze of white circles.

"You'll need more than that!"

Ignoring him, the old man screwed on the lid and placed the tube in his pocket. "Thank you. I have something. Thank you."

Rifling around in the pile of bags, the old man pulled out an old sock and handed it to Fred. A hole had opened up over the big toe and mud crusted the cuff.

"Thank you," Fred said, taking it by his fingertips and placing it in his coat pocket, silently rubbing his hand against the lining as he pulled it out. "I'll try it on later."

Ata smiled and gestured to the plastic bench. They sat more closely this time, shoulders almost touching. Fred's nostrils had started adapting to the smell, and he only had to hold his breath when Ata looked directly at him. As he tried to think of what they could talk about, he remembered something he had been meaning to say.

"Catchy drawer and sticky door, coming rain will pour and pour."

Fred did not look up. He just studied Ata's shoes; a slither of banana skin clinging to one of the laces heralded the only sign of change. Ata turned towards him and stared hard. Fred stared back. At such close range he could see a grey cornea, with tiny lumps of dried mucus hardened into the corners. Then the man laughed, lifted his arm, and patted Fred's shoulder with a heaviness that surprised him. Feeling pleased, Fred started to talk about his home — not the house in Winnipeg, but his real home, the one in London, the one that was now filled with strangers, sleeping in his bed, brushing their teeth in his sink, and marking their heights on the doorframe in his kitchen. Or perhaps they had painted over that already. He described his friends, his gang, one by one: Johno, with his curly hair; Tommy, smiling with teeth that looked green; and Simon, who was always bumping into things and getting into trouble with his mother. But he hesitated when he realized he could not remember what Sam looked like. Sam was tall, of course, with black hair and a beaten-up jacket, but he could not recall his face. The square forehead and thick eyebrows were clear in his mind but lower down was blank. Nothing.

Ata stopped knotting some string around the handle of the shopping cart and sat perfectly still. Fred had never seen a person sit so still. Turning to face him, and proceeded by a puff of foul breath, the old man began to tell a story of his old home. Listening was hard work — an unfamiliar accent and a lack of teeth hampered clarity but, leaning in closer, his ear angled to catch the story, Fred began to get the gist of it.

And a story it was. The hero was Ata as a young boy. He lived in the far north where it was cold every day of the year. They ate raw meat, sliced warm from the backs of seals. His mother had a large tattoo running beneath her chin; he liked to stroke it with his finger. She sang to him, too, a warble that came right from the back of her throat. He knew that because Ata demonstrated how it was done. They both laughed, then Ata made a laugh come from the back of his throat, and they both laughed some more. Then he described the hood. Ata grew up inside a hood. Naked. Fred honestly did not believe it, but Ata spent his whole babyhood naked inside his mother's hood, coming out at night then returning in the morning before the family moved on. The old man knew the shape of the back of his mother's ears better than anything in the world. Fred wondered what the back of his own mother's ears looked like.

Suddenly Ata was on to something else. He was talking about clothes — clothes made of skin. After the hood came the suit, the skin suit killed by his father and sewn into a special little boy outfit worn over bare skin. Fred lost the thread of the story, suddenly worrying about the lack of underwear, not even a vest, generally considered the most important weapon in the battle against the damp of the British winter. But the old man grew up in a hood and wore no underwear. Fred did not believe a word of it, but it was a good story, especially with Ata as the hero.

The mall was closing. He could see the woman with the cloth hovering in a doorway.

"I'll be here tomorrow," Fred said.

Ata raised his eyebrows.

CHAPTER

II

"I'm sick of it."

"I don't take much notice, Ray's got the generator out at the farm."

"But, June, that's miles away."

"Yeah, well, maybe we'll bring it into the city one of these days."

"Let me know when you do and I'll know where to go during the next blackout."

"Just buy a few candles. Makes everything a bit romantic."

Poppy met the cashier's eyes with a blank look that said nothing and something at the same time. She picked up a gossip magazine from the rack, scanning through the list of indiscretions. "Whose cellulite?" seemed to be the most taxing question on people's minds, with "How to shed six pounds in one day" following a close second. But then the headline of a more sombre magazine, *World Weekly,* drew her attention away from the droves of dishevelled celebrities staggering out of night clubs. "Global warming: the new breed of storm."

"Hello there," said the cashier. "How are you today? Did you find everything you were looking for?"

Poppy slipped the magazine back on the shelf and skimmed her list. Everything crossed out, except wine. But candles, should she get candles? The cashier began to swipe her items through. No, not enough time. "Yes, thank you."

"Parcel pick up?"

"No, thanks."

"Bingo card?"

"No, thank you."

"Gas coupon?"

"Yes, please, could I have several?"

"Sorry, only one per customer."

"Oh."

"Will that be everything, Mrs. Forester?"

Mrs. Forester. How did she know her name? "Yes, thank you." She glanced at the name tag pinned on the blue smock. "Tracy."

As she rummaged in her handbag, Poppy mused over the exchange. Twenty years with the same bank in London and no one had ever bothered to learn her name. Thirty years with one dentist and she still had to spell out "Forester" every time she booked the next appointment.

"That will be one hundred and eight dollars, fifty-five cents," said the cashier.

"Are you certain that's right? Could I see the receipt?"

"For sure."

She scanned the list, clicking her tongue at each item. "Did something go up?"

"Everything did."

"Pardon?"

"Everything went up. It's the gas prices. Everything went up."

She pulled out her list and, pressing the paper onto her palm, crossed out the wine and wrote "candles" instead.

CHAPTER
12

Fred had tattoos on his mind as he stepped out of the mall. He turned left at random and strode up the street, the speed of his steps belying the vagueness of his purpose. He veered right at a deep-red fire hydrant, mentally earmarking it as a landmark for his return journey, and marched across the road. It seemed darker in this part of town. Warehouses crowded out the sky and skinny alleyways punctured the blocks, enticing passersby with their promises of shelter and things unknown. He was looking at objects dotting the snowbanks — a stiff mitten, a chocolate wrapper edged with frost — so he did not notice the antiques warehouse until he stubbed his toe into a sign buried in the snow. MCINTYRE'S ANTIQUES.

He looked up. A smudged note was pinned to the door. Only by bending back the corner that had blown free from the glass could he read the hours of operation: 2:00-6:00, Monday-Friday. Ignoring the finger of wind stroking his wrist, he looked at his watch. Half past five. There was still time. He pushed open the door, battling an unseen object lurking within, then turned sideways, sucked in his belly, and entered the store.

"Hello there." The voice was muffled, its owner out of sight.

"Hello?"

"Can I help you with something?"

A woman emerged through the door of an inner room, followed by a wave of warm air.

"I'm just looking, thanks."

"For sure. There's six floors, knick-knacks on the first, chairs on the next, tables, office furniture, lighting. I'm not sure what's on the top floor these days, never go there." She smiled. "The elevator's round that corner. Alan will go with you if you like." She flicked her head back towards her room.

Alan sat in the inner sanctum. Represented only by a tightly stretched newspaper held aloft, a pair of legs, and slippers that looked as if they had been worn outside, Fred struggled to gauge who was being offered up as his guide.

"I'm fine, thanks, I'm just browsing."

But Alan was on his feet. "Come on. I'll show you the way

up. Some people don't make it back from the top floor." He grinned at the woman; she grinned back.

The elevator looked distinctly dodgy. A shuddering floor was unnerving enough, but soon it emitted a cry like nothing he had ever heard, wolves chewing on iron filings being the image that came to mind. Furniture packed every square inch of the large elevator floor, almost obscuring the panel of buttons on one wall. His travelling companion settled himself down on a spare chair, brushing crumbs of perished foam off his trousers before tilting his head upwards.

"Looking for something special?" Alan asked.

"No. I was just passing. Is this building very old?"

"Eighteen ninety," he said.

"Where do all the things come from?"

"Oooh, everywhere — auctions, house clearances, you wouldn't believe what people throw out."

"What used to go on in this place?"

"Grain storage. Which floor?"

"Top please."

As Fred stepped out onto the listing boards of the top floor, he felt the rush of a forgotten pleasure. Second-hand goods filled every inch of space, their mass only punctured by tunnels running through, just wide enough to accommodate a pair of human hips. Dust was stacked high, accentuating the curves of bentwood screens and damping down the sheen of the velvet sofas. He accidentally kicked a bucket brimming with water. It spilled, only adding to the sodden circle of wood already wet beneath his feet.

"Watch yourself," Alan said.

His escort, showing signs of impatience, set off, burrowing through the piles, ducking table legs and climbing what appeared to be a dead end by scaling a pile of chairs stacked into a pyramid. Fred scurried behind, unwilling to be left alone amongst the army of drawing boards closing ranks around him. Retrieving a finger that had become trapped beneath the lid of an old school desk, his guide turned around victorious, waved a bruised digit in his general direction, then disappeared behind a row of mannequins.

The room was suddenly quiet. So quiet he could hear pigeons cooing from somewhere on the other side of the vast space. He sat down for a moment, wrapped in the arms of a fine board-room chair. A shiver shot down his spine as he looked around. The room felt colder than outside, a penetrating, damp cold that quickly discovered the gap between his trousers and shirt. He rested his head on his hand, and during that pause in his life, during those few seconds of doing absolutely nothing, thinking in a void, he spotted something. A pair of snowshoes. They lay inside the partly opened drawer of a maple wood desk, which matched the chair he sat on. He picked one up and poked a finger through the webbing, inspecting the bindings that trailed down over his knees. The workmanship was flawless. Wooden cross members merged into the frame through invisible joints, and a stiff lattice of triangles in the centre collapsed into lazy pentagons as they met the edges of the shoe. But there were gaps, large ones, some wider than a fist.

"Want a price on those?"

Fresh from a reconnaissance along the west wall, Fred's chaperone was back at his side, breathing warm air onto the back of his neck.

"Yes please, how much are they?"

"Forty-five dollars."

"Oh, I think I only have forty."

The man frowned. "I suppose they are damaged. You can have them for forty."

"Right. Thanks, thanks very much."

As the proprietor rummaged in the back of the drawer to

find a missing length of binding, Fred gazed over his shoulder towards the massive semi-circular window at the far end of the room. He stared out at the view, convinced he could see the sun drawing diagonal shadow ladders across the buildings outside. Forgetting the shoulders bobbing in and out of his vision, he studied the city blocks through the window. Old stone threaded its way through the buildings, framing windows, protecting corners, and holding up arches. Towering words stencilled the facades: WESTERN MILLINERY, MANITOBA WHOLESALE, GARY'S AUCTION. Some were faded, some scratched, some frozen and thawed, then frozen again, but all told a story of his new city that he had not yet heard.

CHAPTER
13

A new type of quiet filled the house. Tiny echoes and impromptu clicks, not normally heard in the general rush of things, became discernable as the building heaved and strained, slipping minutely out of shape, then realigning itself under the pressure of frozen soil and ripple-bellied icicles that draped the edges of the roof. Charlie's absence always created a sombre mood. Not that he was a noisy man, but his presence always generated activity: lots of rushing about to find his shoes, calling out jokes to Poppy while brushing his teeth, or insisting that Fred taste his latest culinary experiment.

Charlie was the cornerstone of the family triangle. If he went on a trip, they always needed a few hours to adjust to the quiet, falling into new patterns of doing. He was the one who stirred up action, leaving a deluge of disturbance behind him, while Poppy was the one who absorbed the consequences. She was the calm one. But she was also the worrier, camouflaging her anxiety with shortened smiles and snappy remarks. Not saying anything meant she had something to say.

Fred kneeled down, laid the snowshoes out neatly beneath his bed, sat down at his desk, and pressed a button on his computer. It hummed to life, spreading a greenish light into his room. He typed fast.

What is the origin of the name Frederick?
Frederick is of German origin, meaning "peaceful ruler."

Then came another question.

Who lives in northern Canada?
Inuit, plural of Inut. Inuit, meaning "people."

He typed faster, grinning.

What is an Inuit hood?
Traditionally, infants were carried for the first two to three years of their lives in a roomy back pouch.

A paperclip skidded beneath his keyboard as he smacked his fist down on the desk. It was real. The stories were real. Ata grew up in a hood. A light tap on the door interrupted his exclaiming, and his mother's face appeared. She looked flushed.

"I'm making bison stew. Want some?"

"You what? Bison? Are you serious?"

"You're not going to be picky, are you?"

"No, but bison? What does it taste like?"

"You'll see." She smiled.

"Hey, Mum," he said, turning towards her. "Have you heard of the Inuit?"

"The Inuit? Of course. They used to be called Eskimos, but

people don't use that word anymore. They come from the far north but some moved south to the city. Why do you ask?"

"I just heard the word and wondered who they were. It's not important."

"Right. You coming downstairs?"

"Sure."

He followed his mother down the stairs and settled himself on a stool next to her before prodding at the assembled ingredients, looking for something to scrounge. Cooking was one area of Poppy's life where she achieved good order, and Fred could see today was no exception as he noted the precisely measured food lining up on matching saucers.

Unable to find suitable pickings on the kitchen top, he rummaged in the fridge, which was almost empty as usual. His mother had not yet mastered the North American art of bulk buying, unable to think beyond a single meal plus a few cornflakes. Attempts at persuasion by his father had been met with a dogged resistance not usually witnessed in a person that preferred to fit in with the plans of others, and several recent shopping expeditions had been cut short as she made irritable allegations that if they bought more food they would only eat more. A claim of likely accuracy, but as a person prone to skinniness, he could not see the harm in that.

Nibbling on a shrivelled carrot, he returned to his position on the stool and watched her prepare the meal, slicing the onions at an angle and squashing the stock cube into a glass of water with the back of a teaspoon. Next came the bison meat, shining and raw. Miniscule drips of blood stained her fingertips as she sliced. Slices of meat were lobbed into the waiting bowl of flour, flicked and rolled, transforming into soft white pebbles in dusty coats. A slither of meat remained on the board, too small to bother with. With no plan in mind, he picked it up, put it in his mouth, and, omitting to chew, swallowed it down whole.

"Fred! Did you just eat that?" His mother stared at him.

He had, but he was not sure why. He felt ambivalent about meat. Just the smell of a Sunday roast would have him hovering around the oven, burning his finger as he captured blobs of juice dripping off the gravy boat, but sometimes when he sat down at the table, starving, he was unable to eat a thing as he examined the blue-veined flesh.

"I just thought I'd try it," he said. "It didn't taste like anything."

And it didn't. It slipped down and that was that. No resemblance could be found to his mother's delicious creations with their long, slow build up — the gathering of ingredients, the warming of the pan, the aggressive sound of frying, the glorious smell of onions wafting over the house, the churning of the hungry stomach, the slow serving, the delicate dividing up with knife and fork, the last-minute holding back, and finally the eating.

"Oh ... well, I suppose some people like raw meat. Dad adores steak tartar. Raw egg mashed into raw beef. Perhaps we should try that some time?"

"No, thanks," he said with a small smile.

She continued cooking. A high ponytail held her hair in place and he could see her ears; there were faint freckles on the backs of them. He had never noticed that before.

CHAPTER
14

Poppy hated sleeping alone. The missing toothbrush she could cope with. The empty coat peg ignored. But the cold sheet was more than she could bear. It stretched across her bed forever, and she felt like a child in its parents' bed, ill fitting, scaled down. The mattress felt strange, too. When Charlie was away it reacted oddly, bouncing back a bit higher than normal, quivering a bit too much. After years spent sharing a bed with another person, her muscles were tuned to a precise distribution of limbs. Their absence vexed her.

There were ways around her loneliness, of course. Chocolate helped. Eaten in great quantities, on the cold sheet. And a slug of whiskey at bedtime could always be relied upon to take the edge off. But she could not help imagining what could go wrong in the house when Charlie went on a trip. Great, imaginary plumbing disasters would have her sitting bolt upright at three in the morning, wondering where the stop cock was located. Her childhood fear of collapsing ceilings would return to harass her on a nightly basis. It *was* possible. She had read about it in the newspaper. But, lovely Charlie. He had found three huge textbooks dedicated entirely to why ceilings *don't* fall down, and she was now well versed in the faintly obscene language of structural engineers: bending moments, trusses, sockets.

And the worst thing of all, she thought as she studied a crack in the ceiling that she had never noticed before, was that the cold sheet was still cold in the morning.

CHAPTER
15

The moon had forgotten to eat. It was true. Ata said so.

The bench in the mall had become theirs over the past few days, and Ata was always in position when he arrived, eager to talk. Fred's ears had become tuned to the old man's chopped way of speaking and he anticipated Ata's tales with great enthusiasm.

He leaned back and stretched his arms behind his head. There was no need to speak, no need to hold eye contact, no requirement to nod. He just had to be there, and listen.

Ata knew all about the sky. Brother moon had chased sister sun right across it, but they never met. She was too fast. Then the moon forgot to eat. The old man paused as Fred sniggered.

"Sorry, Ata, carry on."

"He forgot to eat. Too thin." Ata pointed a finger towards Fred's stretched-out belly. "Like you."

"Hey, I'm not thin," Fred said, rubbing his hand across his stomach, searching for the muscles he had found the day before.

"Thinner and thinner every day," continued Ata, "then, he disappeared."

"What happened?" asked Fred.

"He came back."

"When?"

"Later ... three days later."

Fred changed position, unfolding his ankles and trying to sit up straight. Ata had an amazing capacity to sit still. It seemed like hours between movement, and Fred envied his rod-like shoulders and complete dearth of itches. He scratched his nose and settled himself into a new pose.

"Ata, did you live in an igloo?"

Suddenly animated, the old man turned his whole body towards him and beamed. A fresh torrent of words gushed forth, slipping into sentences. Fred struggled to keep up as an igloo took shape inside the mall. Saliva-coated saws sliced through blocks of compressed snow, ice dust rose up, backs ached, and cold, white light pierced the joints. As Fred listened to the staccato stream of words, a swathe of images formed in his head. Then a new tone tinged his friend's voice, and he realized Ata was no longer talking about slivers of light filtering through igloo walls. He was talking about the Aurora, the great, shimmering curtain drawn across the night sky. He was talking about his fear as the curtain danced and spat colour, of his sheer terror as the spirits put their feet down on the ice. Then, he did not want to talk anymore.

CHAPTER

16

"Minus twenty-eight degrees Celsius. Windchill factor, minus thirty-five."

The voice on the radio seemed to relish the numbers, extracting extra effect where none was needed. Fred stood in the kitchen looking out at the backyard. *Yard.* It was another word that he had failed to fully grasp. Local dialect demanded "yard," not "garden," but surely everyone knew a yard was a place where you roughed it, kicked up dust, washed the dog, and turned your bike upside down to oil the chain? This yard had grass. He had never seen it, but he guessed it was down there, beneath the snow. Plus two baby trees, held up with stakes.

He sighed. A momentous decision had been reached in the previous five minutes. He was going to build a snow cave, determined to find out what it was like to sleep in a "quinzhee," as the boys at school called it. For some reason, their descriptions of burrowing into snow heaps with frost-burned fingers were strangely tempting. Would it make him feel like a real Canadian, he wondered, to do this one thing, likely considered insane by his friends back home, who thought temperatures below minus one heralded a new ice age? It couldn't be all that hard, could it? Ata had told him about snow — about its dryness and wetness. And he had discovered some things for himself — dry prairie snow didn't allow for the construction of snowballs, its powdery flakes constantly defying the squeeze of gloved fingers. A white pat embossed with fingerprints was about the best you could do, and even snowmen evaded construction as their heads flattened to plates and their bodies collapsed to the natural angle of slump.

He opened the back door and scanned the garden, searching for the snow he had heaped into a pile against the fence the previous day. His muscles had already solidified in anticipation of the cold, and the skin on his face tightened as he stepped over the threshold. The moon was out. He could see it through the crystals of ice shimmering in the air.

"See you later, Mum."

"Don't kill yourself," Poppy replied. "I mean it, Freddie. Come in if it gets unbearable."

The hairs in his nostrils were already beginning to freeze as he grabbed the shovel. Work had to be fast. Loitering was an alien concept in his new city; extreme cold demanded extreme activity. Whether you were jumping up and down at the bus stop, running from the store to your car before your fingers froze to the shopping cart, or shovelling snow off the driveway, you had to keep moving.

He began to dig into the pile with the enthusiasm of a navvy being watched by his boss, and he was soon sweating under his coat — but his fingertips were made of ice. "Go in from the side," his book had stated. But which side and how low? At first, no specialized dexterity seemed to be required but as the shape of the heap skewed obliquely, he doubled the speed of digging in an attempt to rescue the collapsing geometry. "Make sure to construct a sleeping ledge," the book had insisted, but he had been unable to understand the diagram and could not think beyond collecting a rough pile of snow that he patted down into a heap.

Suddenly unbearably cold, he had to get warm. Running

SEAL
INTESTINE
RAINCOAT

inside provided glorious and instantaneous relief. He peered out through the steamed glass towards the mound, so innocent when viewed from the heat of his kitchen. The warm air mobilized his frozen brain cells, allowing him to think again. He sat on a chair and gazed around the room, rubbing cold out of his cheeks. It took a while for his fingers to thaw out and it hurt like hell as the feeling returned. Then came the post-thaw itch and, knowing full well it would make things worse, he scratched the backs of his hands in a frenzy, raising a small cloud of dry skin that settled back down on his cuffs.

Girding himself for more work, he stood up, pulled his hat over his ears, plunged freshly thawed fingers into gloves, and ran outside. He worked at double speed, gouging out a cavity until his back ached. It looked small but he remembered Ata's words: "Igloos are never bigger than they have to be." The comment had puzzled him at the time but now as he stood in the frozen garden, the wind teasing out gaps in his clothing, it made perfect sense. The door slammed behind him as he ran inside again. This time he was shaking.

"Back so soon," said Poppy, who had returned to the kitchen. She was stirring a cup of tea at the table.

"It's free ... eezing." They laughed as his teeth chattered like an excited monkey who has lost control of its jaw.

"Want a cuppa?"

"Yes, please."

Jumping from foot to foot, he looked over his mother's shoulder as he warmed up. She was sketching a flat landscape filled with people flying kites, tiny dots in a huge sky with clouds rushing sideways off the page. One cloud was smudged where a drop of tea had fallen off her spoon, and now she was smudging the others, spreading the tea from cloud to cloud.

"Is it finished?" she asked, turning to face him.

"Almost, I just need to work out how to build a door."

That seemed to be the hardest part. How *could* he seal the entrance? Ata had not mentioned igloo doors. A cartoon came to mind, ice bricks drawn with a black pen, a gaping arch with only a set of quivering lines protecting the hapless occupants from hundred-mile-an-hour winds.

"What about putting your rucksack in the hole and stuffing a towel round it?"

"Mum, you're brilliant!"

She smiled, stood up, and threw her tea bag into the sink. A bundle of carrot skin shavings followed.

"Mum, wait, are you sure you're supposed to ram all that stuff down there?"

"Oh, yes. Everything goes down here." She beamed and, bending forward, pressed a switch somewhere beneath the sink. A rasping sound rose up from deep inside the cupboard.

"Look at that thing go!" she said.

⌒

Fred lay outside five minutes later, questioning his sanity. With the temperature hovering at minus twenty-four, there was just enough time to inspect the towelling door before the air tested his pain threshold, forcing him to scramble into his sleeping bag in a panic. As his head crunched over the plastic pillow, he thought of Ata and his igloo.

The old man had endured a lifetime of living in ice rooms, bedding down every night in this extraordinary way. No warm kitchen to dash into, no emergency hot cup of tea. Fred would kill for a hot cup of tea now. His feet and nose were frozen. His ears were ready to snap. But his brain still retained a pocket of sense, and he suddenly realized what was missing. The heat of another body. Ata had slept with his entire family every night, his mother and sister on the outside, his father and brothers on the inside. That was the way.

CHAPTER
17

"Mum, how about an interesting experience?" Fred had run into the kitchen, breathing fast through a red nose.

"What sort of experience?" She knew what he was going to say.

"The quinzhee. It's ready and ... quite warm. But it's a bit boring on your own."

He was working hard at appearing neutral; she could see that. "Quite warm" were his exact words. That was difficult to imagine while looking at him. He shivered, sighed, and blurted out sounds of relief from between stiff cheeks. She felt them; they were icy to the touch. His shoulders were locked upward in a solid shrug.

"I'll give it ten minutes."

Ten minutes was a long time, but she had said it — there was no going back. As Fred hugged the side of the recently boiled kettle, there was time to consider what she had agreed to. Scurrying from the back door to the car normally took fifteen seconds. That was how long it took to freeze when the temperature dropped below minus thirty degrees. Her family had learned these lessons within hours. If you dashed from the house before warming up the car, you were done for. If you left the house without a cover over your mouth, you were done for. Extreme cold acts fast on your senses. She had felt that rising sense of irrationality more than once. Even now she experienced a fresh flush of guilt every time she remembered the day she had slammed the car door on Fred's fingers in her rush to keep the heat in. Luckily she had only grazed them. But they had learned, learned to park right outside the door of the movie theatre, learned not to meet on street corners but inside the mall, learned that you had limited time in the cold.

She pulled a large sweatshirt over a fleece, sealed by a scarf.

"Mum, that's too much. We have to warm the cave with our own body heat."

She stared at him, searching for spots of irony. "You sure?"

"Yes, keep only the sweatshirt."

"Just ten minutes, Fred," she said, peeling off the layers but flipping a scarf around her neck at the last minute.

They ran into the garden and dived into the quinzhee. Rapidly freezing kneecaps were the focus of her attention as they scraped across the icy threshold, and her buttocks were only spared a similar fate by placing them down on the neat bed of plastic bags spread across snow bumps. She scrambled into the sleeping bag with her boots on, jamming them against the inside of the bag as they slid down.

"We must be mad," she said through chattering teeth.

Fred was too busy filling the entrance to respond. Working fast, he stuffed handfuls of snow into the gaps. Most fell straight off, but he persisted. Suddenly the freezing draft cut out.

"How do we breathe?" she asked.

"I left a gap in the door and there's a hole up there," he said, waving a stick in the direction of the ceiling.

She looked up. A cone of moonlight squeezed through the air hole, spreading white light onto white walls. The desire to draw the scene was strong but all she could think about was the cold, the mean and searing cold that was working on her. She looked at her son, his limbs drawn in like an overgrown fetus, and pulled a blanket over them both.

"What are you thinking about, Freddie?"

"Hot chocolate."

She could hear his smile in the darkness.

"Hey, Mum, let's see if we can stay all night."

"All right," she said, the cold already clouding her judgment.

Now she had something to tell Charlie: a night in a snow cave in the middle of Canada. At minus twenty-eight degrees Celsius.

CHAPTER
18

Ata was licking a knife; it was plastic and covered in blood. Fred leaned over to grab it, but smelling the vinegary ketchup at the last moment, he sat back, feeling foolish.

Three days had passed since their last meeting, and Fred felt strangely happy as he settled himself down on the bench.

"I have something for you, Ata."

The old man, who was now chewing on a piece of beef jerky, looked at him. Fred unwrapped a sandwich. A monster, it bulged with slivers of meat, mayonnaise, pickles, and cheese. Ata stopped and stared, his eyes flickering.

"It's for you."

Usually so restrained, Ata exuded a suppressed hunger, licking the sides of his mouth and twisting the jerky wrapper around in his fingers. Then, without warning, he reached for the sandwich and stuffed it into his mouth, taking a huge, toothless bite. Everything oozed out sideways, mayonnaise bubbled up, and pale-green juice dripped down his chin. Three bites later he stopped, pulled off a wedge, and handed it to Fred.

"No thanks, I've eaten."

Ata continued to hold out the bread, finally laying it on Fred's lap where drips of cold juice seeped into his jeans. He continued munching, his eyes glowing as he devoured the rest of his share. Fred picked up his half and nibbled the edges.

Then, struck by a thought, he split it in half and passed it back to Ata. The old man accepted, swallowing it down in one gulp. They had reached an understanding.

Suddenly, Ata said: "*Inunnguaq.*"

Fred leaned forward, straining to catch even the bones of a word.

"*Inunnguaq,*" he repeated.

Fred tried out the sound, coughing up the crowded consonants. Then, the word had meaning. Ata was describing the landscape of his childhood: the place with no trees. Not one. In a vast, monochromatic world, eyes were shielded from burning light by antler goggles carved with slits. Losing yourself was easy, and getting lost meant death. But they had a clever system. They had the *Inunnguaq:* piles of stones that marked location. Not just any stones, but specially chosen ones placed in specially chosen places, stacked up in the shape of a man. He was the man who showed the way, standing up on stone toes and poking his head out over the drifts. Fred could relate to Ata's problems with orientation. Half the time he could not spot the end of his own street. He had lost count of the number of times they had driven by it, his father cursing, reversing with a screech of the tires, then sometimes missing it again on the way back. Twilight posed the biggest challenge. In the faltering light, their home became almost unrecognizable, melting with the others into a continuous facade, the colour of weak tea. Their only marker was the mound of twigs that he had fashioned into a crude pyramid in the front garden. Occasionally picked up in the car headlights, it now lay buried beneath snow, the shape collapsed underneath weightless snowflakes.

There was no halting the flow of memories once they had begun. Ata spoke of his grandparents and, somewhere within the muddled marriage of two languages, Fred grasped their importance. A coffee cup hitting a saucer on a nearby table drowned out their names, and the old man's finger-licking spliced more pauses into the story, but through all the disturbance, Fred managed to form an impression of people that were treasured. Not only were they the keepers of family history, but the elders also framed a story tracing back over countless generations. Thousands of small incidents were filed in their memories, and during a lifetime of shared cups of tea and hugs in caribou skin beds, they passed them on to their children — small morsels of knowledge building up to create a template for survival. They had both died a long time ago, and Ata lived alone in the city. Fred strained to hear the old man's final words but caught only the closing sentences, clogged by a mixture of tears and rusty Inuit vowels, ending the story in a graceless silence. Fred felt miserable.

But just as Fred started to think about his own grandparents, Ata sat upright, staring into space. Then he stood up and ferreted about in his cart, unearthing new items. Reaching right down to the bottom, his armpit pressing onto the rim, he pulled out a flat, lozenge-shaped parcel secured with string. Fred had never noticed it before.

"For you. A present. For you."

Fred took the parcel and laid it on his lap, surprised at its lightness. He sniffed it; it smelled old and faintly fishy. He squeezed it, sliding a thumb beneath a knot.

"Thank you, Ata, I'll take a look at it when I get home."

He knew better than to open it there. His companion's generosity had already spawned a large bag of collectibles that were stashed beneath his bed. One-inch pencils, stinking goose feathers, and plastic pillboxes posed a constant threat to his reputation as a normal boy and would have without a doubt alarmed his parents should they ever feel the need to run a vacuum cleaner beneath his bed. Ata stared at him. Fred sensed something was different today. Something was bothering his companion.

"Ata, are you all right?"

The old man hesitated then turned, raising his eyebrows. He leaned forward, patting the parcel on Fred's lap. As Fred looked down at Ata's wrinkled knuckles, the lights in the mall snapped off.

He sighed. "Not again."

Darkness turned up the sound. Parents felt for children, coffee-sipping shoppers groped for bags, and the sound of anxiety, disguised as laughter, filled the mall. He turned to Ata. "S'pose we'd better try to find the way out."

But no reply came. Fred peered towards his companion and laid his hand on the bench, rubbing his fingers over the warm plastic.

"Are you there, Ata?"

He stood up. "Ata, where are you?"

Ata was gone.

He would catch him tomorrow.

CHAPTER

19

Poppy was bored. The lineup looked even longer today, winding through the forecourt in the ragged shape of an S. She had been marooned for ten minutes, and with the engine switched off, the temperature inside the car was plummeting. They'd gone and bought a Jeep soon after they had arrived. A thirsty American beast, the sort she'd sworn never to drive. The driver's seat was on the wrong side and her first two days behind the wheel had been nothing short of a nightmare, scything close to parked cars and drifting to the other side of the road at junctions, her hand groping the air after a lifetime of gear sticks. She pulled her blanket around her shoulders and buried her face deep into the folds, trying to seal a bubble of warmth around her mouth. She gazed at the gas gauge. The arrow said empty.

A police car appeared, smugly bypassing the lineup before coming to a halt at the door of the pay booth. Discernible sparks of interest rippled down the line of cars. She watched as two doors flung open up ahead and red-seamed legs poked out. Buried inside their matching parkas, two policemen emerged, gripping their clipboards with fat gloves. She imagined guns inside their coats, clipped to the back of their belts. Funny how she felt nervous, guilty even, at the sight of the police. Charlie always teased her about that. The slightest whiff of authority, he said, and she would be overcome with groundless guilt, ready to rush out a confession or offer up her trunk for inspection.

Splitting up, the officers began working their way down the line of cars, bending forward to tap on each car window in turn. The news was clearly bad, bad enough to tempt the drivers out of their cars. A throng of people gathered in the officers' wake, their shoulders bobbing with cold. Fearing she had become part of some terrifying mass arrest, Poppy searched for her cellphone, only to be interrupted by a face at the window, followed by a sharp tap. She switched on the engine and pressed the open switch; a mixture of cold and complaining voices rushed in.

"Excuse me, ma'am. The gas station is closing now."

"But I don't have any petrol yet," she said, a little girl's voice coming out of her mouth. "How will I get home?"

"I'm sorry, ma'am. The gas station is closing. The whole city is having problems with its supply." Then, turning to a man tugging at his sleeve, "Just *wait* a moment, sir." Lowering his head until the window framed it again, he continued to Poppy, "There'll be announcements in the media. Thank you for your cooperation."

With a brief touch of his hat, he left, ignoring the trail of frustrated drivers striding through the snow in a line after him, placing their boots in his every footprint. She stared at the gas gauge. How long had it been like that? She couldn't remember.

Leaving the gas station was a slow process. Just one abandoned car was enough to thwart the mass departure and only by driving dangerously high over a snowbank did she manage to get back onto the road. Even here her fellow drivers seemed jittery, forgetting to signal, breaking at random, and it was not until she had sat in a jam for five minutes that she realized the traffic lights were out. The arms of a volunteer traffic controller flapped up ahead. She gave him a grateful wave as she glided slowly by only to be halted at the next block by another jam, another blank traffic light. Waiting her turn, she pondered her predicament, mesmerized by the windshield wiper of the car in front of her, sloughing snow off the freezing glass.

What used less gas? She tried to recall. Should she cruise at a constant speed? Should she drive fast, or should she drive slow? Should she try to find another gas station, or should she go straight home? They were all practical questions, all demanding her attention, all needing answers, and all helping her ignore the most important question that plagued her.

How would they cope without gas?

CHAPTER
20

Fred wore his coat under the duvet, too cold to recall, let alone heed, his own convoluted advice on clothes, insulation, and bedding. Dubious of his chances of ever reaching a comfortable temperature again, he concentrated on forgetting the tortuous journey home from the mall that had led him to understand his grandmother's favourite expression, "chilled to the bones," for the first time in his life. At least the electricity had returned. He heard the study door close and, braving the world above the covers, leaned down sideways and pulled the parcel out from under his bed.

It was larger than most of Ata's gifts, and the knots encasing the package lacked the elegance of those seen on the shopping cart. The wrapping paper was brown and woolly, collapsing into pieces as he worked at the knots. Inside he found a strange piece of cloth. Small at first, it unfolded and unfolded, until five or six feet of fabric were spread onto his bed. He stared. It was a garment, of sorts. Two arms the colour of ancient rubber bands, a body, and a hood wide enough for several heads. He picked it up and held it towards the window, puzzling over the feel of it, so dry in the body yet damp at the seams. The skin on sausages came to mind. Grabbing a swatch of the material, he scrunched it up in his palm, dredging up boyhood memories of balloons, shaken from the bag, their bodies cruelly stretched. He made a fist, stretching the soft part of the cloth over his knuckles, increasing its transparency. Then he rubbed it over his face, beneath his chin, across his upper lip, down his cheek. He noticed the seams — the stitches were tiny and even, sewn with a slender twine, the colour of flesh. Gripped by a boyish curiosity, he stood up, shook it out, and put the coat over his head. It fit, floating down and clinging to his body like a brand-new skin.

Unconcerned by the surreality of the sight that might greet a visitor entering the room at that moment, he sat at his computer, still coat clad, and scrolled through the search engine: "Inuit clothing, coat, animal skin, waterproof, intestine, transparent, seal." The hunt narrowed to a handful of words: "gut, arctic, annoraaq." He knew then that Ata's wondrous gift to him was a traditional Inuit garment. A seal intestine raincoat.

Tomorrow, he would return it.

PART TWO

CHAPTER

21

Twenty-four hours later the lights went out again. Poppy had just reached a highpoint in her book, hanging by her nails onto a cliff of enthralling text, when the page turned yellow, illuminated only by the light from the fire.

"Hey, Fred. Do you know where the torch is?" she yelled from her chair. "Did we put it back after last time?"

Footsteps sounded on the stairs, toes felt for treads.

"I'll look."

Cutlery rattled in the kitchen drawer. "Got it."

A beam of light danced into the room before landing on the sofa. "Scary storytime again, I suppose," Fred said, sitting down, grinning.

Seeds of a tradition had been sown during the last two blackouts, and without further discussion, they took their seats by the fire, searching their minds for fresh ghost stories. She could never retain anyone's interest for long but Charlie was superb at it, scaring even Fred, and it would be a relief when the lights came on before the punchline. As the fire spat and an invisible hand dislodged the embers, she looked at her son. He appeared older in the firelight. It flickered, drawing reedy eyelash shadows across his face and sculpting gauntness into well-nourished cheeks. Fire dots reflected in each eye. She felt relieved he was with her.

"Fred, you've got that old battery radio in your room. Let's check it for news."

"Good idea," he said, jumping up.

Returning to his chair a minute later, he twisted the dial until a serious voice barged into the room.

"...has been hit by a power blackout. I repeat, a large area of the Prairies has been hit by a blackout, extending from western Saskatchewan across Manitoba as far as Thunder Bay, down to the Dakotas and across the entire Minnesota region. The government are advising people not to leave their homes unless it is absolutely necessary. Gale force winds and blizzard conditions have ..."

"Bloody hell!"

"Fred!"

"Sorry, but that sounds bad. And big."

"You're right, it's a huge area."

"Yeah. And part of the States."

They looked at each other.

"Fred, have we got much wood outside?"

"What, to help us survive the night?" He was sarcastic these days.

"It might be good to know ..."

"I'll check," he said, jumping up, the flashlight skimming the walls with renewed enthusiasm.

Adopting the pose of someone about to get up and help, she was relieved to see him reappear quickly, his ears edged with red. He clutched a pile of logs pressed into his stomach. The wood looked damp.

"It's all right, there must be more than a hundred logs out there. We're not going to need that many."

"Phew. I can't believe we're so organized," she replied, settling back into her chair. "Mind you, I wish I had bought those candles at the shop."

"I've got some in my room."

"You do? What are they doing up there?"

"Oh, nothing. I'll get them."

He thumped up the stairs, returning moments later with two half-burned candles.

"So that's where the matches went."

"Yeah, let's light one up."

The smell of sulphur irritated her nose as he struck the match. Wax dripped as he began melting the bottom of the candle.

"Ouch, mind my feet."

"Sorry."

She leaned forward and scraped the wax off her felt slippers, folding back a warm tongue of it into a ball and dropping it back into the flame.

"You okay, Mum?"

"I wish your father were here," she said.

"Don't worry. It won't last long. It never does."

"But the petrol shortage, Fred. The station had run right out. *We've* run right out."

"They'll get some more, won't they?" He touched her shoulder. "They always do."

~

Fred stoked up the fire, trying to tease it back to life with balls of scrunched paper. Poppy could see steam escaping from the curls of birch bark, confirming her suspicions of dampness. A brochure at the top of the paper pile caught Fred's attention just as he was about to throw it in. He stopped scrunching and studied the photograph of an asymmetrical building dominated by double garage doors and a roof piled with snow.

"Hey, Mum. This is our house!"

She came towards him and looked over his shoulder, reading on the slant.

"They've got to be joking," he said. "Living room, thirty feet by twenty-five feet."

They both looked around the gloomy space, trying to guess its dimensions. Taking the brochure from him, she read the details aloud.

"'Brand-new, three-bedroom, two-storey home. Two thousand square feet, asphalt shingle roof, designer kitchen, double-glazing, landscaped, double garage, wood-burning stove. Ready for immediate occupation.'"

"Yeah, right."

"It *was* ready," she said. "They just failed to mention the neighbourhood wasn't quite finished."

"Not quite started, you mean."

"Shh! Let me finish. 'New subdivision, quiet neighbourhood, much sought-after location, closet organizers ...'"

"Closet organizers? Do we have those? What are they anyway?"

"They're those things in the wardrobe in my bedroom. I think."

"And where's the landscaping? Is it those two sticks out the front?"

She hesitated. "It's buried under the snow, isn't it? Just needs a bit of time."

"Why did we buy this house, Mum? It's so ... boring."

"Come on, Fred. Think of all the space we've got now. You couldn't swing a cat round your old bedroom. Isn't it lovely having new floors, a brand-new bathroom, new everything? And I bet you never dreamed we'd have one of those things in the kitchen sink that eats rubbish, did you?"

"No, Mum, I didn't."

⌒

Poppy was biting her nails, wondering why the electricity was taking so long to come back on, when someone thumped on the front door. She was instantly alarmed. Visitors were a rare species in the subdivision, and they usually turned out to be a sales representative shoving a well-polished shoe in the door, or the postman pressing an electronic notepad into her hands, making her sign her name with an electronic pencil. No one ever called at night.

Together they crept towards the door and peered through the glass at the top. Several heads at different heights were visible. A seasonal reflex took hold, her mind irrationally believing them to be carol singers. But this group was not singing — they were thumping, hard.

"Fred, should we open the door? We don't know who's out there."

"Mum, it's freezing. We've got to see who it is at least."

"I'm not sure if Dad ..."

Without waiting for her to finish, he clicked the latch and heaved the door open, cracking the freshly formed ice seal that lined the frame. An abrupt drop in temperature accompanied a group of strangers into their hall. They pushed forward as the last person slammed the door behind him.

"Thank God!" came a voice from the back.

Six people stood on their doormat — no preamble, no introductions, no small talk. Poppy could feel cold air coming off their bodies as they moved, little rocking motions passing back and forth through the group, shifting them from side to side, up and down. For a second no one spoke, then a large man at the front interrupted the silence. "Do you have a way to heat this place?" His voice was louder than she expected.

An apology came from somewhere behind him — another man, slightly shorter.

"We're sorry to show up like this. We had a collision; both cars are in the ditch. It's a slippery corner out there. The kids are frozen."

Pieces of children were just visible behind the large man — half a head here, a sliver of leg there.

"Come in and warm up by the fire," Fred said without hesitation.

The word *fire* perked them up, and after struggling out of their boots, ripping at Velcro and flipping biscuits of ice onto the mat, they hobbled after him on numb heels, displaying all the eagerness of abandoned chicks.

"Careful, Buster," the female stranger reprimanded the smallest boy, who had darted up to the stove and was holding his hands too close.

They refused to take off their coats but agreed to sit as Fred made a half circle of chairs around the fire. The shorter man began to talk.

"I won't shake hands, too cold, but my name's Dwayne Kress, this is my wife Rennie, and these are our children, Ryan," pointing at a boy sitting next to Fred, "Marcie, our daughter, and Buster. Or Brian," he added behind a cupped hand. "We're sorry to turn up like this but as I said, our car got tangled up with Mr. Grabowski's truck." He glanced at the other man. "You won't believe how slippery it is out there." He looked at the man again. "Oh, this is Mr. Grabowski."

Mr. Grabowski was not listening. He had closed his eyes and was resting his head on the back of the chair. Poppy watched, mesmerized, as he rubbed his fingers, cracking each joint in turn. The chair he had commandeered looked too tight for him, and she felt an unreasonable fear coming over her. Would he ever get out of it? He looked about fifty years old, but it was hard to tell. Not much older than she was. She glanced down at the back of her hands, then at the stranger's fingers that were still cracking, noting telltale signs of self-neglect: loose-thread buttons threatening to detach and serrated lips in urgent need of moisture.

"Any chance of a drink, ma'am?" said Mr. Grabowski, opening his eyes.

"I'll get it," replied her son.

As Fred stood up, she could see the children's eyes follow his back into the darkness. None of them had spoken yet. They sat upright in their chairs, unwilling participants in an untried situation: strange people, strange house, strange dark. The boy, Ryan, looked younger than Fred, and was still very much a boy. Wide shoulders had not yet arrived, and his head was small and round with tight black curls on top that looked as if they never needed trimming. As his gaze reached her he smiled, peeling back his lips to reveal a vast expanse of pink gum. The girl was more striking, her back exhibiting a notable straightness usually absent in the spines of sofa-loving teenagers. Seemingly oblivious to the beauty of her posture, she had devoted her efforts to her eyes, which were outlined in thick black eyeliner, ineptly applied. But what must make casual passersby throw her a second glance was her hair. The colour of an over-ripe tomato, it seemed to crush the exuberance out of surrounding tones and glowed in the light from the fire. The little boy, Buster, sat on his sister's lap, almost asleep from the heat of the stove. He still retained the white blondeness of babyhood, but with an arm covering the side of his head, he was keeping his face to himself.

"Do you mind if we take our coats off now?" It was the wife, Rennie, speaking.

"Oh, of course, sorry."

Poppy stood up, feeling embarrassed at the quality of her hostessing skills. The general confusion that ensued did nothing to contradict this self-criticism as coats, gloves, scarves, fleeces, and down vests piled up on the coffee table before she had time to remember if they had any coat hangers.

"Who would like some juice?" Fred had returned, balancing eight glasses on a tray.

"Got anything a bit stronger?" enquired Grabowski, winking at Poppy.

"Oh ... I'll get something else," replied her son.

Fred disappeared, returning a moment later with a bottle of scotch. He began to pour a shot into a glass with the enthusiasm of a trainee innkeeper. Poppy was just beginning to wonder how he knew where the alcohol was kept when Rennie spoke.

"We couldn't see a thing out there. The wipers were jamming up and then we were in the ditch, then we got cold, and then we got so cold we couldn't stand it. Dwayne saw the smoke from the chimney and said we should leave the car and then I said we shouldn't and ..."

The length of the narrative allowed Poppy time to inspect the narrator. Rennie reminded her of an old physics teacher — the same neat haircut, fresh with highlights, and an identical nose, thin, with nostrils sucked inward. During the breathless and eternal sentences, she regarded her guest's clothes. Flight attendant couture came to mind, and it was obvious a great deal of time had been spent laundering, ironing, and mobilizing to create an enviable, colour-coordinated assembly. Cream shirt and cardigan above complemented purple velvet trousers below. Magenta gloves represented a daring diversion from the colour scheme only to be brought back into line by an elegant cream trim. As the woman ploughed on with her description of snow up to the dashboard, she pulled out a perfectly pressed handkerchief from her pocket, the iron lines still visible, and attempted to repair her makeup, dabbing at invisible imperfections on her cheeks.

During the speech that would not end, Rennie's husband inadvertently diverted the attention of his wife's audience by searching for something in the folds of his clothes. The listless audience freshened visibly at the sight of him as he patted his hips and crammed fingers that were too large into his narrow suit pocket. His wife was several sentences further down the line when he beamed with triumph and pulled out a set of business cards, opening them out into a perfect fan shape and offering them to Poppy with a showman-like flourish.

"Please take one."

"Oh, Dwayne! Not now," said his wife, interrupting herself.

Looking hurt, he folded up the fan just as Poppy picked one out of the centre. He instinctively tightened his grip but she gave a strong tug, sending the cards flying onto the floor. While he poked his head under the sofa looking for strays, Poppy studied the card she had captured.

"So, you sell golf carts?"

She attempted what she thought was a sophisticated double-edged tone, hoping it was within the boundaries of politeness yet signalling there was no need for a reply. But the rhetorical nature of the question was lost on Dwayne, who launched into a detailed account of the "Green Baby Kress," which apparently featured a lightweight chassis and detachable roof system that had to be seen to be believed. Poppy listened, concentrating all her attention on Dwayne's upper lip, which had that fresh pink quality of a recently shaved moustache.

"Dwayne. They don't need know all that."

"I'm just letting them know who we are."

"They know who we are. I just told them."

He did not reply but sat back, flashing her a cheerful smile, identical in shape, she noticed, to the one on Ryan's face.

"So, Mr. Grabowski," Poppy said, turning to face the man sitting in her best chair, "where do you live?"

"St. Norbert's."

"Oh, and what do you do?"

"Do?"

"What do you do for a living?"

He hesitated. "Sort stuff out."

"Oh."

"What sort of stuff?" asked Dwayne.

"You know, old stuff."

"Oh, you mean second-hand goods?" Poppy asked.

"Yeah. Look, I'm a bit tired, I'm gonna grab a snooze."

"Of course, be my guest."

Poppy looked out of the window, then at her watch, then at her son. "I was wondering if you'd all like to stay the night?"

Fred glanced at her.

"It's very late and without a car there is no way to get around."

"Are you sure?" asked Dwayne.

"Absolutely, we have enough beds. I'm sure everything will be back to normal in the morning."

CHAPTER
22

Three people slept in his bed that night. Ryan couldn't stop giggling as they bumped the mattresses down the stairs, trapping themselves against the wall on the turn and repeatedly throwing off the youngest Kress, who had quickly discovered the joys of bed surfing. As their living room evolved into a dormitory, heaps of clothes appeared at the end of each mattress, thrown on top of unmatched bedding dragged from cold cupboards and smelling of laundry detergent. Coats were folded for pillows and small piles of clothing at the end of each bed marked embryonic patches of territory. Nothing involving electricity worked. No television, no lights, no phone, no internet access, no heating. The toilet refused to flush and the fridge had ceased its endless humming. Fred pointed his flashlight towards the calendar fixed to the door with magnets. He could just read the date on the sloping page: Thursday, December

7. "Pearl Harbour Remembrance Day (US)" was written in red beneath the seven — eighteen days until Christmas. A pencilled note marked the next day: "Get car serviced."

He returned to the living room to a barrage of complaints for taking the only flashlight.

"Which way up will I sleep?" asked Buster.

"Whatever way you like," Fred replied, patting down the corners of his pillow.

"I like your house," said the little boy, lying back and slapping his arms down on the outside of the duvet.

"It's bigger than ours," Ryan said, "but we've got a pool." He grinned.

"In your house?" asked Fred.

"No, in the yard."

"You have an outdoor pool in this climate?"

Ryan grinned again. "When did you guys get here?"

"Um ... middle of November. Why?"

"It's boiling here in summer. Over thirty most days."

"What? You mean centigrade?"

"Er ... yeah. I think."

⌒

Fred knew he was in for a long night. Knees knocked thighs, shoulders chafed, and he fought to hold onto a corner of duvet. He lay back on his pillow and thought about Ata plunging his hand down through the ice into the freezing sea, dragging out snared fish. Icy toes brushing against the back of his heels interrupted his thoughts. He pulled up an elbow, rested his ear on his palm, and looked around the room.

The next mattress held Marcie and Rennie, and beyond them lay his mother, alone. Dwayne winked at him from the sofa, settling in for a long night of fire tending. Beside Dwayne sat Mr. Grabowski, resplendent up on the armchair, whistling through his nose and smelling of whiskey fumes.

As the group dozed off, Fred looked at Marcie; her hair was spread over her face. It must itch, he thought, suppressing an urge to blow a handful of hairs off her forehead. She resembled a sleeping dog, flat on her stomach and pressing maximum body area onto the sheet. Unlike Ryan, whose knees were twitching against his elbow with a randomness that broke all chance of sleep. He continued to look at her. She turned over and he could see her face. He was not sure if it was the light or the act of sleep, but she looked about six years old, not the sixteen that she had told them. She was wearing earrings, four altogether, funny homemade ones made of papier-mâché. "Saw it on TV," he had heard her tell his mother, "but I didn't use enough glue."

He was not sure how he felt about sleeping so closely to strangers. Their breathing changed the atmosphere of the room; Ryan's chest moved up and down in a regular rhythm, Marcie breathed fast, Buster sniffed a lot.

He wondered: how long would they stay?

CHAPTER
23

The rumbling of a stranger's stomach can break the deepest sleep. Mr. Grabowski had a loud, grumpy belly, and Fred gave up trying to regain his lost dream after a chorus of noises fizzed across the slumbering guests for the umpteenth time. The man trod on Fred's hair as he strode not so nimbly across the sea of mattresses, heading for the kitchen. By the time Fred joined him he had poured cereal into a large mixing bowl and was drinking milk straight from the carton.

"Is that the last of the milk?" asked Fred.

"Oh, yeah ... oops."

Putting down the carton, Grabowski held the cornflakes in place with the back of a spoon and tipped yellow milk back through the spout. "There you go," he said, a cracked tooth peeping through his lips. The early morning forager proceeded to scoff his food and was wiping the last drip of milk off his chin when Dwayne and Rennie padded into the kitchen. Puffy-eyed and sniffing, Buster trailed in behind them. "I'm cold," said the little boy, pressing his toes into his father's pockets as he lifted him up.

"Let's get a hot drink and ... oh." Dwayne trailed off.

"I'll just make some toast and ... hell, what *can* we do?" said Fred.

"Get breakfast for a start," said Rennie, running a well-manicured hand over the pile of bowls in the top left cupboard. "Then we can work out what else needs doing."

"Going out to see what's happening. That's what needs doing," replied her husband.

"In this weather, don't be ridiculous, Dwayne."

"We can't just hang around here all morning."

"Why not?"

"I have an appointment at eleven for starters. I'm under the gun at work."

"Dwayne, no one's going to be there. Look outside."

Fred followed Rennie's gaze and was startled by the size of the snowflakes colliding with the window. Big as babies' thumbnails, they were tearing downwards in three-dimensional sheets, closing down the view of the street.

"It'll ease off soon, Rennie. Look, I can see a patch of blue coming up over there."

"Oh, Dwayne."

⌒

No one likes to listen to an argument between married couples. But the only alternative was to loiter in the chilly kitchen, so they stuck it out. Pimples on the backs of hands were suddenly fascinating, a crevice down the side of the sofa required urgent cleaning, and as Fred discovered, clearing the glasses from the coffee table offered up the dual benefits of both noise and activity.

While trying not to, he listened, absorbing the gist of it. Dwayne wanted to go out to find out what was happening; his wife was not having any of it. Warnings were mashed as they sparred, surfacing into politeness when they remembered their reluctant audience, then submerging again beneath the rising levels of acrimony. Fred sensed a subtext emerging. Rennie was ostensibly the one in charge, but Dwayne was dogged and, with quiet replies disguised as compliance, ended up getting his way without his wife even realizing it.

Snow still raced out of the sky when Dwayne started the layering ritual, dressing himself for work in a show of normality. Watching from the end of his bed, Fred observed a salesman persona being reassembled — creases smacked out of a suit jacket, a tie knotted, hair slicked down using implements from a handy emergency grooming set. Dwayne seemed uncannily proud of this unlikely possession, a "freebie from a trade show," making efforts to use every obscure piece during his long session of waterless ablutions. Obviously forgetting the scarcity of potential Baby Kress customers in a city struck down by a blackout, he tidied his brief case, composed a cheery face, and settled himself into a ready-to-help posture, in the way that he had probably done every morning for the last twenty years. At last, with his turtleneck pulled snugly down, he was ready.

"Where did you get *those* things?" demanded Rennie, pointing at the ski goggles on her husband's face.

He lifted the goggles and tapped the side of his nose. Rennie tutted, then followed him to the front door. Fred was dimly aware of Grabowski hovering in the background as he trailed behind them. The door seemed stiffer than usual, and slivers of waiting snow collapsed into dust as it popped open.

"Dwayne, you'll come right back, won't you?" said Rennie.

"When I find out what's happening I will."

"And Dwayne, don't forget we have to get a tow truck out for the car."

"I won't."

"Hurry up and shut the door, you're letting all the heat out."

He scuttled out, turning back to face them at the last minute. "Maybe unplug the TV and stuff, you know, just in case."

"Why do we...?" said Fred.

"And drain down the system."

"Wha ...?"

"The pipes, drain the pi —" The wind caught Dwayne's words and threw them up into the air, whipping out the sound. Then his back disappeared inside a small vortex of snow. Fred raised his hands to his face, cupping out a megaphone. "See you later!"

But Dwayne did not hear him; the snow was too thick.

CHAPTER
24

"Get your ass off my chair!"

One sentence, loaded with contempt, entered the circle around the stove and their newly born world, still damp from its birth, changed.

"Sorry," said Ryan, jumping up and scurrying towards the sofa.

"Now get me a drink. And no fucking baby juice this time."

Grabowski was looking straight at Poppy. It was not a joke. Too much time had passed for it to be a joke.

"I don't understand," she said.

"What don't you understand? I want a drink. Now."

"But ..."

"Mum, I'll do it."

Her son was hardly out of the room before he was back, bottle in hand. He tipped a generous portion into a glass and handed it to Grabowski before sitting beside her, his shoulder touching hers.

No one spoke as the new and unfamiliar person who had entered their group slurped and belched his way through half a bottle of whiskey. Voices collapsed into whispers, noses sniffed the alcohol fumes drifting around the furniture, and their circle lost its integrity as they edged away from the soused body sitting amongst them. In a final act of encroachment, he rammed his feet into Poppy's slippers, lifted them onto the coffee table, and fell asleep.

CHAPTER
25

Fred felt an unrefined fear as he watched Grabowski across the room. Was he an alcoholic? Was he dangerous? Or was he just an obnoxious bloke they could ignore? He studied his sleeping lips, crusted with remnants of the last meal, looking for signs of malice. Just as he was inching closer to examine his eyes, a lid flipped open.

"What are you looking at?"

Fred jumped back in his chair. "Nothing, sorry."

"Get out of my face. And bring me a drink."

"Yes, what would you like? Whiskey or...?"

"Look, kid, as long as it has a kick to it, I want it."

"Right."

He hurried into the kitchen and was reaching into the back of the bottom cupboard when he felt warm breath on the side of his face.

"Fred, what's happening?"

He turned to see his mother kneeling down beside him; strands of hair hung across her face.

"I don't know, Mum, he just ... changed."

"What shall we do?"

He paused. "Keep him happy, I suppose."

"How?"

"This?"

As he held the bottle of whiskey towards her, he glimpsed feet coming into the kitchen — four pairs wearing thick socks.

"What's happened to that man?" whispered Rennie from the doorway. Marcie stood behind, her arm around Buster. Ryan's head was just visible.

Before Fred could reply, they surged forward and he felt a prick of claustrophobia as they surrounded him, pressing him into a corner of the kitchen with a barrage of whispered questions. Why is he...? Should we...? What if he...? He tried to think, distracted by the ice-cold fingers touching his wrist, and just as the soufflé of anxiety was reaching a pitch, a figure appeared at the door. The room fell silent.

"Where's my liquor?"

⌒

The rapid metamorphosis of an adult was a new experience for Fred. He was trying to recall what Grabowski had been like when he first entered the house when another change occurred, just as abrupt in its arrival.

They were eating breakfast on their beds later the same day. Dry cereal with no tea. Rennie had organized it, rummaging through the cupboards with all the energy of a fired-up furnace, sharing out the cornflakes, insisting on napkins on laps. But just as she tucked herself beneath a blanket, ready to eat her first spoonful, she sagged visibly and covered her face with her hands.

"Mom, are you feeling all right?" Marcie laid a hand on her arm.

Her mother dropped her spoon into her bowl and gazed out of the window.

"Mom?"

Rennie looked at her daughter, murmured something in her ear, then stared out again.

"She's worried about my dad," announced Marcie, as if translating for a three year old.

"He'll be back soon," said Poppy, touching the woman's shoulder.

But Rennie drooped further and did not reply. A moment later Buster muscled in, widening the gap between the two women with a well-judged wiggle of his hips before settling a hand on each of their knees.

Fred observed from a distance. "Shall I get something?" he asked, unable to imagine what the something might possibly be.

"It's all right," said Marcie. "She just needs a moment."

He looked at his own mother. He could tell she was cold. She had been cold since the lights went out and she was missing his father. He could see that.

"Don't worry, Mum," he said. "Dwayne will be back soon." She nodded.

Fred felt tired. The atmosphere was bearing down on him more than the cold. He distracted himself with a stupid thought. All their hopes of finding out what was going on had settled on a thin man equipped with nothing but an emergency grooming kit. A small laugh slid out of his nostrils — but it was not funny.

CHAPTER

26

"Take a pee in the garden in this cold? You've got to be joking."

"But, Fred. It's a tradition." Ryan's gums were stretched to their limit.

"I'm not exposing my bum to that wind."

"Fred, the loo's blocked, we all have to do it," said Poppy.

Poppy leaned against the kitchen top, working out the logistics. Coping with five guests, a blocked toilet, and arctic temperatures right outside the back door required some planning. They'd turned off all the lights, unplugged their appliances, and after struggling to locate the tap, had even managed to "drain down the system" as best they could. But the bathroom already smelled like a kindergarten cloakroom at the end of recess and something had to be done.

"*And* you have to write your name in the snow."

"Shut up, Ryan," said Marcie.

"Mr. Grabowski will be gone some time," said Ryan, eyes smiling.

"Ryan, shut up."

"I can't spell my name," said Buster, tears welling up in his eyes.

"Okay, let's just use a bucket and throw ... everything out in the garden," said Poppy.

"Can I have my own bucket?" Fred said, belligerent.

"What?"

"My own bucket."

"Oh, Fred. We only have a couple but maybe we could use something else."

rosie chard   95
SEAL
INTESTINE
RAINCOAT

"Cereal bowls?"

"Ryan, that's gross," said Marcie.

"Actually, it's not a bad idea," Poppy replied. "Let's choose. Buster, you can have the yellow one."

The boy stretched his hands up onto the kitchen top and pulled down a bowl flecked with pebbles of old cereal. He smiled up at her.

"So," said Fred, rubbing his hands together. "Who's volunteering to explain the new system to Grabowski?"

Grabowski. The name sunk lead into Poppy's chest. Somehow she had managed to forget, for a moment, the man lying comatose in the living room. Even while unconscious he exerted a powerful hold over them. The tiniest movement from the direction of his chair was enough to send a ripple of anxiety through the circle, and she was experiencing the beginnings of a minor obsession, staring at folds in his bedding, looking for signs of a knife. Or a gun.

Suddenly tired, she gazed at the floor. Only the sound of dried cornflakes being picked at with a thumbnail broke the silence of the chilly kitchen.

CHAPTER
27

Little boys are fussy eaters. Fred remembered that as he entered the kitchen later that day. Inspired by the big man in slippers, Buster searched the fridge, groping the greyness and sniffing at remnants that had been rejected by Grabowski. He was hard at it, passing over perfectly good lemon halves and chucking dried knobs of parmesan into the bin.

"This juice is smelly," he said, turning towards Fred.

"Oh, come on, Buster, we gave you the last of it," said Ryan, entering the kitchen.

"It's got chunks."

If he were honest with himself, Fred would agree the last bottle of orange juice did look thicker than usual, but he was past caring about expiry dates. He had been so busy watching Grabowski wolf down most of the food that he had forgotten about drink, and by the time he checked the cupboard most of the bottled water had gone, too.

"We can melt some," said Ryan, swaying from side to side on his toes in an exaggerated way.

"What, you mean, drink snow?" Fred asked.

"Yeah, grab a load from the yard and heat it on the fire."

"Fred." A small hand tugged the back of his fleece. "Fred. Fred."

"Okay, Buster, you can come, too."

"Come where?" said Marcie, coming into the kitchen.

"The gar ... yard," said Fred.

"Oh, yes, we can get away from that smell," she replied under her breath.

They wrenched open the front door; it took two to open it.

"Holy moly. Let's do this quickly," said Ryan, jumping up and down.

Fred closed the door behind him, chasing the others into the yard, laughing as their layers cramped their ability to run. Snow was coming down in sticky chunks and the quinzhee was completely buried, a sad lump in the corner.

"Let's have your glasses," Fred said, snatching the goggles off Ryan.

"Hey, give me those."

Forgetting the cold, they wrestled, rolling over on the ground, oblivious to the snow working its way beneath the collars of their fleeces.

"Ryan, Mom will kill you if Buster gets too cold," said Marcie. "We're supposed to be getting snow in the bowls, not in our pants."

Ignoring her, they rolled some more, crashing into Buster before tripping up Marcie in an unexpected about turn. They laughed until they coughed.

"Hey, you guys," said Fred. Now *that* sounded Canadian, didn't it? "Where's my bowl?"

Remembering the reason they were outside, Fred grabbed the shovel, prizing it off the top of the snow cave, and began digging up snow, patting it down into his bowl with his hand.

"Aaaah," he cried, as Ryan slid a fistful of snow down the back of his neck. "Let's go in, it's too cold."

"But we've hardly started," Ryan said.

"Come on, you guys," said Marcie. "Buster's getting hyper. I'm going in."

They followed her inside, basking in the heat of the icy hall. There they waited for the pain. They knew it was coming. Even newcomers to an extreme climate knew the only way back to normal fingers from frozen ones was through that wall of pain — in one end and out the other.

The two mothers were sitting side by side on the sofa when they entered the living room, one talking, the other not listening. Rennie's stare was fixed, slightly madly, on a cup beside her knee. For some reason Fred noticed their clothes. Rennie's were as neat as the day she arrived, but his own mother's appearance was more dishevelled than usual. Switching his glance from Rennie to her, he realized she had never been too bothered by her appearance. Her thick hair always needed combing, her ponytail lost its grip throughout the day, and she forgot what she was wearing.

His gaze wandered back towards his new companions,

who had rushed onto the sofa, fighting to squeeze each other out. They were all focusing on him, Marcie doing a silly wave, Buster holding up a picked-off scab for him to inspect, and Ryan pointing out the tide mark on his wet jeans. That moment left him with a new feeling. Maybe not new, just forgotten. For strangers, he knew a lot about them — he knew Ryan's legs juddered when he lay in bed at night, he knew Buster wore socks with polar bears on them, and he knew Marcie brushed her hair exactly one hundred times every morning. They had a bit of a history together, didn't they? But would they be friends in real life?

He did not know.

CHAPTER
28

"Are you feeling all right?" Poppy looked at the carpet, wondering how long she should wait before speaking again. "Rennie?"

"Yes."

"Are you feeling okay?"

"No." Her voice continued in a whisper. "Where is Dwayne?"

"Don't worry, Rennie," said Poppy. "He'll be back soon. Look out there, the snow is already easing off a bit. What could possibly happen?"

A wet sheen appeared on Rennie's eyes.

"He'll be back soon. Rennie, he will."

Rennie stared at the floor. Poppy watched in silence as the woman beside her pressed a crude pleat into her trousers, just above the knee.

Something profound was happening to the woman sitting beside her, but Poppy could not tell what it was. Did her sad guest always cease to function without her husband? She thought of Charlie. Four thousand miles lay between them. Would she stop functioning, too? But she was lucky; she knew where her husband was. She had the precise location. He would be sitting in a chair at his father's house. By the phone. He would have a list of phone numbers on a pad on his lap. A cup of tea on the side table. But poor Dwayne. He was out there somewhere, coordinates unknown.

As she touched Rennie's shoulder, Buster joined them, arriving with a great deal of commotion, forcing his backside into the gap at the end of the sofa. He shoved his mother's hand off her knee. Rennie responded with a tepid hug, then returned to her pleating, adding a second ridge beside the first.

"Mom, I've got Fred's shoe on." He dangled an oversized shoe in front of her face. Rennie attempted a half-baked smile.

"Poppy, I've got Fred's shoe on," he said, turning towards her. She smiled. Then she felt a gentle tap on her shoulder followed by a murmured request to go to the kitchen.

"It's happened before, you know," said Marcie.

"What has?"

"This ..." She paused, frowning. "This thing with my mom, going all quiet and being weird."

"When?"

"Ryan had an accident. Years ago. Fell off the garage roof and broke his leg. Mom was all right about it at first, you know, called the ambulance, got a blanket. Then she went quiet, closed right down. She couldn't even tell the paramedics what had happened. Couldn't remember our phone number, couldn't even remember Ryan's middle name."

"What happened?"

"Nothing. Ryan had a huge plaster cast, we all wrote our names on it, and she came back."

"But where had she been?"

"I don't know."

CHAPTER

29

Fred stretched a sock over his knee. Pulling on the layers was tiresome, and tucking an extra T-shirt into his jeans only made things worse as his waistband dug into his stomach. By the time his coat was on he felt hot, irritable, and bloated, the feeling made worse by an itch that wasted no time creeping down his neck. He was in a jittery mood, too. The conversation half an hour earlier within the circle had invoked a trajectory of random emotions that died down as quickly as it had begun. All he could remember of the final moments was an image of Buster, biting his lip through salty tears. But it was decided. He would walk to the store.

The cold hit hard as he yanked open the door. Snowflakes tore in and he could only just make out the drifts of pristine snow that invited his first step. Using a gesture perfected during his childhood, he took a huge leap off the doorstep and sank into powder five feet from the house. Regaining his balance, he looked around. Fields of white had buried his suburban world. Everything looked different. The paths had vanished, the curb had gone, and the scale was confusing, all benchmarks obliterated. Much guesswork would be needed to identify the blobs and mounds that littered the street.

He began to walk, feeling annoyed by the snow weighing down his feet and finding its way over the top of his boots. Squinting towards Grandma Knuckles' window, he saw it was empty. He stopped, stood up on his toes, then, stretching his neck, tried to see a face in the window. Only his own reflection flickered back. He trudged around the side of the house and whacked on the front door with his fist. It shuddered inside its frame. No one answered. Finally, convinced that she was out of town, he strode back up the road.

It felt good to be outside. He enjoyed the squeak of the snow. As he trudged to the edge of the subdivision, towards the city proper, he thought he glimpsed an occasional figure on cross-country skis, skimming the horizon, but he met no one. He had a poor sense of the length of a mile and grew tired of lifting his feet higher than usual when he spotted a cluster of dots moving up ahead. Watering eyes hampered a clear picture but, walking closer, he realized it was people, lots of them, clustered around the entrance to the grocery store. A low-pitched hum drifted from the clumps of colour. The level of noise was comforting, but reassurance was short lived. It did not take much to realize that the normal suburban scene, cars in neat rows, shoppers rattling their carts out of the store, had been replaced by a disturbing tableau of high tension.

Several vehicles had docked near the entrance, parking at random. A small crowd surrounded a large truck, its rear panel folded down. The source of the noise was not immediately obvious, but as he walked closer he could see the doors of the store were open. Nothing unusual in that, but there was something in the way people were carrying their groceries that suggested things were not quite right. In spite of the deep snow, shopping carts were being taken off the premises, worked on by whole families, pushing, pulling, and cajoling the skidding wheels in unison. He sidled up to the entrance and, resisting the temptation to pick up a basket, slipped past a trio of men carrying jumbo-sized cereal boxes and went into the store.

People were slipping all around. Blown snow carpeted the entrance, melting into puddles by the pressure of hordes of hurrying feet. They slid without warning and he nearly tripped trying to avoid a falling man clutching a soggy pack of diapers.

"Do you want a hand?" said Fred, catching the man's elbow as he wavered on the brink of a second fall.

"Thanks, buddy."

"You okay?"

"Yeah, just wet."

Fred turned. And gasped. The store had been breached, its interior overrun by people rushing, shoving, climbing, crying. He could see them in the borrowed light at the front of the store; he could hear their racket from the shadows at the back. Natural courtesy had given way to something else.

He ducked as a box of beef burgers flew through the air. Then distraught voices jumped out of the crowd.

"Mavine, hold the bag up. Higher, higher!"

"Mom, where are you?"

"Holy shit."

"Higher."

"Mom, Mom!"

"Catch it!"

"Get bread. Bread!"

"Fucking insane."

"Grab those cookies. There. No, *there*."

"Aaron, don't!"

"Mom."

"Catch."

"I'm okay."

"Under there!"

"Catch."

"Shit."

"Watch out!"

"Get it!"

"Ouch!"

"Hold it, can't you?"

"Jesus."

"Catch."

A new species of customer had emerged. Everywhere, in the aisles, behind counters, wedged beneath displays. Supple-limbed teenagers scaled the high shelves, perching on the edges, sweeping armfuls of cans down into the mouths of waiting gym bags. Thick-waisted men straddled the freezer cabinets, heaving out great white frozen turkeys, oblivious to their uselessness in an ovenless world. An elderly couple grazed the periphery, picking over the debris: sugar granules spat from bags, abandoned onions, fish fingers cast adrift, and candy bars crushed out of all recognition. In the midst of the scrum, a young woman stood very still, the hem of her print skirt sucking up water from the damp floor like blotting paper. She was handing out apples to a row of children, their obedience tested to the limit as they were jogged and shoved by passersby.

Fred stopped for a second, thinking. To join or condemn. That little clip of time held him for only a moment before the fever took hold, and he grabbed what was closest — one cucumber, four cans of tomatoes, three bags of pasta, and a tube of garlic spread. Then he remembered Grabowski, the man now in charge of his house. He had to find a liquor store.

The tills sat silent as he slipped through the checkout. He glimpsed a question, "Whose cellulite?" and a small mound of coins spilling over the counter. Ignoring them, he left the building.

The liquor store was closed and shuttered. He walked towards it, disturbed by the ease with which he had become a thief and wanting nothing more than to climb into a warm bed and eat the cucumber he had stashed in his bag. A window was broken down near the pàvement; glass splinters marked the snow. He peered in, glimpsing neat rows of liquor. Pushing his hand through the hole, he touched a small bottle of vodka with his fingertips. It fell over, making an unexpected din.

He tried again, stretching his arm until it hurt at the elbow. The second bottle tipped as he touched it, but by some happy fluke it fell towards his waiting fingertips. Stretching through for more, he manoeuvred a miniature bottle of whiskey into his hand, gave it a stupid kiss, then pushed it down into the pocket of his ski pants.

Returning to the store, he found his way barred by two uniformed men guarding the entrance, arms crossed.

"The store is closed," yelled one through cupped hands to anyone who might listen.

Absorbed by the crowd huddled around the entrance, he peered through the doors with them, waited with them, and, finally, turned sadly away with them, before moving off alone to the edge of the parking lot. A weary-looking couple stood next to him; they rocked with cold. The woman sobbed through a red nose, wiping away tears with the back of her mitten. The man held her shoulders, whispering into her ear.

"Do you know what's happening?" Fred said, meeting the man's eye.

"Looks like a riot to me."

"But where's the manager? Where are the police?"

"No idea. I think the cold has driven everyone out of their minds. People are fighting in there, you know. Fighting over a damn box of burgers."

"Are you going in?"

"We tried. My wife needs her prescription but that security guy threw us out."

"Have you heard when we might get the power back?"

"You know what? I think we'll all be frozen in our beds before they get this mess sorted out."

"But someone must be in charge?"

"I'd go home if I were you. Come on, honey, let's go." He turned back towards Fred. "Good luck."

Luck. Is that what he needed? He looked at the people around him, heaving bags onto shoulders, churning snow to flat ice. He felt bewildered. The place he was just getting to know was changing by the minute. The smiling citizens of his first days in the city, so friendly, so eager to help, were disappearing into a blur of shoving and angry shouts. He brushed a snowflake out of his eye and wondered what to do next. Waiting any longer seemed pointless, so he made his way to the back of the crowd and turned towards his neighbourhood, eavesdropping shamelessly, absorbing the stories, the forgotten generators, the broken ankles, the abandoned cars.

"Where's the mayor?" yelled a woman.

"I'll give him a kick," said a voice from nowhere.

CHAPTER
30

In the space of fifteen hours Poppy had become a surrogate mother. Yes, her. The woman who could not remember the last line of Humpty Dumpty, the woman who had washed a complete set of team autographs out of her son's football shirt, the woman who did not really like children, except her own son. She could only come to the conclusion that children are hard-wired to identify an alternative provider, regardless of their qualifications for the job. Buster's mother had entered that lonely state of extreme worry and, although she did not know Rennie very well, Poppy could see that the woman the children knew as their mother was not the woman sitting on the sofa, staring at the carpet. Rennie's fear for Dwayne seemed to overwhelm her, and she had sunk into a deep melancholy, unable to concentrate on her children's questions and oblivious to her young son's demands. Why Buster had earmarked her as his new temporary mother was something she could not fathom. Being motherly was not a quality she had ever heard people attribute to her, but somehow his childish intuition had identified her as the one most likely to pay him attention. And he was right. She had been unable to refuse his requests for help with cutting up his food, and she had almost lost her voice reading stories from Fred's remaining collection of children's books. She now had a second shadow and, as she tried to prepare some food in the kitchen, he stood watching, an expectant smile on his face.

"There's not much here, so it's going to be a baby salad," she said.

"Baby salad, baby Jesus," said Buster.

Poppy looked down at the boy beside her; he was wearing one of Fred's fleeces and trying to raise himself onto the counter with his elbows. She found it hard to understand other people's children. She always had. Her own son presented enough of a challenge, especially now that he was changing so quickly, a new person crawling out of bed every morning. But other people's children were a complete mystery. They had their own set of sayings and jokes, evolved in the privacy of the family home, and they could not see that strangers did not understand. Unable to think of an appropriate reply, she chopped a piece of cucumber into tiny pieces, followed by half a tomato diced into cubes, then placed them on a saucer. It was like feeding a baby bird.

"I don't like the seeds," he said, wrinkling up his nose.

"Well, Buster," she said, feeling strange using his name, "I think your mum would be very pleased if you ate the seeds, just this once."

"Will Fred bring back candy?' he asked, catching her hand and rubbing it across his cheek.

"I don't think so."

A tiny pout appeared, then vanished. "Thanks, Auntie

Poppy," he said, pushing the tomato seeds to one side with his finger. Then he disappeared into the living room. She wiped the knife and chopping board with a kitchen towel and followed him in.

Buster was fiddling with the radio when it blasted to life. Endless turning had left the dial on maximum, so a loud and important voice burst into the room, waking even Grabowski, who looked around, blinked, then glared at the little boy.

"...extreme weather warning. Fifty centimetres of snow is expected over the next forty-eight hours. Temperatures are forecast to remain at minus twenty-eight but with the windchill factor will feel like minus forty. I repeat, do not leave your homes. The army is being mobilized but is currently hampered by several blocked roads, drifting snow, and damaged power lines. Attempts to re-establish power in the Prairies have been unsuccessful so far, but the emergency services are confident ..."

"Buster, turn it back!" said Ryan, jumping forward. "Give it to me."

Grabbing the radio from his brother, he tweaked the dial as if cracking a safe. "You idiot! We've lost it now."

Buster glanced at Rennie, worked up a look of contrition, then looked towards Poppy. But, preoccupied with thoughts of her real son, she could only muster minimal solace, squeezing out a weak smile. This seemed to satisfy him, and he flopped into a chair with a book on his lap.

No one spoke after that. Poppy sat on the sofa, prey to a fresh set of worries. She fretted about Fred, mentally kicking herself for letting him go out. She checked her watch. She nibbled a rough fingernail. She even rubbed a greasy spot off the arm of her chair with a tissue she found in her pocket.

The smallest events had taken on new significance within the cloud of boredom that had descended. Grabowski, snoozing in his chair, displayed a wealth of tiny activities that distracted her. He had a habit of scratching a fold beneath his chin, loosening white flakes of skin that settled onto his chest. She noticed his boots lying beside his feet, the lining thick with animal hair. She wondered if he had a dog waiting for him at home, or a wife, or even a child. He was like a newborn baby himself, she thought, sleeping, waking, eating, sleeping again.

She looked at her watch again; she flicked through a book; she looked at her watch. One comfort was to think about Charlie, but the happiness of the envisioned reunion, with kisses and tears and lingering hugs, was tossed out by other images – Charlie wringing his hands as he waited by the telephone, or Charlie yelling at airport officials as he tried to board a plane.

At last she pulled her sketchbook out from under her cushion and opened it to a fresh page. No one looked at her as she scanned the circle of visitors and began to draw. Rennie came first. Her limp air of despondency called for a hard lead, and after rummaging in her pencil box, Poppy located a sharp 6H. The sadly curved back and drooping shoulders grew clearer with every stroke, and she had to sharpen her pencil twice to capture the crisply ironed pants threatening to blur at the edges. She felt a twinge of guilt as she looked at the wretched figure appearing on her page and rubbed out the mouth before pressing on a smile with the licked end of a pink watercolour pencil. Two sharp dots for irises completed the sketch.

Capturing the essentials of Marcie's form took a little more effort. She observed her for a few moments. The young girl sat on the sofa, playing cards with Ryan, her hair falling over her face as she leaned forward to pick up the pack. She sketched out the slim figure in grey then worked on the hair with coloured pencils, blending a mixture of pimento, blood orange, and ginger, spiced up with a dash of lichen green. It was tricky to catch the reddish glow but eventually she was satisfied. Matching the skin colour was even more difficult and she laboured hard, trying out combinations of pale peach and pink, only to rub it out and rescue it with a faint wash of antique white flecked with scarlet. Buster, jogging her elbow and forcing himself up onto her lap, forced her to stop.

"I want to draw."

"All right. Draw the people in the room."

Taking him by the elbows, she removed him from her lap, settling him onto a cushion on the floor with a scrap of paper and pencil. She returned to her drawing, opening a new page. Ryan was her most challenging model. By any standards he was amicable and even tempered, but any characteristics of greater interest were camouflaged by an overwhelming sense of the ordinary. He liked to tell jokes; he liked to make people laugh. But what were his vices, where were his transgressions? Had those large ears overheard secrets he would not tell? Did those lips ever bad-mouth those who least expected it? She studied his profile further. She stared at her blank page, pencil poised for action, then gave up and turned her attention to her easiest and most dangerous muse: Grabowski. Shielding the paper with a cupped hand, she easily captured the huge bulk with generous sweeps of a marker pen. The double chin was soon unmistakable, followed by the great feet, finished off with a speech bubble filled with Zs.

Closing the book and hiding it beneath her cushion, she leaned forward to look at Buster's drawing over his shoulder. It was instantly recognizable — seven stick figures with their arms in the air, standing in a boat.

CHAPTER
31

"That it?" said Grabowski.

It is usually easier to stomach criticism from people you hate than those you respect, but the comment from across the room stung in a way Fred did not expect. Things normally look bigger when viewed indoors as opposed to outdoors, but his heap of supplies broke the rule, looking distinctly meagre and unsatisfactory as he laid it out on the coffee table. He launched into a spirited defence, describing the mayhem, the empty shelves, the carts dragged through the snow.

No longer listening, Grabowski commandeered the liquor and sat back in his chair. Fred continued. "The shop was being ransacked and ..."

"You mean these are stolen goods?" said his mother.

"Stolen goods," repeated Grabowski, in a girly voice.

"Yes, they are stolen," replied Fred, ignoring him. "Everyone is stealing."

The hero's welcome he had expected was rapidly evaporating. He found himself questioned. Why he had not tried to pay for the food, why was there not more of it, and why had the army still not taken over the city?

"I don't know what's going on," he said. "It's chaos up at the shops. There's no police around. It's a free-for-all. I got what I could."

"This can't be happening," said Poppy, inadvertently squeezing the tube of garlic spread; it bulged up against the cap. "Where are the authorities? Are you sure there is no one telling people what to do?"

"Mum, I told you. There's no one."

Ryan stood up and went over to the window. "I've never seen flakes this big. Look, Marcie."

His sister stood beside him. "It's so thick," she said. "I hope Dad's got himself inside."

Rennie shifted in her chair but said nothing.

"I can't see any sky," said Ryan. He pressed his nose against the glass. "The snow looks odd."

"What do you mean?" asked Poppy.

"I dunno, it's not like Winnipeg snow — the flakes are fat and ... well, fatter. It's weird."

"And the colour's wrong," said Marcie.

"Let me see," said Poppy, joining the siblings at the window. "You're right, it has a purple tinge."

"It can't have a purple tinge," said Fred, heaving himself out of his chair. He was shocked by how much snow had fallen in the last few minutes. His footprints had vanished. He could not see purple but he did think the snow looked strange, almost grubby. "You're right," he said. "It's different."

"A new breed," murmured Poppy.

CHAPTER
32

"Garage," said Fred.

"No garage," said Marcie firmly.

"Garage," said Fred again, trying not to laugh.

Marcie grabbed his lips, pulling the corners into a fake smile.

"Garage. Slow down at the end. Now go. Garage."

"Garage?"

They both laughed. Marcie was sitting next to him on the sofa, teaching him Canadian. He was enjoying the lesson. He could forget the chill lingering permanently around his kidneys, he could laugh out loud, and best of all, he could feel her fingers touching the corners of his mouth. He leaned forward and whispered in her ear. "Can I show you something?"

"What's that?" she replied, using the half-crushed voice of someone who has never learned to whisper.

"Get your coat and follow me."

"You mean outside?"

"No, I mean upstairs, to my bedroom."

"What for?"

"Don't worry. You'll see."

Marcie stood up, pausing only to flip her hair over her shoulder before pulling the curls together into a bunch with an imaginary elastic. She was soon perching on the edge of the bedframe, her eyes sparkling and her shoulders shivering. Kneeling down beside her, Fred reached under the bed and pulled out a package; it was badly wrapped, the paper loosely held with string.

"What have you got there?" she said.

"Well ..." He stopped, thinking for a moment. What *did* he have here? Pulling out the raincoat, he laid it on her lap, unfolding the sleeves until it straddled her knees like a man collapsed in prayer. She glanced at him then felt the material, stroking it with her fingertips, just as he had. Next, she ran her finger along the seams, just as he had, feeling the stitching. Finally she held it to her nose, and sniffed.

"What is it?"

"It's a seal intestine raincoat."

"A what?"

"A seal intestine raincoat."

She stroked the material, her hand rounding back and forth over her knee. "What's it made of?"

"The intestine from inside a seal."

They giggled.

"I can't see how they made the seams. Can you see?"

"I think it's made of something called sinew."

"Where did you get it?"

He began to tell her about Ata; he had decided he would. The oddness of his friendship with the old man struck him for the first time as he told her about their first meeting and the terrific smell. Expressing thoughts he did not know he had, he revealed his worry that he might never find him again. She looked so enthralled that he started on some of Ata's childhood stories, describing as best he could the old man's world of rotten ice, hungry bellies, and fish skin gauntlets sewn together with grass. She seemed mesmerized, gently stroking the coat on her lap.

"His life was hard, you know. Every day he had to find a way to survive."

"That must have been tough." Her expression said nothing.

"Yes," he said, nodding. "Really tough."

The fire had shrunk when they returned to the living room. Small logs replaced large ones and the far corners of the living room seemed even darker than before. The circle had shrunk, too, as chairs were dragged closer to the stove.

Fred looked around, noticing for the first time that everyone in the room had earmarked their own positions in the room. Grabowski had the biggest and best chair, his incontestable rights over its soft cushions and large seat remaining unchallenged. Poppy sat in the old armchair, the one Charlie had lugged from house to house since his student days. Impossible to clean, it was imprinted with a dark patch at head height, and should anyone ever be hunting for lost items beneath it, they would be certain to catch a graze from the forest of springs bulging from the bottom of the frame. Rennie had developed a liking for an upright dining room chair. First it had acted as a superb foil to her straight-backed poise, but now it only functioned as support for the sagging shoulders of a dispirited woman. Ryan and Marcie shared the sofa in an amicable state of sibling rivalry while only Buster roved and fidgeted from lap to lap. Occasional self-inflicted dares would send him closer to Grabowski, where he gazed up at the bristles on the underside of the up-turned chin with a childish recklessness that terrified them all. Sensing his secondary ranking in the pecking order, Fred had taken possession of the blue recliner with the tassels strung along the bottom; it seemed to fit him nicely. As he ran his nails under a loose piece of piping he saw Rennie stand up, a look of worry on her face.

"Where *is* he?" she said.

Although confident of the identity of "he," no one had an answer to "where is" and, just as Poppy began mustering her hundredth reassurance, Rennie picked up her cellphone and tried to call her husband, hammering out the numbers with the persistence of a woodpecker searching for ants. Fred knew the sequence of tones by heart. He fought not to hum it. Two days had passed, Dwayne had not returned, and Rennie was getting desperate. Fred was getting desperate just watching her scatter stress about the room. But it did not seem the right moment to comment that her youngest son's eyes were watering as she threw down the phone and began ruthlessly brushing his hair in a brief and skewed return to motherly love.

Blocking out the sounds of the frenzied tidying that had ensued, Fred returned to thinking, trying but failing to unscramble the muddle of logs, seals, and hairbrushes that filled his head. What the hell were they going to do if the power did not come back soon? How many logs were there left? Grabowski put on another one as he watched. And where was the tin opener? Despair rushed in as he watched his least favourite guest adjust the air flaps on the stove, sending flumes of warm air into undeserving corners of the room.

Then, for some unknown reason, the bureaucratic side of his nature managed to climb out from beneath the layer of hopelessness that threatened to envelop him. He would make a list. He ferreted out a piece of paper from beneath the heap on the coffee table and began to write.

Seven names appeared on the page, Grabowski last. A catalogue of condiments followed: marmite, pickle, mayonnaise, pepper sauce. Long-term residents of the cookie jar represented carbohydrates, in addition to three bags of pasta. But the list shortened as he wrote; a bag of pasta splashed into luke-warm water, and three became two. To make things worse, he was forced to observe profligacy in action as the youngest Kress squeezed out the garlic spread and smeared it over his cheeks as if it were the funniest thing in the world.

"Buster," he said, grabbing the tube. "We need that. You're going to stink."

"It tickles," said the boy.

"Well, it's also our dinner."

"When's dinner?" said Grabowski.

"It's nearly ready," answered Poppy in the flat tone of a disgruntled housewife.

"Better had."

Grabowski returned to his snooze. Fred returned to his list. Logs, what about logs? What about alcohol?

Alcohol. That was where a crisis could emerge. Gauging the level of liquor left in the house had become his private mission. The boyish part of his nature longed to draw black lines around the bottles, but his fear of Grabowski made secretly measuring the levels with a ruler and recording them in his notebook the only safe option. What he was going to do with this pool of data was not clear even to him but, with his newfound spirit of readiness, he wanted to know when Grabowski would grow more volatile. As he considered the ugliness of future scenes, the much-maligned man, prompted by the sound of food slopping onto dirty plates, woke up. They ate in silence.

"Where's the cheese?" said Grabowski.

"You ate it," replied Fred.

Grabowski shot him a dirty look then resumed eating, licking off the residue with a hideous tongue. They all watched spellbound as it swirled around inside the glass plate.

"Saves on washing up," he stated.

"Certainly does," replied Fred, struggling to keep the sarcasm out of his voice.

"You want the last of it?" said Grabowski. "Marcie?"

Fred stared. He could see Marcie's profile, her guard up so high it was almost visible. She wiped orange sauce from the edge of her lips with her sleeve before speaking.

"No, you have it."

Fred watched Marcie as she stood up. He watched the remains of her meal slump downwards into the man's bowl; juice flicked onto the back of her hand. Grabowski had said her name. He had acknowledged the existence of a fellow human being. He had asked a polite question. That must be a good thing, surely? So why did he want to push the words back through those wretched lips and poke them down that wretched throat with a stick?

Marcie returned to her seat and began whispering to Rennie. Fred continued to look at her. She wore a bracelet made of paperclips, wound around her wrist three times. It flashed in the firelight each time she pressed a stray curl behind her ear. Clumps of her hair had been plaited into tiny braids held at the end with elastic bands. When had she done that? He brooded over the possibilities, looking around for other small changes he might have missed. His mother looked down at her food, deep in thought and scratching her neck where the collars of two fleeces rubbed her skin. Her hair looked unbrushed, flattened on one side and curling beneath her ears on the other. Eating seemed an effort and she rested her head on one hand between mouthfuls. Buster sat at her feet, shaking tomato sauce off his pasta while holding his nose with each swallow. Ryan looked exactly the same as the moment he had arrived — same clothes, head tipped at the same angle, even the same curl irritating his left eye. Rennie stared at the fire, her bowl of food untouched.

"You finished," said Grabowski. More a statement than a question.

Not waiting for an answer, he grabbed Rennie's meal out of her hands and tipped the contents onto his plate, returning the empty bowl to her lap. No one said a word.

CHAPTER
33

"Mr. Grabowski?"

Two eyes cracked open.

"Mr. Grabowski?"

"What?" An eyelid slumped.

Poppy swallowed. "Don't you think we should go and try to get some help?"

Grabowski opened his eyes wide and looked straight at her. "What for?"

"Our wood supply is going down fast."

"So?"

"It's going to get terribly ..." How not to sound patronizing? "...cold."

"You'll think of something." He snuggled his shoulders deeper into the cushions. He belched.

Then she realized. He was enjoying himself.

CHAPTER

34

In prairie cities, the passing of communal time is not marked by the clang of church bells but by the hoot of trains as they lumber through, never changing speed, never stopping, always going somewhere else.

The absence of that reassuring *toot* was deeply felt as Fred sat on the sofa later that evening, gazing out of the window. He tried to remember how much time had gone by since the power went off. But he couldn't. He stood up and went to find his watch.

"Hey, Fred, while you're over there could you grab a tissue out of my purse? Buster's got a giant snot." It was Marcie speaking, filling the mother void while Poppy visited the kitchen.

"You mean this one?"

Fred had a thing about touching women's handbags. He felt a twang in his stomach as he picked up the pink container, the target of Marcie's pointing finger. Holding it up by its edges and avoiding the strap, he experienced feelings of embarrassment and curiosity in equal parts. The pinkness only served to heighten the response that washed over him, but his fear of looking not quite himself was tempered by the promise of touching and exploring the contents of Marcie's bag. And if he were completely honest with himself, he would admit that he was as eager as a freshly praised puppy to sift through its interior. His hand brushed against a bundle of graphite pencils tied together with a rubber band. They were all blunt with teeth marks chewed into the ends. He longed to sharpen them. Delving deeper, he disturbed a scent of lip balm then felt specks of tissue dust settling onto the back of his hand. He pressed on, discovering more wonderful things: moisturizer that had been rubbed on her lips and perfume that had been dabbed behind her ears. Finally, he felt a perverse joy as an open lipstick smeared a streak of red onto the back of his hand.

"Hurry, it's about to drop."

The pretence of speeding up masked the actual slowing down of his search as he savoured the last few moments amongst Marcie's possessions. The bottom of the bag was lined with a layer of broken staples, their ends bent back like trampled spiders. Pulled from long-discarded papers, they were half an inch deep and buried the last item he had time to discover — a small, nut-brown pine cone. With no chance to consider the meaning of this unexpected layer, he yanked out the handkerchief and dived forward, just in time to catch the plummeting mucus before it hit the deck.

"Good save," remarked Ryan from the comfort of the sofa.

⁓

Bent nose, torn foot, split belly. The worst attempts at origami he had ever seen. Two days had passed since the lights went out, and with boredom merging into cabin fever, they were making a family of paper frogs. Marcie finished first. The poor thing resembled a sickly mouse and they all laughed, Marcie the loudest. Undeterred, she produced ten more squares of paper, folding the sheets torn from a notebook into triangles. They all tried, following her instructions to fold and press then fold again, with varying levels of success. Fred's frog was perfect. He could hardly suppress his delight as they passed it around, almost causing a crisis when Rennie absentmindedly went to pass it to Grabowski to admire. Ryan cut in just in time, grabbing the legs and flicking the creature back onto the table. Rennie's attempt was a disaster, nothing but a loose ball of unsharpened folds and ill-judged flaps, and she withdrew from the game, preferring to watch or to "think Dwayne" as

Fred had started to call it in his head. Poppy and Ryan made passable attempts but Buster gave up altogether, preferring to practise spelling his name with a marker pen that soaked through onto his jeans, leaving green dabs. Fred felt inspired, and under the proud direction of Marcie, made another frog and placed it beside the others.

"Buster, Fred, Marcie, and Ryan," said the little boy, in a singsong voice.

"Let's put them to bed," said Poppy, passing Buster an empty tissue box.

As the little boy set the new amphibious family inside, covering them over with a hankie, Poppy prepared their beds, shoving the mattresses as close to the fire as the heat would allow. Fully dressed, they crawled under the duvets. Marcie began a round of tucking in, helping her younger brother into his sleeping bag and kissing him on the forehead. Busy with all-night fire-tending duties, Ryan thought he had escaped, only to be caught unawares by a mock kiss, and he emitted a grunt of sibling disgust. Fred felt a tingling in his toes as she turned to him.

"Now, *you.*"

He could hardly breathe. She smoothed the duvet down over his legs, sealing the edges down with a lingering pat of her hand. Next she straightened out the top and tucked it beneath his chin.

"Night," she said, flicking aside a few hairs that covered his eyes.

"Goodnight," he replied, with a voice that croaked.

⌒

The house rocked that night. Wind swirled over the roof and down the walls, hitting the windows with what sounded like handfuls of gravel. Fred heard that lonesome windy howl from far away, the one that makes you think of something from way back. When he least expected it, squares of snow slumped off the roof, waking his fellow sleepers. He thought of Ata. He thought of the cart stuck in the ice, the bags buried. Was he lining up somewhere with other old men, waiting for a hot drink, his hands too numb to hold the cup, his feet too frozen to feel the ground? But he was tough, wasn't he? He grew up in a hood. He knew how to keep the family on the move. He knew the cold. Fred sat up. Someone must help him. Someone must bring him inside. But looking out of the window at the snow rushing up into the sky, he realized it would not be him.

CHAPTER
35

Ryan's knees woke Fred early the next morning. Bony and fidgety, they had eked open gaps in the bedding that left the small of his back stiff with cold. Only his right ear felt warm, caressed into comfort by Marcie's warm, rhythmic breath that crept across the gap in the pillows. He was well placed to examine her freckles from where he lay. Hundreds of them covered her face, only thinning out on the sides of her nose where small patches of skin lay bare. She had that look of someone who was pretending to be asleep — eyelids a little too firmly closed, breathing not deep enough, and the mouth solid, without the slightest hint of a dribble.

"Did my dad come back?" she asked, opening her eyes without warning.

Fred moved back an inch. "No, but he will. I'm sure he will."

She looked over his head, gazing at the fire. Then she glanced at Grabowski, still asleep and wheezing through unwilling lungs. She moved her lips close to his ear.

"He's like the tiger who came to tea."

"Who?"

"Him," she said, peeping back at Grabowski, who was now farting in his sleep. They giggled silently.

"What do you mean?"

"Didn't your mom read you that story when you were a kid? This tiger turned up on the doorstep one day, uninvited. He came in and raided the fridge; he ate every single thing. Then he ate all the food in all the cupboards. Without a word."

"And then what?" said Fred, suppressing a laugh.

"He drank all the water in the taps!"

They laughed, blurting out spit, then stopped, stuffing handfuls of duvet into their mouths. Ryan twanged a curl off his eye but did not wake up.

"I don't agree," said Fred.

"You don't?"

"No. I think he's more like the bishop who ate his boots." The end of the sentence dissolved beneath the covers.

"Was he really real?" said Marcie.

"Oh, yes, back in nineteen hundred and something. He was trapped in the Yukon, starving and almost frozen to death. Then he had a brainwave. He could eat his sealskin boots. And he did, ate them both. He boiled them, toasted them, even chewed them raw. But the tastiest bits were the laces, saved as a treat for breakfast."

It was too much; the duvet rocked.

Then Marcie stilled. "Fred."

"Yes?"

"My dad will come back, won't he?"

"Of course."

⌒

A boy under pressure needs some solace, a little bit of something that takes the edge off. That was his excuse and he was sticking to it. Fred sneaked up to his bedroom later, rummaged at the back of his closet, and pulled out a small bottle of vodka. Finding himself trapped without power in one of the world's coldest cities was one thing, but sharing a duvet with a dazzling red-headed girl was of a completely different order. Something strong was called for.

He was not used to girls in his life and felt aggrieved that no one had explained quite how bad things could get when someone like Marcie got near you. He couldn't stop thinking about her, even though he had other important things on his mind. But plans for collecting wood or retrieving food from the garbage kept taking second place to thoughts of touching red hair.

He took a noisy slurp. It stung the back of his throat, just as he had intended it to. Then he lay back on the slats of his bed, waiting for the warm glow to circulate through his body; he knew it would not be long. Another mouthful forced him upright as a coughing fit began. A third swig calmed his throat and he remained seated, waiting to warm up and staring at nothing.

CHAPTER
36

A loud hammering on the front door woke Poppy just after eleven o'clock that night.

It came at the end of a long day. Frustration had simmered throughout the afternoon as they played endless games, watching small hands drop the playing cards again and again. Tempers had twisted up into a peak by the time the Jack of Diamonds' head was torn off and the King of Spades' sword broken in two. Only sleep promised to break the tedium, and grateful for the chance to join Buster's bedtime routine, they had crawled under the duvets at a quarter to eight and lain still, aching for the oblivion of slumber.

Poppy clutched the cold sheets and trembled as the banging came again. All thoughts of rescue left her head, replaced by the prospect of a second Mr. Grabowski squeezing a large backside onto her armchair. Rennie was not scared, however. She jumped up, leaping across the mattresses like a schoolgirl. Fred followed. The sound of someone struggling with the front door floated into the room, and Poppy reached for her fleece. She stood up on cracking knees, but before she could move, a speeding Grabowski pushed past her. Yelling.

"Get away from the door!"

He owned a booming voice that comes straight from the gut, vibrating eardrums to the verge of pain. Hopping on stiff legs, Poppy followed him into the hall. Three head shapes bobbed in the glass. Rennie was tugging at the door handle with Fred standing beside her, fixed in a moment of indecision. Grabowski took charge.

"*Away* from the door."

The big voice was quieter this time, releasing a sinister resonance. Rennie, glancing at Grabowski, let go of the door handle and took a step back. The thumping intensified, rattling the door on its hinges, and Poppy could see the dark figures moving outside, up and down.

"Fuck off!" boomed Grabowski.

"It might be Dwayne," cried Rennie. Her whole body pleaded with him, her eyes begged, her hand touched his shoulder. She shivered uncontrollably.

"It's not fucking Dwayne and it's not fucking help. It's just some bastards trying to get their hands on our food. They're not coming in!"

"We have to let them in," Fred said in a low voice. "They might freeze."

Grabowski turned. His cheeks billowed and, without warning, he lifted his fist and punched Fred, full on the chin, knocking him backwards. A groan of pain rose up from the floor. Forgetting the cold, forgetting the bully, forgetting the people at the door, Poppy dashed forward.

"Fred!"

He lay flat on his back, his blinking out of control. Her knees clicked as she kneeled down and took his hand; it was icy cold. But before they could speak, Grabowski was bending over them, poking a finger into her son's face. The smell of stale whiskey made her want to retch.

"They're not coming in."

CHAPTER
37

The moon had forgotten to eat. Fred could see its thin waist as he gazed up at the sky. Wiping the sheen off the window he stared up the road, trying to see a sign of them. He jumped as a block of snow slid off the roof, big as a wardrobe. Their footprints had disappeared, rubbed out by the snow. They were out there somewhere. Those people. Were they going from house to house? Were they shouting? Were they freezing? He pictured Ata abandoning his bags in the snow. Then, a final question entered his head. Who would let in a filthy old man when their supplies were running low?

He returned to a bed full of boys. Ryan's socked feet were on Buster's nose and the little boy was talking in his sleep, eyelids fluttering as he spluttered out commands and swallowed questions. Two mouse-like squeaks followed faint words: "Mom banana two banana." Sliding his legs down Ryan's back, Fred sighed to himself, savouring the borrowed warmth that seeped into his limbs. He suspended his frozen feet one inch behind the younger boy's body, stealing his heat. Finally he pulled his coat over the deadly gap that had opened up between duvet and mattress.

Marcie lay next to him, moving around in the deepest of sleep. He held his breath as she moved towards him, lifting her arm and sliding her coat closer to his shoulder. He did not move, just looked. Her earlobes looked naked, only tiny pink holes where earrings had been. The urge to wipe the grease on her forehead was immense, but he did not. His unfocused eyes drifted towards the fire.

"Bugger. It's my turn."

His words sent a small wave of restlessness across the sleeping bodies. He let it subside before dragging himself out of bed, placing a log on the embers and flopping down onto a chair. He felt a hundred years old as he tucked a blanket over his knees.

Sleep leaned heavily on his shoulders as he struggled to stay awake. He slapped a cheek, he rubbed an eyelid, he pushed his fingers back through his hair, then he held his head in his hands, pondering its weight. Flicking on the flashlight, he checked his watch.

"One o'clock and all is well," he muttered under his breath.

CHAPTER

38

Only the sound of Grabowski, whistling through his nose, disturbed the dead air that folded over the sleeping group early the next morning. Fred had woken from a brief nap with an unidentified worry sitting at the bottom of his stomach. He mentally sifted through the contenders: they were running out of logs, they were running out of food, they were running out of time. And no one was coming. That was the nub — no one was coming. How he yearned for a policeman to rap on the door, shout commands to minions, write notes in a stiff little notebook, take complete and absolute control. And when not longing for policemen, he fantasized about rescuers clad in green cotton and staggering behind towers of plastic boxes, exuding meat-scented steam. He thought of Ata. The old man had spent his whole childhood in a group of seven people without outside help. Seven was the number of mouths connected to hungry bellies, seven was the number of caribou parkas stitched each winter. And seven was the number of people that worked together, to get through life. No hour could slip by without calculations being made, blubber levels checked, ice floes prodded, and fish counted.

A rough reckoning totted up in his head. How much food do people actually need in a day? No tenth-grade math formula seemed applicable to the complications of appetite, body size, and teenage growth spurts, and any attempt at fairness would be skewed by Rennie's absence of appetite and Grabowski's greed.

Grabowski. He was the essence of the problem, wolfing down most of the food and hogging the fire. Could they overpower him? Could they throw him out of the house? Could they get him drunk and stab him with the long kitchen knife? Fred pressed his forehead. Those deep, secret, evil thoughts were pouring out now. He saw blobs of blood on steel, toes blackened by frostbite, and slices of human face served up on a plate, boiled potatoes on the side. There was no stopping them as they crowded into his head, hijacking his reason and crushing his last shreds of rationality.

"Stop," he said out loud. He had to get a grip on things. He pulled his list from beneath a cushion, read it, and frowned.

People:
Me, Mum, Marcie, Ryan, Buster, Grabowski

Food in the fridge:
Half jar mayonnaise, three quarters jar chutney, jar curry sauce,
bit of cottage cheese, two half lemons

Food on shelves:
One bag pasta, two tins tomatoes, one onion, two tins baked
beans, one bottle Tabasco sauce

Firewood:
Thirty-five logs

He ran a finger down the names. Something was not right.
Someone was missing. Six people. Six. But it was not six; it was
seven. Rennie was missing. With his heart pounding he rushed
to correct the mistake, pressing his pen deep into the paper as
he wrote her name, only allowing himself to stop when the nib
scratched through onto his fingers. Feeling satisfied there were
no more errors, his eyes lingered on the last line and a rough
timescale took shape in his mind for the first time: thirty-five
logs, burning night and day.

CHAPTER
39

Poppy was convinced she had been awake all night. So how
come she had just woken up? Saliva lined the surface of her
tongue like glue. Some had seeped out of her mouth and dried
into crumbs on the corners of her lips. The memory of the
long night spent staring at the window, watching snowflakes
smearing the glass, was now mixed with the confusion of an
early morning dream that ended with a jolt as her conscious

brain switched on. Her first thought was of Charlie; it made her want to cry. But she could not cry here, not like this. Not surrounded by strangers. She blinked fast, forcing the water back down beneath her eyeballs, ending with a sniff and a swallow.

Looking across the lumps of bedding, she saw Fred sitting up in bed, writing. He was frowning and flicking hair off his eyes with the end of his pencil. She had been unable to see it before, but he looked a lot like Charlie: same nose, same way of raising his eyebrows, leaving a pale patch of skin just visible above his eyelid. She watched him get out of bed, patting down the edges of the duvet, saving its precious warmth for later. He glanced at Marcie then stretched his arms lavishly, revealing an inch of belly beneath the creased hems of four T-shirts. Muscles loosened, he picked up his notebook and left the room.

She turned her eyes to the fire and was just about to shift a half-burned cinder with the poker when a contemptuous question broke into her thoughts.

"You getting the breakfast yet?"

She managed a neutral reply, aimed at the duvet. "I'll see what there is."

Fred was already there when she walked into the kitchen, shivering beneath the cold fabric of a recently added fleece. Relief replaced the minute look of guilt lingering on his face.

"Oh, Mum, it's you. I thought it might be *him*."

"Fred, what's that under your fleece?"

He gesticulated for her to come closer.

"Don't worry now, but we don't have much food left. I think we should start being a bit careful, you know, make sure *he* doesn't get it all. I'm putting a couple of tins upstairs just in case. Gives us a bit more control over the situation. What do you think?"

"Well, I'm sure Dad would ..."

"Look, Mum," he said, louder. "Dad isn't here. We have to deal with this ourselves. Our situation is getting worse. We can't just drift along and hope it will turn out all right sometime soon."

"But ..." A parent under attack is allowed a moment's hesitation, and she took full advantage before replying several seconds later. "Just don't let him catch you. Have you left something for breakfast? He's asking for it."

She saw a patch of her son's cheek, pulsating in and out.

"God. He's like some sort of stupid dictator. I just want to chuck him out into the snow. Maybe Ryan and I could somehow ..."

"Freddie, remember what he did to your jaw. We have to be careful. He's strong. He's unpredictable."

With almost comic timing, Mr. Grabowski appeared in the doorway, brushing his shoulders against the doorframe. Without a word, he pushed past, opened the fridge door, and bent forward. He went on to reveal not only the much-depleted stock, but also the crack in his backside, which lengthened as he reached inside.

"Garbage," they heard him mutter from inside the fridge.

He emerged holding several bottles, which he set down on the kitchen top. They watched in silence as he picked up a bowl lined with smears of old milk then placed it next to the bottles. Snapping the lid off the mayonnaise, he stuck in a finger, turned a half circle, and pulled out a lump. It quivered as he stuffed it into his mouth. Next, he found a spoon in a drawer, muttered "garbage" again, and emptied the mayonnaise into the bowl, whacking the bottom of the jar with his hand. Chutney followed, the bottle emitting a small popping sound as a jellied lump came unstuck from the base and fell out as one, forming a transparent castle. Even with the benefit of large hands he had to struggle with the curry sauce, but eventually the lid came off. He shook it over the bowl so violently that flecks splattered the back wall and dripped down onto the open drawer below.

"That's a new one," said Poppy under her breath.

"What did you say, Mum?"

"I was thinking of Charlie," she replied. "Chutney and mayonnaise."

"Who's Charlie?" demanded Grabowski.

"My dad," said Fred. "This is his house."

"Well, tell him he needs to get more stuff in his fridge next time."

Next time. She almost sniggered at the absurdity of it.

Picking up the cottage cheese, Grabowski clicked off the top to smell it, pushing his nose inside the carton. A bubble of vomit popped to the top of Poppy's throat and she worked hard to stifle her gag reflex. He threw the carton onto the floor and, ignoring the need for frugality, took a bite from one of the lemons. She could not dispel the image of a cat bringing up a hairball as he spat it out, whooshing a spit-drenched blob onto the floor. He returned to his creation, stirring it with a dirty spoon. Then he left the room, crushing the heels of her slippers as he flip-flopped down the hall.

"Fred, no!" Her son had kneeled down beside the discarded cheese carton.

"Why not?"

"It's disgusting."

"Mum, does it really matter if it's disgusting?"

Not waiting for an answer, he picked up a teaspoon, positioned the carton at an angle, and scooped the grubby curds back inside, scraping up the juice, only stopping to extract a long grey hair that had wound itself around the handle of his spoon. He clicked the top back on and slipped it into his pocket. Finally, he rescued the calendar from the floor and, stretching the attached pencil to its most taut, circled the day, Sunday, December 10, adding "Day four" beneath.

He took out his notebook and began writing a list. She looked over his shoulder, reading as he wrote.

Food in the fridge:
Cottage cheese (not much), half lemon

It read like the ingredients of a crash diet. Lose ten pounds weight in less than a week.

Guaranteed.

CHAPTER

40

Fred sat alone in his bedroom as the sun struggled to rise, balancing on the bare slats of his bed. His forehead hurt and the walls shifted a fraction whenever he moved his head too fast. He looked around. Winter seemed to be encroaching on his bedroom, painting ice ferns on the inside of his windows, blurring the boundaries between inside and out.

He spread Ata's coat on his lap, stretching the fabric over the nails of one hand, trying, yet not trying, to puncture it. He wished he could be more like Ata. This tight-skinned mammal had been the old man's life source, its skin moulded into boots, its flesh eaten, its fat melted for heat, and its gut sewn into a garment so perfectly adapted to its purpose that even its tiny stitch holes swelled and closed on contact with water. How comforting it felt to spread the coat over his lap, letting it push the cold from his legs.

The texture felt different this morning. Rubbing the cloth

SEAL
INTESTINE
RAINCOAT

in his hands, he noticed a loss of suppleness and a hitherto undiscovered hint of crunchiness to the edges. He spat on his finger, smearing the saliva over one sleeve, musing over its origins. How old was this coat? Years might have passed since it was last filled with swallowed fish, swilling around in a porridge of digestive juices. This most internal of organs, cut from a damp, dark place had become something external, a simple coat, which protected human skin from killing cold and wet. Was it possible Ata made it himself? As he toyed over thoughts of Ata's mother, sewing sinew into the seams, he realized. He sat bolt upright. Of course! Ata's family used what they had to make what they needed. It was as simple as that. They must do the same; use what they had to make what they needed. He said it aloud, "Use what we have," then stood up, repeating himself, "Use what we have to make what we need!"

A voice booming up from the bottom of the stairs broke his solitary speech. "Where you hiding the booze?"

Fred manhandled the coat into a bundle and threw it under his desk, trying to ignore the inexplicable guilt washing through him.

"Oi! Freddie boy."

He stepped out onto the landing and, from the top of the stairs, felt the full force of Grabowski's glare from below. Poppy stood a couple of feet behind, the familiarity of her face blurred beneath a layer of apprehension.

"I'm not hiding anything."

"What the hell are you doing up there?"

Without waiting for an answer, Grabowski clambered up the stairs. Fred could smell him as he came closer.

"There's nothing up here."

"Yeah?"

He took a step backwards as the man entered his bedroom

and sweeped in stenched air. Grabowski began searching — touching, shoving, tipping, and spilling with the insensitivity of a police raid. Lovingly created order was disturbed, drawers pulled, shelves swiped, and trays emptied with no regard for the territorial rights of his unwilling host. Nothing was sacrosanct. Fred felt he could almost take no more when Grabowski pulled out a crumpled bundle from under his desk, took a quick look, and threw it down amongst the pile of clothes and papers strewn on the carpet.

"Mr. Innocent, are we?" said Grabowski, stretching an arm to the back of his closet and pulling out a half-empty bottle of gin. "Bet mommy doesn't know about this."

Fred watched in silence as he unscrewed the top, held it to his lips, and drank the bottle down in one. Poppy, who had remained by the door, said nothing.

"I'll take these, too," said Grabowski, bending down to pick up two large dictionaries before disappearing out of the door. Fred grabbed the raincoat and shoved it to the back of his wardrobe. "He probably wants to look up the word 'polite,'" he said.

"Oh, Fred, this is all so horrible," said Poppy.

"Come on. Forget him. Let's go and warm up."

⁓

When Fred entered the living room, he could see that something was wrong. It was not so much the faces but the body language that gave it away. The relaxed slouch of the occupants of a family den nearing the end of a long film had been replaced by the upright postures of a dentist's waiting room — backs were stiff, hands held in laps, expressions solid.

"That's what I call a decent fire," he heard Grabowski say, rubbing his hands.

Peering through the stove window, Fred could see flames flapping over the sides of a book, the pages already edged with black. More books were piled up beside the fire. He sat down on the sofa beside Marcie, feeling anger rising up inside him yet unable to prevent his body from basking in the extra warmth. He turned to his mother; she looked back at him, shaking her head. Ignoring the body language being shouted across the room, Buster spoke. "Can I burn the frogs?"

"Course you can, kiddo," replied Grabowski. "Chuck 'em on in."

Nervous at being addressed by Grabowski for the first time, the young boy obeyed. He picked up the cardboard box, opening the stove door with a cloth over his hand, and threw in the paper frogs, each receiving the simplest of epitaphs.

"Goodbye Marcie, goodbye Ryan, goodbye Fred, and goodbye me."

Glancing around to make sure they were all watching, he threw in the cardboard bed with a giggle, curtailed by a tug at the back of his fleece as Poppy pulled him towards her.

"Poor frogs," she murmured into his ear. "Let's not burn anything else."

As if receiving invisible instructions, Grabowski hauled himself out of his chair and headed up the stairs. After much thumping from the room above, he reappeared at the doorway, balancing a pile of books beneath his chin. Fred could see his school notebooks sandwiched between novels, their yellow Post-it notes curling off the edges. *Migrating Birds of North America* went first, followed by a battered French-English dictionary. The fire blazed, sending growls of delight up the chimney.

"You can't burn those," said Poppy, jumping out of her seat.

"Who says?"

Poppy sat down again. Fred could see her twisting her wedding ring — round and round it went.

It was almost too late by the time Fred realized the danger. That magnificent, soothing, glorious fire, warming their outstretched toes with its delicious heat, made him forget what he should have been remembering. He had to act. Now.

While Grabowski was distracted, forcing a copy of *Canadian History* into the stove, Fred slipped back upstairs.

The air in Poppy's study was bitter, but disconnection from the grid had not impacted the room beyond a drop in temperature, and the piles of dusty chaos — dried-up apple cores and coffee cup rings dotting the desk — remained untouched. The sight of them comforted him. He stood for a moment, relishing the familiarity of the black notebooks, their chronology scrambled. Then he looked at the shelves and felt a horrible premonition burrowing into his stomach.

The early sketchbooks, bulging with pressed flowers and newspaper clippings, were on the left. Fred knew them intimately, never growing tired of browsing through, sniffing the ancient rose petals pressed between the pages. Unfolding the photographs clipped from magazines brought particular pleasure, and the random scattering of brown seeds into his lap was always an unexpected delight. Black notebooks filled the middle section of the shelves. They were crowded with sketches and notes, some written on the diagonal. His mother had encouraged him to add to them, so squeezed between her drawings of pollen dusted stamens and old men snoozing on benches were drawings from his early world: Daddy with an enormous head and hands for ears, a tiny family inside a giant car and embryonic sentences, "mummy hat" and "hammy sleep." The right hand end of the shelf held Poppy's published collections, ten in all, with a copy of *Wildflowers of Hampstead Heath, illustrated by Poppy Forester* acting as a bookend.

Grabowski was coming. Fred's heart felt like a tiny fist

trying to punch its way out. He scooped books off the shelves at random, swinging around with an armful, desperate for a hiding place. The sound of footsteps ceased then resumed with a change in tone: moving off the stair carpet and onto the wood of the landing. Three notebooks had been stuffed into the drawer of the desk by the time the man appeared at the door, with Poppy two steps behind and Buster holding onto her leg.

"Aha, more kindling," said Grabowski through a nasty smile.

Caught up in desperation, Fred slammed the desk drawer shut then headed back towards the shelves. Struck by yet another thought, he stopped in mid step and veered back towards Grabowski.

"Get out of my mother's room!"

He had never shouted so loudly in his life. It hurt. He swallowed in quick succession, trying to soothe the pain in his throat. Grabowski hesitated, his arm raised, then lowered it again and stepped back.

"Garbage, anyway," he muttered, sloping out of the room and leaving a sweaty smell behind him.

CHAPTER

41

Their final meal stank. Tepid pasta, slimed with starch then soaked in tomato juice, turns a grotesque colour. But only to the well fed. To the ravenous members of the circle, this was haute cuisine at its peak. No food was left in the house and everyone knew it. Everyone except Buster, that is, who was piling his tomatoes to the side of his plate and riddling pasta bows with fork stabbings. Grabowski licked out the can after Poppy had turned the tomatoes into the pan, cutting his tongue and swearing obscenely. No one commented. No one dared.

The children's teasing and roughhousing had died down, replaced by a tired irritability bordering on petulance. They were stewing, hoarding up silent grievances against Grabowski but not daring to voice them. Rennie had become dumb, occasionally flicking open her cellphone without even looking. But she mostly stared into the fire. Now and then she fiddled with the radio. Poppy had tried to coax her listless houseguest into eating, but she had refused. Now it was too late. The cupboards were empty.

The evening of the fourth day stretched in front of them. After cards came Monopoly, then more origami, but Poppy could see that Fred was not concentrating on the game. He was watching the fire and he was watching Grabowski. But before she had a chance to work out what was going on, he suddenly stood up and left the room. He returned with a familiar bag; she recognized it from their last camping holiday. Grabowski, looking more alert than usual, started to laugh. Fred ignored him. He loosened the drawstring, revealing a wedge of grey canvas folded into creases.

"A tent," said Buster, hugging his own waist in delight.

"Going on a holiday, are we?" said Grabowski.

Not listening, Fred turned towards Poppy. "Look, Mum. It may seem mad, but we have to try to preserve heat. Do you remember the night in the ice cave? I was freezing until you came in, but we felt almost warm with the two of us. Ata said that's how they survive in igloos."

"Who's Ata?"

Fred hesitated. "Oh, just a friend." He began heaving the canvas out of its bag.

"Hey, did I hear the words 'night in ice cave'?" said Ryan, a smile on his face.

Still mulling over igloos and people named Ata, Poppy smiled, too. Of course it sounded ridiculous, messing with survival shelters without a clue.

"It's true, isn't it, Mum?" said Fred. She nodded.

"Well, I see you survived," said Ryan.

"I'll show you the missing toe later," replied her son, smiling.

Between them they shook out the fabric, dislodging chocolate wrappings, a flat sock, and a comic, dated July 1998. Ryan seized the final item, stuffing his prize inside his fleece with a look of supreme happiness. A new smell of old grass and mildew floated around their circle.

Deep in holiday thoughts, Poppy failed to notice that Grabowski had got up out of his chair and left the room. His return was made obvious by a scrape of wood on wood, and a small African carving entered the circle. Before she could react, he threw it onto the back of the fire, gave a mock sigh, sat down in his chair, and closed his eyes.

Please do not do anything, please do not do anything, she pleaded in her mind. Unperturbed, Fred continued to unpack the tent at the same pace, and with Marcie's help, soon had it spread over the mattresses.

"Wow, this thing looks prehistoric," said Ryan. "And metal pegs?" He dangled a peg between his fingers, dislodging a clod of soil augured along its length.

"Woolworths, 1979," Poppy replied. Ryan looked blank.

"How are we going to get it to stay up?" asked Marcie. "There's no soil to stick the pegs in. And where's the pole?"

"I can be the pole," chipped in Buster. He burrowed his way into the pile of cloth then, standing on his toes, stretched up his neck until a head-shaped bulge appeared at the front of the canvas.

"Have you got any instructions?" said Marcie, fingering a tangle of knotted nylon.

"We don't need instructions," replied Fred, "but I could do with a little help."

They swarmed over the tent, rummaging through the parts like a family of inquisitive chipmunks.

"We need some sort of triangle," added Fred. "Something with three legs that's stable."

"What about Dad's tripod?" said Poppy. "I'll get it."

Poppy could see the excitement on Fred's face as the dormitory turned refugee camp. Only Grabowski remained on the periphery, watching them in silence.

The tent was eventually erected, with a tripod at the front and a broom handle at the back, its end jammed into an obsolete set of weighing scales, with a hole cut into the top. Gaps were stuffed with the flat sock, freshly plumped for the job. Then they brought in the bedding, and Poppy felt a small slot of pleasure as she and Marcie punched up the pillows and smoothed down the duvets, giggling and knocking elbows like a couple of busy hotel maids. Sleeping positions were bagged and they sat back to admire their work only to see it demolished as Buster, taking a short run up, launched into an inaugural dive towards their new sleeping quarters.

CHAPTER
42

Six people lay in a tent, listening. An hour had passed since they moved into their home within a home, and a muffled bevy of obscenities not yet entered into Fred's Canadian dictionary drifted down from the ceiling. Grabowski moved from room to room, sniffing and grunting, grunting and searching. With whiskey levels resting at zero, the situation Fred feared had arrived.

He stared at the cloth ceiling, scrutinizing every crease in the dusky light. A tired brown stain streaked from the pole hole above his head. It rippled as Buster fidgeted, knocking the broom and shaking the cotton ceiling. Then, a flashlight flickered on the canvas wall. Grabowski was coming. What should he do? Would the man come into the tent? Could he stop him? He felt increasing dread as the beam of light dancing across the side of the tent grew smaller. And smaller.

A loud whoosh of clothes on upholstery erupted close to the tent, then silence. Fred could see two feet through a gap in the tent flaps. Fred sat up, shimmied forward, lifted up the tent flap, and peered out. Unbelievable. Grabowski was asleep already, chucking out snores through a blocked nose. Relieved, Fred returned to his bed and pulled the duvet up to his chin. Savouring the warmth, he tried his hardest to dismiss the dizziness that threw the brown stain across the inside of the tent. Someone muttered in the dark; he could not tell who. Then a child's voice piped up: "When are we having dinner?"

Silence followed; someone's lungs drew in a breath.

"We're not having any dinner tonight, Buster," replied Poppy, at last. "We're camping and the bears have eaten all our food."

Another silence.

"Did they eat everything?"

"Everything," she replied.

"I'll wait 'til breakfast."

"Yes, Buster. You wait."

Fred had fallen asleep when someone tugging on the hem of his jeans woke him up. No sooner had he become aware of what was happening, it stopped. Then it started again. Someone was pulling on his duvet; he could just make out a huge hand coming through the flap of the tent. It floated, lowered, then grabbed. The duvet left the tent. He lunged for the disappearing corner, grabbing at air, but missed. Before he had time to react, the hand reappeared, floating towards his mother. With fresh determination, Fred snatched at the fast-receding blanket, but it was wrenched out of his hand before he could get a decent hold, leaving his fingernails smarting.

"What the hell are you doing?" he whispered.

"I'm cold," said Grabowski.

"Look," said Fred, pushing his head through the opening. "Why don't you just come in with us. It's much warmer in here." He could not believe he had said it.

"What, with you unwashed kids? No way."

"It's up to you," Fred said, throwing an encouraging smile at Ryan, who had managed to be so wrapped up with rearranging some wood on the fire that he had evaded all involvement.

As far as one can in an armchair, Grabowski turned over and tucked in, leaving only a ragged tail of hair poking out of the top of the bedding.

Fred returned to the tent, slipped beneath his mother's remaining duvet, and savoured the warmth from her back.

CHAPTER
43

Poppy was desperate. Even the thought of the blocked toilet bowl, layered with coils of excrement, could not subdue the ache in her bladder. She sat up, pulled on a fleece, and poked her head through the tent flaps. Ryan was just visible, a blurred lump snoozing on the sofa, punctuated only by the black hole of his open mouth. The sound of a book snapping shut drew her attention to the best chair, and she squinted towards Grabowski. A flashlight shone in her eyes.

"Were you watching me?"

"No."

"What are you doing?" Grabowski's voice sounded tired.

"Visiting the bathroom."

"Huh, enjoy yourself."

Pulling the zip of her fleece up to her throat, she crawled out of the tent, then stepped across his outstretched legs.

"Wait. I'm gonna need more liquor soon."

"I know."

"Have you hidden any?"

"No."

"You swear?"

She saw his lips pressing together, his neck thickening.

"I swear."

"Well, piss off then."

⌣

She scuttled past him and hurried down the hall, succumbing to the dark and fetid sanctuary of the bathroom. She groped her way towards the toilet, stubbing her toe on the towel rail, then sat down on the lid. Unable to face exposing her skin to the freezing air, she remained in position, elbows on knees, thinking. Why had she allowed things to get this bad? She thought of Grabowski, then she thought of the piercing cold waiting for her on the doorstep. Finally she thought of Charlie, waking up without her, already basking in the warmth of tomorrow.

CHAPTER

44

Something was different. Some infinitesimal change had occurred in the room, but Fred did not know what it was. He sat up and looked across the sleeping bundles — pointed clumps of hair on pillows, clothing scrambled into knots. Rubbing his jaw, he braced himself for the trip to the freezing bathroom, but as he poked his head out of the tent, he could see that Grabowski had beaten him to it. The best chair, hardly worthy of its title, was empty, occupied only by a jumble of blankets, a soup can licked clean, and an empty vodka bottle, which had been forced into the gap between the arm and the cushion. A tiny earring lay on the arm of the chair. Leaning back on his haunches, he looked over at Marcie, whose face had pushed out from under the covers. He leaned forward, examining her closed eyes.

Watching someone when they are asleep is always an odd thing, intimate and precarious at the same time. There is always a chance that they will open their eyes and catch you, a little closer than you should be, a little too familiar with the minutiae of their skin. She had a tiny cold sore on her top lip, which quivered as she breathed a whispery feminine snore. Her hair was lovely, the curls knotted over each other; he longed to touch them.

Then he remembered Grabowski, whose long absence failed to square with the arctic temperatures of the bathroom. Fearing a repeat raid of the study, he pulled his fleece over his head and stepped out of the tent, almost falling over as Marcie's blanket snagged his foot.

"Ryan, where is he?"

"Whorrr," replied the woozy fire tender, rubbing his eyes.

"Have you seen Grabowski?"

"Um ... wha ... no."

He strode towards the kitchen. Empty. Then he went upstairs, tiptoeing along the landing then running from room to room, feeling his spirits soar with every scan of the deserted bedrooms. Tips of toes forgotten, he thumped back down into the empty kitchen and, with a boldness brought on by excitement, poked his head around the door of the rank bathroom — it was empty. Only the cupboard under the stairs remained unchecked and he sprinted towards it, threw open the door, and groped foolishly in the cold, dark space. Finally he ran up to the hooks lining the hallway.

Grabowski's coat was gone.

CHAPTER
45

Everyone had an opinion. Poppy was convinced that Grabowski had gone out looking for more alcohol then lost his way in the storm. Buster thought he had been kidnapped by the abominable snowman, while Marcie suggested he had experienced a cold-induced epiphany leading to the selfless act of leaving the house so he would no longer be a burden to them. They had all laughed at that one, but stopped when Rennie wondered vaguely if he might have gone to find Dwayne. Marcie pressed her mother's hand as she spoke.

Whatever the reason, Grabowski's tyrannical reign was over, and a mood of elation verging on hysteria took hold. Buster practised impressions, wrapping himself up in blankets, banging his feet onto the table, and snorting through his nose. He became so raucous that he had to be told to shut up so they could hear Ryan's convoluted joke about smelly feet, slippers, and being trapped in a chair.

"Now that he's gone we can work out what we're going to do," said Poppy.

"I'm getting the best chair," said Ryan, flipping himself up onto the seat and stretching out his legs. "Lovely," he sighed, running his hands down the sides of the cushion.

"What's that?" said Marcie, looking at the envelope that had appeared in Ryan's hand.

"Dunno. A letter I s'pose."

The new occupant of the best chair pulled a sheet of paper and two photographs out of the envelope. It was creased on both sides, with the corners folded inwards, looking like a paper frog that had been trapped beneath the rug. He held the photographs up for all to see. Age had washed out the colours; Fred noticed his mother putting on her glasses.

A large dog stood in a field. It could have been anywhere. A leafless tree grew beside a road. The second photograph showed a little girl of about three years old. She sat on a person's lap, the owner of which could only be guessed at from the disembodied knees and hips.

"Should I read the letter?' said Ryan.

"You might as well," said Poppy. "I mean, he's not here anymore."

Ryan cleared his throat. "'Blueberry Farm, September 19. To Rusty Grabowski. After what happened yesterday I am taking Caitlin and the dog away. We are leaving this place and we are leaving you. Don't try to find us, you never will. I am letting you keep these photos so when you are an old man you can look at them and remember what it was you lost. Cathy.'" He paused. "The end."

"Is that it?" said Poppy.

"Yes. No, wait, there's something else."

He poked his tongue out of the corner of his mouth as he forced his hand beneath the cushion. After a brief bout of squirming, he dragged back his arm and pulled up a book.

"What's that?"

"Wait, let me read the front." He flipped the book over. "*Winnie the Pooh's Little Book of Wisdom.*"

A terse silence hung in the air.

"You know what?" said Marcie, frowning. "Maybe we should have tried harder to be friendly to him."

"Come on," said Ryan. "He was an ass."

"I know," said Marcie. "But maybe something made him like that, eh?"

⌐

Fred did not join in the conversation. New possibilities were opening up; they needed careful thought. He would bring the hidden food downstairs, he would ration it, he would find more wood, he would melt more water, he would improve the tent, he would ...

"Can we get a dog?" said Buster, leaning on the arm of his chair. "We could train him to go and find food, like pigs."

The sarcastic reply forming in his head collapsed as he was struck by a new imperative. He had to go out. Of course, he had to go out again to find wood and food. He did not want to die here, his body buried in the strange smelling soil or his ashes scattered in the fractious prairie wind. Yes, he had to go out.

"Mum, I've got to go out to find more fuel," he said. "The wood pile is right down."

An odd expression crept across her face. "Freddie, you can't go out in this weather." She lowered her voice. "Dwayne didn't come back."

"I know that. I'll only go to a couple of houses along the street. No further, I promise."

As he finished speaking, he remembered Grandma Knuckles. She was out of town, but there could be wood and even food in her house. Would she mind? An abrupt thought punched him with guilt. She was away, wasn't she?

"Mum, I have to go out, now. It will be dark soon. I promise, no more than fifty yards from the house."

"I'm coming with you."

"No, please, no. There's no need. Really. What's the point in both of us getting colder than we already are? Fifty yards. I promise."

It took massive effort to pull open the front door, but a foot placed squarely on the wall did the trick. It opened with a hollow pop. With freezing air pouring in, he said goodbye quickly, slamming the door behind him. Certain that a row of eyes would be watching his back through the glass, he fought to retain his dignity amongst the random snowdrifts, which tricked his judgment and upset his balance, sending him staggering sideways the moment he crossed the threshold. The shovel, frozen to the wall of the house, further thwarted his attempts at dignified heroism. It refused to budge, but several kicks later, it snapped free and he began to clear a path in the direction of the street.

The snow was deeper than he had ever seen it; it clung to the trunks of baby trees, it balanced on twigs, it wrapped the frames of half-built houses. But he enjoyed the digging. It kickstarted his sluggish blood, and ten minutes later he reached the road, blinking snow off his eyelids and feeling warmer than he had for days. He looked up and down the street and felt a twinge of anxiety; no reassuring tread marks, no footprints, just a sprinkling of pine needles dropped in a pile on the snow. Wary of the risks of stopping and cooling down, he continued, picking up speed with a shoulder-jarring swipe as he threw the snow over his left shoulder again and again. Soon a rough trench followed his advance.

The entrance to Grandma Knuckles' house was almost unrecognizable in its fresh coat of snow. He nudged the steps with his toe and, deceived by the fresh strata of ice layering the surface, misjudged the height and almost fell before regaining his balance. He pressed the defunct doorbell. He pressed again. With raw air bruising his senses, he rang again. The cold was making him angry and irritated, and stupid. Then the hammering started — his fist pummelled, his shovel sliced ugly grooves in the bottom of the door. He strained to hear a noise but could catch only the sound of his lungs rasping out freezing air. Then a new thought came to mind, and moments later, a lateral trench was driving towards the front window. Standing on frozen toes, he pressed his face against the windowpane and a deep feeling of horror sliced into his body. She was here. Grandma Knuckles was here. He could see her, there inside the house. But before he could react, misted breath closed down his view, and he wiped, he smeared with gloves, he frantically scraped with his nails to get it back.

The old lady sat in an armchair facing the fireplace. Tucked beneath her elbow was a small dog, lying motionless. Relief surged in, then panic, as he noticed there was no fire. Two slippered feet pointed towards nothing but a cold black hole. He rapped on the window, vibrating the glass. He banged, but not even his loudest thump disturbed the peaceful occupants.

"Hello! Hey, there!" he bellowed, dragging off a glove and banging with his bare fist. "Hello!" As much as he longed for it to do so, the little dog failed to lift its head from its neatly folded paws. He hesitated. Then, without thinking of the consequences, he lifted the shovel and smashed it into the windowpane. The crash made him jump, sending him snapping sideways to avoid the fallout of flying glass. He picked a shard off his hood, then peered back through the hole.

"Hello!"

The old lady had not moved. Slippers still pointed at the black fireplace. Paws were still folded. Breathless with adrenalin, he heaved himself in, leaving footprints in the opportune layer of snowflakes already gathering on the carpet. He tiptoed towards her and stared into her face. The rigid mouth and glassy eyes confirmed what he had already guessed: Grandma Knuckles was dead.

He started shaking then, a rhythmic pulse juddering up from his elbows then crawling into the muscles at the back of his neck. He had never seen a dead body. Not in real life. He moved closer and stared down at the lifeless face, trying to see remnants of the wistful look that had followed him down the street. But all he saw were frozen eyelashes glued to grey cheeks, and nothing could stop the guilt that was now buckling up inside his abdomen. She had died alone, a hundred feet from their house.

He looked around the room, shocked by its austerity. A single chair furnished a small wooden table and an old-fashioned display cabinet stood empty. No blankets, no coffee cups, no trace of food. Glancing around he spotted a postcard on the table and picked it up, overwhelmed by the sudden brightness of the blue sea off Florida. He turned it over.

Dear Mom,
I hope you're coping all right without the rest of your furniture.
Brian and I will come by with the truck as soon as we get back. It's
thirty-four degrees; we're nearly dying of heat. Kevin's been stung
by a jellyfish. He's okay. See you on Thursday. Take care of yourself.
Love, Christie

He pretended it was the cold making his hand shake as he put the card back down on the table, engulfed by that most unforgiving of emotions — regret. But low temperatures do not allow a hiatus, even one with such depths, and soon the card was propped up against a small vase and he was running up the stairs, poking his head into the empty rooms. The only place showing evidence of life was a back bedroom. It contained a neatly made bed, a small wardrobe, and a chair with a green jacket folded over it. A small bottle of pills sat on the bedside table. He picked them up, sniffed inside, and put them into his pocket. Back downstairs, he returned to the kitchen and searched through the cupboards, feeling cheated by the contents: three small cans of dog food and a jar of gherkins. Cheated or not, he slipped the jar into his pocket and inspected the dark fridge, which harboured nothing more than a carton of milk, swollen with cold, and some old, grey cheese.

Returning to the living room, he walked over to the woman and looked down at her. The absence of blankets was nagging at him. He walked over to the spot by the window where he imagined she had stood when she was alive. He could see his house; he could even see part of the inside of his bedroom. His family was in there now, wondering where he was, waiting for him to come back.

With the cold browbeating him into action, he began to break up the flimsy table with the pleasurable high of wanton vandalism, only just managing to block out intense feelings of self-reproach that were threatening to overwhelm him. A hard kick was all it took to detach the legs, and he gathered them together into a bundle fixed under his arm. He watched the tabletop make a perfectly straight imprint in the snow as he pushed it over the window ledge, wishing he could be on the other side to catch it. The unbearable cold hectored him again, forcing him to hurry, numbing his cheeks just below his eyes, hurting him. He returned to the old lady for a final look. No words came, but a gesture seemed possible. He picked up her dangling arm and tried to place her hand on the dog's head. Stiff at the elbow, it slipped from his fingers, slapping back down onto the frame of the chair. He picked it up again, holding the stiff fingers in his, then wedged them beneath the dog's belly. They stayed, and so did the memory of that moment, the memory of that feeling, human and canine skin merging into one, cold as dry ice.

Heaving the broken furniture back across the street nearly finished him. Legs were dropped, legs were found, ice built up on the tips of his gloves. Halfway across he stopped and scanned the street, scrutinizing the empty houses, looking for signs of chimney smoke. But there was nothing, just a blank sky and the closed mouths of double garages lined up along the street. He was ready to give up by the time he dragged the last piece of wood up onto the threshold and banged on the door.

What joy it was to see faces pressed on the glass. What delight he felt as eager hands pulled him in. And what pleasure it was to have his boots eased off, one by one. Someone was massaging his feet, pressing delicate fingers into the gaps between his toes. He succumbed to a deep feeling of exhaustion as Marcie rolled the balaclava up over his mouth. She was smiling and, without asking his permission, undid the knot in his scarf, folded it up into a rectangle, and set it on the stair beside him. The zip of his coat jammed as she started to pull it down. He wanted it to. He wanted it stuck, broken beyond repair, anything, anything to prolong the time he could spend in the sensual new world into which he had stepped.

"I'm glad you're back, Fred." There was a whiff of cough mixture on her breath.

"So am I," said his mother, who suddenly entered his

consciousness, brushing snow off the bottom of his jeans. "What happened?"

He could not think what happened; something was affecting his brain. "I ... er."

"Where did you go, Freddie?" His mother's face moved closer.

"I went to the old lady's house."

"What old lady?"

"The one on the corner."

"Which corner?"

"The brown house."

She stopped brushing. "Is she all right?"

"No ... she's dead."

CHAPTER

46

A grey face, chiselled with shadows, stared back from the bathroom mirror. How old she looked. Light shone from below can crush life out of the healthiest features and, as Poppy held the flashlight beneath her chin, she thought of the old lady. The one she had never met. The one that was dead. Usually discreet areas of her face were springing into focus as the light glared upwards: the prickly ring of her nostrils, the underside of her chin studded with tiny hairs, the freckled underside of her brow. She watched her features slump into grotesque angles as the light flicked around, and she felt an ache in her chest, sadness threaded with guilt.

How could it happen? Forgetting her coat, she had run into the street after Fred had told her about the old lady. She remembered the wind slicing cold blades beneath her collar as she scanned the street looking for human traces: smoke from a chimney, footprints, even a face in a window. She surged towards the closest house, chopping through the snow with heavy legs, only to be captured by her son persuading her back to the relative warmth of their living room with murmured assurances and an arm around her shoulder that felt like Charlie's. How could it happen? How could an old lady die alone?

The bathroom cabinet was full. She plunged both hands in, famished anticipation briefly burying her lingering feelings of remorse. Here was one of those moments when ordinary items take on a new meaning. She could not remember how many times she had casually flipped open the mirrored door without a thought for its contents. Reduced now to a new level of hunger, she salivated at the mere thought of passion fruit lip gloss, and there it was now, right in front of her, the miniature tub on the bottom shelf, promising so much. She had no problem stuffing a greasy fingerful into her mouth, and she completely forgot she had a family, just one floor below, as she pressed the tip of a nasal spray into her left nostril. A single sip of cologne had to be urgently neutralized by a swig of cough medicine rattling with purple ice cubes, then another and another, until she spotted a travel-sized tube of toothpaste that she squeezed into her mouth, gasping at its mintyness. Poor stomach, she thought, grinding under the strain of the apothecary's meal. She felt sick. But sick or not she continued, taking a bite right off the top of a lipstick, spitting it into the sink, then biting again. She slurred and guzzled some more, convincing herself that hand cream tastes good, and only stopped when she found a large jar of iron tablets that cried out to be shared.

"We can share that," she said aloud.

Wiping the lipstick off her teeth with a sleeve, she closed the cabinet door and went downstairs with a satisfied stomach for the first time in three days.

CHAPTER
47

Fred could not remember if they had an axe. Ryan had helped him search the cupboard under the stairs, but the only set of blades they could find belonged to a pair of hedge clippers. How pathetic could one family be? No food in the fridge, no axe, hardly any wood. The stolen table legs had given off a fierce heat but died down abruptly to a melee of complaints followed by a scraping of furniture as they all shifted closer to the fire. The last remaining logs were now displayed on the coffee table, being dusted down by a dreamy-eyed Rennie. He watched her trying to straighten out the curls of bark, bending and flattening without success.

"We need more fuel," said Poppy suddenly, lifting up her shoulders as if she was saying something none of them had thought of. "We'll have to start burning our furniture if we're going to keep the room bearable." Buster gripped the arms of his chair. "What else can we do? Look outside."

Fred glanced at the snowflakes rushing down the windows. "I should try to get some wood from somewhere up the street," he said.

"I don't want you to go out again, Fred. Last time you found a dead body."

The bluntness was uncharacteristic. He was not the only one to turn and look at her.

"Do dead people get cold?" said Buster.

"No ... yes," said Poppy, twisting her wedding ring.

"Schoolbooks burn great," said Ryan, verging on a wink before checking himself.

Fred shuddered. He could hardly bear the thought of more

books burning. Too much emotion was bound between those pages. So he stared at the carpet, dragging his nails across his scalp, thinking. Hard. Then a breadboard came into his mind. Square and small and wooden. Hitching up his jeans, he rushed out of the room.

The board lay on the kitchen counter, its final crumbs licked off by persons unknown. He picked it up, put it down again, then began trawling through the drawers, searching for anything made of wood. Spoons, mallets, and rolling pins were soon piling up, and he cursed as he worked to prise out a spatula that was wedged at the back of the drawer. Then he began a deeper search, whooping with delight as he made other small yet flammable discoveries: the slender columns of the egg timer, the finely sanded handle of the corkscrew. He returned to the living room and, sweeping a space onto the table with the back of his hand, laid out his hoard.

"I think …" He stopped as the circle settled itself, ready to listen. "I think we should find everything that burns and bring it here, then we can work out what we've got and what should go on first." His voice had taken on a different tone. He could hear it himself, a bit bossy, a tiny bit patronizing. "If that sounds all right to everyone?"

They all nodded.

"Let's go!"

~

Fred was the first back to the living room. An unexpected fear gripped him as he walked in. Something about the circle of empty armchairs, still warm from recently removed backsides, unnerved him. He placed a pestle and mortar on the table and sat down, feeling the temporary absence of the others so deeply that he had to make himself breathe.

"Hurry up," he called up to the ceiling in his loudest voice.

The scuffle of feet in the room above calmed him down, and he laid his head on the back of the chair, twirling the egg timer over in his fingers. It seemed immoral that only he sat by the fire. He was convinced he could see the precious heat climbing the walls and drifting across the ceiling, seeping through invisible cracks.

"Hurry up," he yelled again, into the empty hall. He was rewarded by the sight of Ryan feeling his way down the stairs, his view ahead blinded by a pile of board games. He clasped a cricket bat between his knees.

"Outta my way!" he said on leftover breath.

Fred grabbed a travel chess set that was about to slip from the boy's clenched elbows and laid it onto the table, beside the last two logs.

The pile continued to grow, looking increasingly like preparations for a Saturday morning yard sale. Picture frames, pencils, and pepper mills vied for a place on the table with items of dubious flammability — spectacle cases, handbags, and plastic soap dishes. Furniture seemed to walk into the room as Marcie and Poppy carried in the dining chairs, one by one.

"Brilliant, just brilliant," Fred found himself repeating, unable to contain the intense feelings of pyromania that were creeping under his skin.

"Let's burn the small things first."

A footstool was the first to go, its legs ripped off and thrown into the flames without ceremony. A cookbook was next, thick with photographs. He could not help but drool over the prawn cocktail on its cover, and no amount of holding in his stomach could suppress the Pavlovian response brought on by the sight of a faded crustacean lying in a silver dish. Most hope of long-term heat rested with a piece of skirting board, the only remaining casualty of a war his father had waged with a dead cable and broken television. Buster spotted an ancient piece of gum, stuck to the back of it. Not caring if it had been spat from the mouth of a long-forgotten builder, he popped it into his mouth before anyone could stop him.

As the heat poured out they rocked from side to side like a posse of excited penguins. Fred's cheeks burned deliciously and the muscles gripping the back of his neck loosened, allowing him to think.

In the space of a few days their lives had boiled down to three simple essentials: food, water, and heat. He looked at the fire and pondered over the embers glowing in the hearth. How long would it last? He had no idea. Then a thought arrived; he wanted to kick himself for not having it earlier. He checked his watch, noted the time, and drew a sketch of the burning logs on a corner of his notepad, confident that he would soon know how long it takes to burn a single log. Then he could work out how much time they had left.

He mulled over possibilities. Their furniture supply was small; the limitations of a transatlantic shipping container had seen to that, with only the most treasured items fighting their way onto the boat. His mother had a large collection of poetry anthologies that she had been building up for years. His father had a pile of magazines that he dearly loved, insisting on bringing his stockpile of *Car Weekly,* every copy ever printed, with them when they moved. Fred tried not to think about the burning of these treasures. Nevertheless, he *must* think about it. He must plan. He must measure, he must calculate, for every minute, of every hour, of every day.

How could they not own an axe?

CHAPTER

48

Poppy had never liked the dining room chairs. She could not even remember why they bothered to keep them when they moved. The feet scratched the wooden floor and she was tired of having to lift the heavy frames every time she wanted to move one. As she watched their possessions pile up around the coffee table, lining up to be burned, she felt her eyes glaze over. What do people rescue from fires? What treasured belongings do people take if the whole house is burning down? Children, of course, and the dog, but if forced, what is the one thing that must be saved beyond all else?

Her pocket was full of photos. What a cliché. Charlie hitching up bell-bottom jeans, newborn Fred glaring from beneath a sagging brow, her mother forcing out a sad smile.

She sighed as a spice rack hit the flames. Canadian maple. Brand new.

CHAPTER

49

Fred wondered if he needed glasses. The circle collapsing into an ellipse persuaded him so as he ringed Wednesday, December 12 with a blunt pencil. A ragged "Day six" further confirmed his suspicions. His handwriting appeared to have lost the idiosyncratic slope that he had spent years perfecting, and he noticed his words were now composed of childish, squat letters, badly spaced. Squashed up against the Tuesday was a tiny note in red: "Doctor, 12:00. Physical — no breakfast."

He had never gone three days without food before. Even during bouts of flu his father would bring him warm drinks of honey and lemon, often spiced with a few drops of whiskey, the illegal nature of which added to the healing effect. Dry toast with marmite would follow, deceiving his hungry senses into rating this simple meal as one of life's greatest gastronomic experiences.

Now he was hungry. A balloon inflated inside his stomach, stretched to its limit. He should have been thinking of logs, but he could not stop thinking of food. He could not stop picturing the cookbooks burning. It hurt to remember the pies ripped in half and cabbage shredded as they were fed to the fire. What a tease that last book had been, taunting him with its deep-fried chicken legs and lemon meringue pies. Page seventeen had pushed him over the edge. Grabbing hold of the spine of the book just as it was about to be thrown on the fire, he had torn out the photograph and folded it over into a small square. *For later.* And when later came, he had to endure the cold of his bedroom, just to have a chance to look, and to drool, at leisure.

It was fishcakes — two recently cooked ones. They squatted in a frying pan, shared with lettuce leaves and three pips squeezed from a lemon. He had learned the recipe by heart, reciting the order of work: poaching, flouring, shaping, and frying. Unable to let it go, he had memorized the weights and temperatures before turning the most sensual words over in his mind. *Tender, opaque,* and *skin* swirled in his head while *squeeze, moisture,* and *yolk* dallied on the tip of his tongue. He felt ready to eat the paper as he sniffed the photograph, but was let down hard when all it gave back was the unsatisfying smell of a rarely visited sock drawer.

He stared at the calendar — twelve days until Christmas. He *had* to find something to eat.

"There must be something else to eat in this house. I'm going to look," he announced to the others as he returned to the living room. Without being invited, the circle stood up as one and followed him. They fanned out across one side of the kitchen like a posse of detectives hunting for clues, looking for something, anything, that resembled food. As the distinction between edible and inedible blurred, they all rose to the challenge, chafing the dust off empty flour bags, sucking on avocado soap, and smelling the noxious fumes of grapefruit detergent with the belief that airborne molecules satisfied the stomach. Finally, enticed by the warmth coming from the garbage bin, he bent over and inspected its contents, stirring and rummaging with a reluctant finger, only to be driven off by the rancid smell of old banana skins.

Nothing came close to dispelling the hunger that corroded his insides, and a new low was reached when he returned to the old lady's house and stole the dog food from her top cupboard. Blowing snow had lined his hard-won trench but it was powder, not ice, that stuck to his ankles as he struggled up to the house. She was still there, of course, with fresh snow heaped on the carpet and a few flakes carried by some ghostly indoor breeze visible on her arm. Those harmless specks settling on the sleeve of her cardigan confirmed her demise better than any death certificate ever could. It horrified him, sending him rushing into the kitchen, his heart racing. He grabbed the cans without ceremony and, forgetting the existence of a front door, climbed back through the window, sparing no more thought for the body draped across the armchair. Who knows what made him look back as he walked towards the road, but he noticed a mailbox by the door and stopped to stare at the brass nameplate. The wind had whipped the snow off it, uncovering a name. Jane O'Sullivan.

Back in the living room, the others crowded around him as

he opened the first can, cranking the handle of the can opener around with such speed that he pressed dents into the sides of his finger. Influenced by the meaty smell lodging itself into his nostrils, something happened that he was ashamed of for a long time after. Not caring that the others also craved the boiled offal as much as he did, he put his hand straight into the can, scooped out a fistful of dog food, and stuffed it into his mouth.

"Fred!" cried Poppy.

He paused, but in spite of the nausea rising in his stomach, he dug a second sticky fist deeper into the can.

"What's it like?" said Marcie evenly.

"Disgusting," he replied, handing her the can as he tried to steady his breathing. She took it and offered it to her mother. Rennie shook her head, so she offered it to Buster, who took the spoon and licked it, then cried as he tasted the meat, salted by the little tears running into his mouth.

"I'm really sorry," said Fred. No one replied.

The nausea kicked in then. He could not help licking the remnants of meat that were drying on his hands but he was soon overwhelmed, running to the front door and forcing it open with foul smelling fingers before vomiting the slimy dog food mash onto the ground. In a haze of revulsion and hunger, he picked up brown snow, cramming lumps back into his mouth, then spat it out again, leaving vile, jellied splatters freckling the ground. He could only stare at the mangled slush at his frozen feet.

"Freddie, come in. Please." His mother had come to the door. With a hand on the small of his back, she guided him back to the living room.

"I'm so sorry," he said again, sitting down on the sofa.

He deserved some acrimony, he almost desired it, but all he got as he re-entered the circle and sat down were looks of concern shining out of five faces.

It was much later in the day when Fred went upstairs. Leaden socks slowed the pace, yet they did nothing to help him cope with the dizziness cart-wheeling in his head. Tidying his room had been the last thing on his mind, but he started nonetheless, gathering the wreckage of his bedroom and re-assembling it with an incompetence not previously seen in that part of the house. As it reached a modest resemblance of its former self, he reached to the back of the wardrobe, pulled out the raincoat, and unfolded it. It felt distinctly drier, the sleeves standing to attention as he shook it out. He sniffed it. The smell had faded, and he was rewarded with nothing but the dry scent of the wardrobe.

Something was happening to him that he did not understand. Something that made him lick the arm of the coat — then clamp his teeth onto the collar, and bite.

He laid the raincoat down on his lap, folded a single sleeve at the elbow, sat back, and stared into space.

CHAPTER
50

"Thirty storeys high," said Poppy, "and the doors had gold handles."

Twilight blurred the shapes in the room, and trying to see details in the faces was hurting Fred's eyes. His mother was describing the restaurant; it was one of the best she had ever been to. Charlie had insisted they go somewhere special on their twentieth wedding anniversary.

"Mum, you mean ten storeys, don't you? There's no building in the whole city that high."

Without pausing she continued, launching into a lavish

portrayal of the reception desk gilded with mythical creatures clutching grapes and smelling of polish. A tap on the silver-plated bell had brought the receptionist running. "She wore a pink dress, the colour of bacon."

"What did you eat?" said Buster.

Ignoring his question she carried on, chronicling the walk from the desk to the table in agonizing detail. "It was lovely, with a white table cloth and a vase filled with bilberry blue flowers and orange ..."

"But what did you eat?" repeated Buster. He was at a low ebb, looking miserable that his favourite person was torturing him.

"Lamb chops!" she said, the pitch of her voice rising in triumph.

Ryan fell backwards onto the mattress in a mock faint and struggled to sit up again.

"How many?" asked Marcie.

"Four. With mashed potato and green beans. There was gravy, too. You know, Fred, just like the gravy your grandma makes. We dipped our beans in it. Oh, I forgot, there was mint jelly, too."

"Did you have broccoli?" said Marcie.

"A huge steaming bowlful with butter melting over it."

Fred could smell the lamb, he definitely could. In fact, he could taste it. Just saying the word left a meaty taste in his mouth. Someone was in the kitchen this very moment, basting it in its own juice. A separate dish just for him. He would not have to share it — not with anyone.

"Were there any carrots?" said Rennie.

They all looked at her. He did not want to look too hard; she was not on his list of things to worry about. The list was full. But despite himself, he noticed how exhausted she looked. She had not taken her share of food when they had it, refusing with a persistence that had left her cut out at meal times. She must be hungrier than the rest of them. But what was he supposed to do, force-feed her? Guilt lined his stomach as an image of foie gras came into his mind from nowhere — the long metal tube being inserted into the throat, the fatty grain rammed down, then the goose waddling off as if nothing had happened. He had never touched the stuff; he thought it was cruel. But now he wanted to eat some more than anything else in the world. Spread on toast.

"Can your tummy eat itself?" asked Buster.

"Of course not," said Poppy.

He could see she was not completely sure. Visualizing his own stomach had become an obsession during the last few hours. His head ached as he pictured microscopic tentacles bathed in redundant acids, reaching out, then retracting with nothing. He hitched up his jeans. What day was it? He could not remember. When did they eat the last can of soup?

He could not remember.

CHAPTER

51

Exhaustion crept inside Poppy's lungs. Too much effort was needed to breathe and she almost couldn't be bothered. She felt cold. She felt it all the time — not a shivering cold but something trapped under her skin, making her joints ache and her fingers stiff. And she was worried about Fred. Why did he keep disappearing? Questions without answers were becoming her reality. Come to think of it, why were his nails bitten down to the quick?

They spent all day around the fire. Only Buster still animated the listless circle, taking random leaps onto her lap, begging for stories. She did her best, patting his shoulders and dabbing at tears, acting out the role of tired, neglectful mother. But those stories wore her out. How many times could a black and white badger be expected to stare at the moon?

She observed changes in the circle without comment, although any person daring to sit in her chair while she was in the kitchen would have seen a side of her never previously on public show. Ryan had adopted the chair vacated by Grabowski and now spent most of the day reading. Who knows what would have happened if they had burned that last book, whose life he had begged to save. A boy who loved to read was amongst them, and the thin novel helped him slip through one tedious hour and into the tedious next, as he read, re-read, then read aloud to anyone who cared to listen, his eyebrows flicking up and down like a pair of waltzing canker worms. When not reading, he was collecting, and hiding things, the bulge under one side of his cushion growing daily. She was amused at the boyish trophies, happy to note the model airplanes and empty salt-cellars pressed into secrecy, but she had to restrain an urge to snatch when she spotted a menu from a Chinese takeout being slipped between the cushions.

Fred shared the sofa with Marcie. She watched their listless ritual of re-arranging themselves without comment — head on shoulder, hand on arm, hand on hand. Under normal circumstances she might have felt all the conflicting emotions of a mother whose son was becoming a man, but now all she could do was observe without comment as the hunger hollowed out her abdomen and set up a chorus of rippling and fizzing that no amount of belly rubbing could subdue.

It was pure chance that they caught the announcement. Fred was fiddling with the radio, slumped on the sofa and staring at nothing, when a fresh voice bounced into the room, its perky tone momentarily distracting them from its significance.

"...the prime minister has announced that the state of national emergency continues and calls on the citizens of the prairie provinces to remain in their homes. Rescue efforts have unfortunately been hampered by the continuing storm, and remaining gas supplies are being diverted to the emergency services. By Thursday morning, emergency shelters will have been set up in the following cities ..."

They straightened up as one. Ryan gesticulated to Fred, shaping a "turn up the volume" with his fingers. Unfamiliar names jostled for position in the long list, and Poppy found herself wondering if it was a machine talking.

"Winnipeg ... the St. Germain area, the community centre on Willow and Main, behind the museum ..."

"Food!" whooped Ryan, pressing his palms together and looking up at the ceiling.

The radio cut out then, but they hardly noticed as a medley of voices erupted inside the circle of chairs.

"Sausages!"

"Bacon!"

"Sausages!"

"Let's get our coats."

"It's not 'til Friday, didn't you listen?"

"A hundred sausages!"

"Mind my toe!"

Poppy rested her head on the back of her chair; she felt so tired. Displays of enthusiasm demand energy and she had none. Her lips were smiling without her telling them to, but that was as much as she could manage for now. Maybe later she would be able to bounce on her chair like Buster, or dance a celebratory jig like Ryan, but for the moment she was happy that the back of her seat could hold her head up and she did not have to speak. She did not even have to make decisions. Fred would do that. She watched him across the room, talking to Marcie. They were discussing food at the shelter. She could hardly bear to hear the young girl's description of her favourite meal at Smokey Joe's — barbecued ribs, all you can eat. They would always put too much on their plates and something would fall off the side, staining the table cloth brown. Her son looked animated, nodding and smiling, occasionally rubbing a circle on his stomach. But she could see he was not concentrating. A part of his mind seemed elsewhere. Then, a random thought came into her head.

It was a box of Belgian chocolates. Two full pounds, enclosed in cellophane then wrapped in orange tissue paper. She remembered a curly ribbon around the outside — Charlie's welcome home present, hidden in her study.

No one noticed as she got up to leave the circle. The description of Smokey Joe's had reached a climax and she was relieved not to have to endure Buster's pig eating stories, which were taking exaggeration to a new level.

The sight of the study reminded her of what had happened there. But she did not care about that now. All she cared about were the chocolates. Her heart thumped painfully as she put her hand inside a large flowerpot, stretching her fingers to the bottom.

"Beautiful," was all she said as she felt the smoothness of the wrapping.

Boxes of chocolates are innocuous items in the usual run of things, but this one was implicated in a violent bodily reaction, sending the acidity of her stomach soaring, followed by a blade of pain that carved its way beneath her breastbone and up across her shoulders. Gasping and hugging the box like a baby, she rushed back to the living room, sniffing the paper as she went. Tissue had never smelled so good.

Cold and trembling fingers are the worst tools for undoing small, tight knots. To make matters worse, an eager huddle of people closed in on her, rippling with frustration and absorbing the obscenities taking their maiden voyage out of her mouth. She struggled to untie the knot, stretching the ribbon off one corner, tightening it only further. As tears ran down her cheeks, blotting the tissue, Fred took it from her.

"I'll do it, Mum."

"I can do it!" she said, snatching the box back.

She worked at the knot again, stretching the nylon ribbon with her teeth.

"Shit! Shit! Shit!"

Desperation set in and, summoning the strength of an all-in wrestler, she tore off the tissue and dragged the tray out sideways. Two chocolates fell onto the floor. For a split second, they were all held by something: the thin line between desperation and altruism that had not yet been breached. She picked up both chocolates and placed them back in their rightful positions. Then she shared them out, fairly and squarely, omitting the culinary filibuster that usually accompanies a box of chocolates. Forget agonizing over whether to choose a raspberry ripple or a hazelnut cluster. Ramming chocolates down throats was the order of the day.

But twenty-six cannot be divided by six, and the sounds of chewing were interrupted by Fred running to the kitchen to fetch a knife. He cut straight onto the coffee table and red jelly oozed out from between the chocolate fragments. Only after every single chocolate had been eaten, the final smear of jelly licked off the table, and the remaining molecules of scent sniffed out of the tray, could they think about the announcement.

"Thank God something is happening out there," Poppy said.

"How far is it to the shelter?" Fred asked, turning to Marcie.

"I'm not sure, but I think it's about three miles, it's close to the museum."

Poppy gazed at her son; he looked exhausted. *She* should go, she thought, she was the mother after all. But she was exhausted, too. She closed her eyes, trying to picture the length of a mile.

"I'll go," he said.

"We need to think about it, Fred."

"What's there to think about?"

"Well, you can't go alone for one thing."

"Mum, look. Let's be honest. Rennie can't go out, Buster needs you, and I'm certainly not taking Marcie. The only other person who could come is Ryan and I don't think he has the strength. I'm sorry but I don't."

Oblivious to the wave of hurt feelings he had created, Fred stood up and left the room.

"Will there be polar bears at the shelter?" asked Buster.

CHAPTER
52

Two hours later Fred sat in the blue chair, flicking though Poppy's sketchbook. It seemed to have a life of its own, the well-thumbed pages falling open at will. An ink drawing of himself towards the back startled him. The handful of scratchy lines had caught his likeness well, and he traced a finger over the stipple etched into the paper. Random page flicking revealed food, food, and more food. The density shocked him. Towers of exuberant sandwiches, twenty slices high, were interspersed with lovingly detailed studies of fruit. Gravy dripped from pies, battered fish swam through jelly, and chips danced across the margin in endless lines. Browsing further back, he halted

rosie chard   171
SEAL
INTESTINE
RAINCOAT

at a boldly drawn figure. Mr. Grabowski. With vast shoulders pressed against the edge of the book and a belly spanning two pages, the likeness was chilling.

Then he noticed the text. A primitive red scrawl annotated the drawing. Words were riding down the man's arm, folding down beneath his knees, compressing into illegibility beneath his armpits before petering out at the corner of his elbow.

"Precious Poppy is going to die. Ha ha ha ha ha ha ha ha ha ha."

He snapped the book shut, then glanced at his mother. She was reading a story to Buster, stifling a yawn as she attempted to imitate an angry badger for the fourth time. Watching her closely, he re-opened the book and, pressing a thumb across the margin, ripped the page out, millimetre by millimetre. A second badly suppressed yawn provided the cover he was waiting for, and he scrunched up the page and threw it on the fire. He sat back in his chair, engulfed by irrational fears. Was Grabowski hiding upstairs in his mother's wardrobe? He stared at the duvet, stood up, and stamped down the fold buckled up in its centre, then sat down again.

New thoughts drizzled in, lathering up his paranoia — a boy leaves a house, a man watches a boy, a man hurts a boy.

It was agreed. On Friday morning he would go to the shelter. Alone.

His mother had dug in her heels at first, sifting through scenarios and fluffing up problems, but with her judgment sabotaged by chocolates, she forgot the provisos she had counted out so forcefully on the fingers of one hand and gave in.

They did not lie down in their usual positions when they went to bed. Buster had been crying a few times during the afternoon and demanded that he sleep between the two mothers.

During the enforced reorganization, Fred found himself in his usual spot on the edge of the tent, but he noticed that Marcie was puffing up a pillow by his side. Dust rose up from her duvet moments before she slumped down next to him, some of it settling into his eye. They did not speak; they lay still, face to face. Everything looked grey. Even Marcie's hair, darkened at the scalp from days of accumulated grease, had lost its glow. But there was just enough light to see her face, about six inches from his — she was looking straight at him.

He normally fidgeted in bed, turning over again and again, realigning his duvet and pummelling his pillows into shape, but at this moment his body immediately found that elusive position of supreme comfort. Unable to imagine ever wanting to move again, he lay still, looking at the face in front of him. Her eyes, nose, and mouth were visible but myriad of freckles had faded into the gloom. He found it hard to gauge her expression, or even determine if she was awake. Could that eye looking at him be closed? Any doubt was removed as she suddenly sat up and pulled her duvet over him. It was all very matter of fact — she pressed the folds down along his spine, then repeated the procedure down her own back until they were sealed in together like two horse chestnuts inside a single shell. Then she lay back down on her pillow. Soon a delicate snore drifted towards him. She was asleep, relaxed and untroubled. But he lay awake, his muscles taut, his heart racing.

CHAPTER
53

The morning of the seventh day, a grimly lit Thursday, felt colder than the sixth. Fred had spent the night mulling over his impending trip to the shelter. Darkness had amplified the hazards and increased his doubts, leaving him to wake with a large problem and the seeds of a solution. He could not walk in deep snow. He had to dig his way to the old lady's house, just spitting distance away — if spit did not freeze in the air. Now his hands were shaking with hunger and only consuming an entire horse would calm them. Then he remembered — snowshoes.

He eased himself out of bed, taking care to tuck the duvet back down behind Marcie's body, smoothing it into the backs of her legs with a familiarity he would never have dared twelve hours earlier. Congratulating himself on his stealth, he opened the zip of the tent.

"Ryan!"

His words drifted unheard over the fire guardian, who was snoozing on the sofa, steel poker in hand. In no mood for recriminations, he said nothing more and, after placing a snapped chair leg on the embers, tiptoed towards the storage space under the stairs. This was a lazy halfway house, usually packed but lately denuded, with possessions held in a permanent state of torpor. Falling into that obscure category of "might be needed one day," the contents were either seasonal or of sentimental value, but had mostly arrived there due to the bone idleness of someone who could not be bothered to carry them any further. He scanned the shelves. Only a highly trained eye would note the complete dearth of flammable objects, and it was mainly the likes of screen wash and bicycle inner tubes that had survived the recent pillaging. The bottom shelf held a collection of empty jam jars, their transparent waists revealing shoeboxes of letters and photographs stacked behind. He was struck by the kindness of the person who had left these untouched.

A rustle behind him announced the arrival of Ryan, peering inside the small space. From his crouched position, Fred could see how tired the boy looked, his view from below accentuating the condition of the boy's skin, which sagged into grey bags beneath his eyes. Only the involuntary twitch of a miniscule muscle beneath one eyelid animated his face. "Found any wormholes?" Ryan said, wiping his cheek with the back of his hand.

"Yeah, and a shortcut to hog heaven," replied Fred. It was an expression he had heard at school. He was trying it out.

"What are you looking for?" asked Ryan.

"Snowshoes. I bought them in a junk shop the other day but I can't remember where I put them. They're ancient but they might get me to the shelter."

Ryan moved in closer and their shoulders bumped in the confined space as they peered towards the backs of the shelves.

"Hey, Fred, we could burn these, couldn't we?"

"What, the letters?"

"No, the shelving. Look, the wood is thick. They might last a couple of hours."

"Ryan, you're a genius."

Minutes later they returned to the living room, waving the shelves at the newly awakened campers before laying them on the coffee table with a flashy display that would have even made Dwayne proud, only to realize they were too long to fit into the stove.

"Tell me you have an axe, *somewhere*, please," pleaded Ryan.

Fred had to admit it was incredible. Not owning an axe when you have a wood-burning stove is hard to explain. Back in the storage closet, he hunted for the toolbox that he vaguely remembered placing there when they first arrived. But a memory running on empty cannot be trusted, and the dangerously sharp saw so bright in his mind was replaced by the world's smallest hacksaw. It was blunt. He carried it back to the living room and slammed it down on the floor. The others jumped.

"What's wrong, Fred?" said Marcie.

"Nothing."

Fred went first. Ryan kneeled on one end of the wood and Fred tried to cut it. Nothing happened. He sawed again — still nothing happened. His arm ached like hell by the time he handed the hacksaw over to Ryan, and he watched gloomily as the younger boy sawed and sighed, carving a faint line where he had made none.

"What is this, granite?" Ryan said after a minute, rubbing his elbow and examining the ruler of dust clinging to the wood.

Fred felt lousy. How did Ata do it? With nothing more than a handful of slippery seals he was set. Did he not ever stop, just stop completely and say, "I can't go on"?

It was while he was mopping himself with this damp hankie of despondency that he remembered the snowshoes again. He stepped over the pile of abandoned shelves and returned to storage, ignoring Ryan's complaints of abandonment. Cold fingers let him down yet again as he searched and shoved, not caring a jot when a jar of white spirit tipped onto the stack of letters, dissolving precious words into a grey sheen. He sniffed.

"Come on," he said through locked teeth. "Come on."

He mapped out his recent movements — cupboard, hall, bedroom — then, letting forth a shout, he charged up the stairs.

The low level of the bedframe forced his head sideways as he squirmed his way to the back wall, burning his ear on the carpet. A goose feather tickled, a sock brushed against his finger like a frozen animal, then he felt the snowshoes, pulled them out, and held them up to the window, examining the webbing. But with its usual lack of warning, the cold re-entered his consciousness, bullying him downstairs to the living room. He almost twisted his ankle leaping the last four stairs in one go. He sat down, too close to the fire.

"I need lots of brains," he was saying, "and some leather thong or something like that. Do we have that?"

"What on earth do you need a leather thong for?" asked Poppy.

He knew it sounded odd; he had omitted the explanation. "I need the snowshoes to get to the shelter but they're broken, look."

His mother leaned forward as he held up the battered frames.

"I need to fix them. Will anyone help me?"

"Fred, I've worn snowshoes, my dad has a pair, but you could never get anywhere in those, look at them, the binding's completely shot," said Ryan.

"I'll help you," said Marcie.

"Well, I'll help you, too. Whatever," said her brother.

"All right, let's all think, together."

"What, you mean a brainstorm?" said Ryan, perking up.

Fred felt worn out suddenly. "Yes, Ryan, a brainstorm."

⌒

Fred discovered that scratching one's head does not bring inspiration. Neither does staring at a pile of objects on a leg-less coffee table. They passed the shoes amongst themselves. Nothing happened. They drew a diagram on the back of Fred's hand. Still nothing happened. Buster judged this to be a good moment for his first tantrum and broke their concentration by wrecking his Monopoly city, destroying neighbourhoods and murdering entire families as he swept the buildings onto the floor. It got so bad Poppy was forced to divert his attention to the pile of knives and forks lying on the table, and soon the calming sound of cutlery being laid out for an imaginary din-ner provided the only background noise to whirring brains.

"I have an idea." It was Marcie who spoke. She had been sit-ting with one snowshoe on her lap for several minutes, poking a finger through the holes. "You said your dad has lots of shoes, right? Well, can't we just collect all his laces and use them to fill the holes? A bit like darning a giant sock. They're probably quite strong. It's what they're made for after all, eh?"

Fred thought for a moment. "Let's try it." Then he paused. "Mum, do you mind?'

"No, just do it."

⌒

"Phew," whistled Marcie, gazing at the inside of his parents' closet. "Your dad's got more of a shoe fetish than me."

He smiled, but could think of nothing to say.

They both grabbed an armful, quickly discovering that shoes are difficult to carry in bulk, and soon the route back to the fire was littered with errant footwear: a lone boot nosed the skirting board beside the bottom stair and two loafers mirrored each other by the front door. The growing pile preoccupied them, and it was not until they had sat down to start removing laces that he realized his mother was upset. She sat with a shoe on her lap, turning the laces around in the fingers of one hand. He had never seen her look quite so sad.

"It's all right, Mum," he said, sitting on the arm of her chair. "Dad is safe. We're safe."

"I miss him, Fred. If only we could talk to him, let him know we are all right. We *are* all right, aren't we?" she said, glancing up at him.

"Yes, we are all right. Now get to work," he added, placing a pair of tennis shoes into her lap.

Shoes without laces are ugly. Even the recently bought ones looked set for dispatch to the thrift shop when stripped bare. Street dirt circled the eyelets and rows of imprints spoiled the look of the leather. They threw the denuded shoes into a heap and sorted the laces, testing strength with an impromptu yank before laying them on the table.

"Now what?" said Buster, in a voice that sounded like Fred's.

"We have to repair the holes somehow, make them as strong as possible."

Suddenly they were busy, poring over their task like a trio of elves, aligning knots with the teeth of a fork, threading and tightening, all to the tune of Anglo-Canadian cursing, the blend of which only served to shock their shivering mothers. Tying the lattice was difficult and tedious work, and comparison between the two shoes only increased their despondency as similarities were lost in the idiosyncrasies of repair. They were forced to unscramble their work several times until, with a little help from Poppy, who late in the day announced she had done crochet as a child, they completed the job. Fred examined the finished snowshoes. The knot-work lacked the elegance of Ata's shopping cart, but he felt a huge sense of satisfaction as he bounced up and down on the frames.

"Look, they work."

"Careful," said Ryan.

"They work! Look, we did it! We did it!"

But satisfaction was short lived. Focusing his attention on the final binding, perished out of all recognition, Fred realized the hardest part was still ahead of them. After fixing his boot to the frame, they passed the snowshoe and boots amongst themselves, twirling leather bindings over fingers, ramming toecaps into holes, and longing, just longing, for the shot of inspiration that refused to come.

For two days a new type of fatigue had been regulating Fred's body. It would come suddenly, kicking him down like a mistreated horse and then disappear, leaving behind the zestful gift of false energy. Left in no doubt that food fuels the brain, he nibbled the skin around the ends of his fingers in an attempt to kick start a rare moment of lucidity. He willed the solution to come. And come it did. Not in an explosive way, but after a series of quiet, logical steps and, as with most ideas, it seemed obvious after it had been conjured. Laces were abandoned, the stitches unpicked from the straps on Poppy's rucksack, and a clever binding system, extracted from the collaborative fingers of three hungry children, evolved, connecting snowshoe to boot.

"How do I look?" Fred said, shuffling bowlegged across the floor.

"Idiotic," said Ryan.

"I have something to add." It was Poppy who spoke. By her tone Fred knew something serious was about to happen. Expecting a long speech on the dangers of low temperatures, he was astonished when she went over to her pillow and pulled out a small can of soup. It trembled as she held it towards him. He had never seen mouths drop open before, and if his desire for the soup in her hand had not been so great, he would have laughed out loud.

"Where did you get that?"

"I took it from the kitchen on the second day."

"Why?"

"I was saving it for an emergency."

"What sort of emergency?" asked Marcie, unable to take her eyes off the can.

"This sort of emergency."

She turned to the circle. "Fred is going out tomorrow, to try and find food, food for us. He can't do that on an empty stomach." She stared at each face.

"He won't need it all though, will he?" said Ryan.

"No, he needs ten times more," replied Poppy.

"She's right," said Marcie. "We can wait."

"I can't wait," came a young voice at waist level. "I'm hungry."

It was too much. Fred picked up the can opener and started opening the lid, grinding his teeth as he forced the steel handle around at break-neck speed. Buster was sobbing by the time a fingerful of cold soup was forced into his mouth.

"Stop it, stop it now!" Poppy was shouting, louder and higher than Fred had ever heard.

"Why?" he demanded.

"It's for you and only you. Think, Fred, think, and eat."

What followed would later be remembered as one of the low points of his life. He lifted the can and tipped the contents into his mouth. He did not wait to chew. He barely swallowed the syrupy mass sliding down his throat, settling somewhere in his gut. Without looking at the others, he wiped his forefinger over the lid, pushed the scrapings into his mouth, and laid the can on the coffee table. Hardly a second had passed before a small boy rushed forward and grabbed it, disappearing beneath the duvet.

⌒

There was one more thing to do. Behaving as if nothing had happened, they planned Fred's route. Marcie seemed to know the area better than anyone and set about drawing a map on a page torn from Poppy's sketchbook. No more blank sheets were left, but Poppy waived her hand dismissively as Marcie pulled out a rough drawing of a sunflower. Avoiding the limp petals, she drew a grid of streets, adding a smiley face next to their house and a richly detailed sketch of a steaming pie next to the shelter. They went to bed soon after, and Fred felt a strange happiness during the night, feeling for the map beneath his pillow and trying his hardest to fall asleep.

CHAPTER
54

Clothe, feed, and shelter. Isn't that what a parent should do? For their child.

Poppy lay on the mattress, twisting her wedding ring. It chafed. She dare not move. Turning over would only send a wave of movement through the line of sleepers. But even as she lay rigid, a cold finger of air sliding down her back, she became aware of noises perforating the dark, a head murmuring on a pillow, and the broom handle quivering on its base.

Should she let her son go out? Alone.

Not a single shred of light entered the tent. Stagnant air wrapped her face like a surgical mask.

Should she let her son go out alone? Should she?

CHAPTER

55

Morning was a long time coming. Someone had taken up snoring and Fred felt ready to punch the quivering nostrils by the time light filtered into the tent. But today was a big day, and he eased the cardboard out of his muscles with a series of bends and stretches that even brought a fleeting smile to Rennie's lips.

Putting on the snowshoes wore him out, but he remembered to save some energy for looking brave — for the goodbye ceremony. They gathered around him, their helpfulness scuffing up the tired edges of his well-being that he had spent so much effort smoothing down. He felt annoyed at Ryan for making last minute checks on his bindings with the air of a government official. Even Marcie, tying yet another scarf around his neck, could not ease the block of irritation that formed in his chest. In spite of all that, his shifting mood soared as Buster handed him an imaginary biscuit "wrapped in gold leaf" that he had "baked especially for him." Graciously, he slid the pebble, folded inside a sliver of toilet paper, down into his pocket.

Finally, he pulled his rucksack over his shoulders and turned to his mother. It did not help that she was crying. He gave her a tight hug, making sure not to cry himself. Even Rennie was there, in the background, mouthing a small thank you and nodding, revealing a line of grey roots nesting along the top of her head.

As he stepped over the threshold, Fred felt someone give him a kiss. He moved at the wrong moment; it landed on his hat.

"Be careful, Fred," said Marcie, in a whispery voice.

"Yes, be careful," said his mother, tweaking the edge of his hood. "And, Freddie, come back quickly. You must come back straight away." He noticed her finger, a raw band of skin beneath her ring.

"Mum, I'll be all right. I have to go."

He opened the door and headed towards the road, his boy-hero walk greatly diminished by the shoes. He could only imagine the last view the farewell party had of their saviour, a wan young man shuffling away on cricked legs. The moment they closed the door he got the hang of it, of course, and should any of them have taken the trouble of returning for one final look, rather than tearing back to the fire, they would have seen an upright and purposeful individual, whose control over his feet was beyond any doubt.

He surged forward in the direction of the street, but the rhythm that so soothed his stress was broken the moment he passed the old lady's house, and he fell to the ground as one latticed plate stood on another. It was a struggle to get up, but after pulling on a Snow Route sign, he was vertical. One not quite so cocky step later, he fell again. Driving snow was now sticking to his eyelids then finding its way beneath his collar, making him shudder. He looked down at his feet, studying the shoes. Something was wrong with his method. Then he remembered. He had laughed out loud when Ata had explained about snowshoeing, spreading his skinny legs in a parody of himself, knees kept apart by an invisible rod and feet lifted high like a demented goose. His walk needed adjusting. Hips, knees, ankles, and soles would have to cast aside their familiar gait, honed daily since babyhood, and start afresh, reassembling themselves into an alien collaboration, fit for walking on snow. He arched the balls of his feet; he spread his thighs and lifted his knees high. An inelegant and loopy stride took shape, but he did not care — he was moving and remaining on the surface, his shoes trailing exotic prints in their wake.

The streets were deserted. He missed his extended family badly as he scanned the empty horizon, blinking snowflakes out of his eyes. Freeze-dried mucus dripped from his nose and a sudden gust of wind seemed to scallop pain inside his sinuses. He swept past the wind's victims — twigs, needles, paper, pine cones, then a fallen tree, its jagged insides already filling with snow. It was not until he was two blocks from home that he remembered the single promise he had made to his mother: visit a neighbour.

Unsure of the distance he had covered, he gazed at the house in front of him. Indisputably a cousin of his own, it had the same garage doors, same dark windows, and same grey stucco smoothed into ridges like icing on a wedding cake. Unusually, the front door had a manual knocker shaped like a lion's head. It had a disconcertingly human look to it, and as he wiped the snow off its whiskers, he thought he saw the eye wink and the nose sniff imperceptibly. He knocked hard. Then he knocked again and waited, poking snow out of the lion's nostrils with a gloved finger. A final knock convinced him no one was at home and, accomplishing a 180-degree turn without falling over, he headed for the next house. He experienced a strange feeling that he was approaching the same building — same facade, same lion — but then he spotted smoke drifting up from the chimney and lurched forward with legs akimbo. The knocker had hardly glanced the lion's nose before the door opened, and a palpable torrent of feeling poured out.

"Thank God!" was followed by another "Thank God!" in a slightly different tone.

Two faces stood in front of him. Two faces but one body, wrapped inside a single duvet that was shaking.

"You've come just in time," the left head was saying.

"We're almost out of food," the right added. "Come in, quickly, quickly."

He straightened up. *They* needed *him*. He backed away, locking one shoe over another. "I'm sorry. I can't help you. I'm looking for help myself. I'm sorry."

Without waiting for an answer, he manoeuvred himself into his turn, sweeping a rough semi-circle onto the snow. But he looked back. He wished he hadn't, but he did. Two expressions sagged in unison. Twins.

"Wait," they said together.

"Please help us," added the left mouth. "Please."

"I need to go," he said. "I'm sorry. I don't have much time. I have to go ... I'm so cold."

He tried not to look into their eyes, but they drew his gaze back in, two pairs, pleading.

"I'm going to find help. I'll come back. I promise."

"Wait!"

"I'll come back."

"Please wait!"

"I *will* come back. I promise."

A promise is a powerful thing; it buys you time, it gets you off the hook. Without waiting for an answer, he turned and forged his way back to the road, not listening to the high-pitched voices, not looking back, not even once.

The floor of the city had been lifted up and smoothed out. He skimmed its surface, detached from all the normal detritus of city life — the dog shit, the coke cans, the flattened blobs of gum. Even the drains, usually so busy breathing wet circles of heat up through the drifts, were covered, suffocated by the snow. Much to his relief, Marcie's scribbled landmarks started coming into view. The church was visible from the moment he got to the corner of the next block, but as he set his bearings, a second church entered his sightline, almost identical in shape to the first. Relying on nothing but guesswork, he plumped for the original and set off, picking up speed and scanning the horizon for the next marker on the landscape.

"Look out for O'Malley's," she'd said, "the coffee shop." Hesitating on the second street corner, he felt a twang of panic. From that one spot in the city he could see three O'Malley's, the distinctive red and blue insignia pulling his eyes in several directions. He chose a store at random then walked on, aware of plummeting levels of sugar in his blood, of numbness spreading down his fingers, and for the first time acutely aware that he had only a limited amount of time.

Even more energy had seeped away by the time he came upon the car. Neatly parked but layered with snow. A stack of ice toppled from the wing mirror as he leaned against it to catch his breath, and his shoulder skimmed a hole in the snow that clung to the side window. He pulled the map from his pocket and, failing to unfold it with his padded gloves, pulled the left glove off, wincing at the cold that swooped down on his exposed skin.

"Bugger!" It remained the only word he knew.

He flipped the paper open in one move before plunging his hand back into the glove. Thankfully Marcie had included a school. Riverside Park was roughly drawn, but as he looked from the paper world to the real world, he connected the lines on the page to the symmetrical building one block away.

Under normal circumstances, the back seat of a snow-covered car would have passed unnoticed. But extreme cold, while dulling the mind, tunes the senses, so while he was pushing the map into his pocket, closing the gap between his cuff and glove, he spotted something through the window. It was a lunch box: small, plastic, and pink.

The last drops of adrenalin pumped into his veins. He was Superman. He had the strength to wrench off a car door. But not even Superman was strong enough to get this door off, and after pulling at the door handle, ramming a knee into the side of the car, he flopped down in the snow, too exhausted to care that flakes were melting into his trousers, numbing his backside. But he had a flashlight. He remembered this a moment later and he was up again, swinging it around like an Olympic disc thrower before lobbing it into the side window. It bounced off with a thud and disappeared into a hole in the snow. Almost sobbing with frustration, he scratched about like a ravenous squirrel, found it, then threw again, this time at the front windshield. A crack seared the air with a volume that hurt his eardrums. For a split second the window held, teetering on the brink of collapse, then shattered onto the dashboard, sprinkling seats and snow with glass. He heaved himself through, scraping snowshoed feet across the hood.

His stomach did strange and unpredictable things as he grappled with the lid. The sandwiches were neatly cut and wrapped in cling film, the line of faded pink along the crusts suggesting ham. A carton of juice was wedged in beside the bread, plus a small kiwi, unpeeled and shrivelled. He grabbed a sandwich, hard as arctic rock, and bit.

"Shit!" His teeth throbbed.

He took the sandwich out of his mouth and stared at the bread, still connected to the corner of his lips by a thread of hardening saliva. Unzipping his coat, he rammed the sandwich down onto his chest, settling it between layers of shirts. Cold at his core trebled his misery, but the mere thought of the meat thawing against his skin made it bearable. The kiwi was allowed no such reprieve. He forced it whole into his mouth, sucking vigorously until the skin softened enough for him to devour its delicious green flesh. The effect was instant; his pulse jumped up, he felt sick. Taking slow, even breaths, he managed to prevent the fruit from returning to his mouth and longed for the moment it would reach his stomach and enter his bloodstream. He walked on, stroking the thawing sandwich through his coat in a series of circles, and although the snowshoes prohibited a spring in his step, he felt a certain buoyancy as he turned his attention to the rest of his journey.

The next landmark was not so hard to find. Sliding with a newfound grace towards the school, he let out an involuntary shout as he saw the gas station coming into view. The one and only. He pushed on, past the silent pumps stacked with snow, around the snowbanks, and towards the shelter, doing his best to ignore the fiery aches flitting across his hips. He could think only of food and almost howled in anticipation as he envisaged the sandwich spreading a damp patch across his chest.

Ten minutes later, he dug into the most exquisite meal he had ever tasted: two slices of bread, turned to mush, and ham, studded with ice crystals. Part of it was stuck to his T-shirt. He picked it over until just a greasy stain remained, and only fear of exposure stopped him from shoving the whole garment into his mouth and sucking out the remnants.

Could there be anything more wonderful in life than a school meal in a pink lunchbox? Eight days old.

The results were electric. Aware of sugar levels cresting in his bloodstream, he experienced an exhilarating high, reaching new speeds on the snowshoes, arms swinging and heels flapping, as he surged in the direction of the shelter.

With his confidence soaring like a thermometer dunked in hot caramel, he was unprepared when he fell over one more time, snagging his foot on an object buried in the snow. Hauling himself up, he brushed snow off the lump and revealed a small dog, frozen solid and finely dusted with snowflakes. Its jaw was locked and icy tid-bits clung to its muzzle, testimony to its final moments of foraging. Something about its stiff little limbs mesmerized him, and he could not stop himself from flicking snow off its whiskers and straightening out its tail. Only the ears had any real colour, pale pink, like the skin of a baby rabbit, and as he ran fingers over the top of its head, he felt stupid tears welling into the backs of his eyes.

Then he saw blood. Faded spots tattooed the surrounding snow like lettering on an ice rink floor. This dog had not died peacefully. Skin had been broken. Blood had been let.

He did not like finding the dog. It disturbed him to see the glassy eyes staring at nothing, but if he had not been bending over at that moment, holding the stiff little paws in his hand, he might not have spotted the running man. Any further on in time or distance and he would have missed him.

"Hey!" bellowed Fred, dropping the paw and standing upright.

But the man was far off, scrambling along in an odd way, bent forward with his hands stretched out in front of him.

"Wait!"

The figure continued to run. Fred tried running too, but stalled, his feet tangling over one another. He shouted, he bellowed, he roared. But it was not enough. He could only stop and stare as the figure disappeared behind the corner of a house.

His boiled-down vocabulary stretched to a second and third word. "Fucking hell!"

A deep, deep low now replaced the sandwich-induced high. Pain had settled in a square on the bridge of his nose, and when the wind suddenly roared across the street, he wanted to shriek with the agony of it as it ripped away the last pockets of heat lingering around his body, beneath his armpits, between his legs. Feeling his final crumbs of energy seep from his body, he leaned against the corner of a fence. Then a new thought entered his mind. He straightened up. He began to shout.

"Is there anyone here?"

The snow mounds sat silent.

"Is there anyone *here*?" Louder.

Snowflakes hit the ground.

He pulled his balaclava higher up his nose and scanned the horizon, twisting his neck around until it hurt. He spotted smoke in the far distance, thin columns of it, trailing vertically skyward. He narrowed his eyes and held a hand against his forehead, aware of a crack opening up between his glove and sleeve. More palls of smoke were attached to the western horizon, twisted into zig-zags by a distant breeze. But not a single one was close by. Not one offered him hope.

He gazed upwards; the sky was a mouldy grey, snowflakes pricked his eyeballs.

He had to go on.

CHAPTER
56

A thin layer of gloom had wrapped itself around the circle and Poppy felt wrung out with exhaustion. Since Fred left, the cold felt colder and the freezing air that entered the house as he slammed the door behind him had lingered, chilling the backs of their ankles as it flowed beneath their chairs. Marcie tended to the sofa that she and Fred had bagged as their own, keeping to one side of an invisible line and adjusting the cushion on *his* side, adding plump where none was needed. A dreary listlessness settled over them all, animated only by the fire, which let out spiteful hisses as heat hit damp wood and flicked red at random.

Red. The colour was seeping into Poppy's thoughts. Red flames, red tomatoes, the red arms of a man jumping from a train, so happy, so exhilarated, so carefree. She wanted that feeling now. She wanted that unadulterated feeling of optimism she had seen in his daring leap, but all she could feel as she laid her head back on her cushion was the monochromatic crushing of ominous dread.

CHAPTER
57

Everything was back under control; the snowshoes were holding out, he could see the wide tower of the museum in the distance. But callous thoughts consoled him as he ploughed towards the next block. His mind was now dwelling not on dogs trapped in ice, but on soup, steaming in polystyrene cups, and clean beds with hot water bottles at the bottom.

Gathering speed, he a felt a satisfying burn in his thighs. But soon the snow was slowing him down, racing downwards in cottony clusters. He had to battle to keep it from building up on his head and arms, swiping off scoops as they settled on his body, finding the horizontal in the most minute of places: a tiny shelf where his balaclava met his nose, a frozen fold beside his knee. But he surged on, determined to find a place that offered him what he most wanted at that moment. Heat. He stopped briefly at a junction and looked around. Glimpses of houses weaved through the snowflakes that were now roaring around him in crazy circles. Unable to feel his toes, he pointed his feet in the direction of the closest house and headed towards it. Snow was stacked halfway up to the door handle, and he could only imagine the pile of ice that would land on the door-mat when they let him in. He surged towards it and thumped his fist on the door. Nothing happened. He stepped back and looked up, blinking off flakes. A face looked back from the first floor window — a man, wearing a hat and coat.

For a second, Fred forgot why he was there. Then he waved — a ridiculous wave, the wave of a small child across a playground. The man stared back.

"Do you have any food?" he called. The man disappeared.

"He's coming to the door," Fred muttered. "He's coming." He waited, shaking out his arms, hooting a cone of hot breath in through the top of his glove. The joints in his knees were stiffening by the time he realized the man was not coming. He looked up at the window; the window was empty. He stamped the ground angrily, tempted to bang on the door but could not summon the energy. As waiting was out of the question, he trudged towards the next house, temporarily forgetting how to walk in snowshoes. He fell over. He dragged his body upright and noticed a flicker of light in the front window, a candle caught in a breeze, or a breath.

"Hey!" he shouted, short on eloquence. He hurried towards the front door. Wind had scooped a perfect bowl of snow from the front of this house and even the prickly teeth of the boot scraper were visible as he stomped his feet on the front porch. The door opened before he knocked and a person stood in front of him. The padding of several coats and a thick hat obscured any clue to gender or age. Even the voice was disguised by the overlapping folds of a long black scarf.

"Do you need help?" Damped-down words slunk through wool.

"Yes," replied Fred, pulling his balaclava off his mouth, hairs on his tongue. "Do you have any food?"

"Come in," mumbled the wrapped person. "But I should tell you I only have enough fuel for a few more hours."

He stopped. At that moment Fred realized how it was. He was not alone. Thousands of families across the city were in the same dire predicament. Maybe some had more food. Maybe heat from generators were easing the cold from the shoulders of a few lucky families, but most people were probably doing what his family were doing, the best they could. Knocking on any more doors was hopeless.

"That's kind of you but ... I think I'll head for the shelter. Did you hear about that?"

"Yes, I'm going. I'm waiting for my brother."

An image of Dwayne flashed into his mind. "Okay, right, I'll go now so you don't lose any more heat and ... good luck."

"You too."

A hand slipped out from a glove. Fred whipped off his mitten and shook the sexless fingers. Neither spoke again.

Downcast, he returned to the street and almost walked into a bench. Turned ninety degrees, its feet straddled where he imagined the curb lay. He swished snow off one corner and, sitting down to catch the balls of breath curling out of his mouth, gazed down the long street.

Scanning the white horizon had begun to take its toll on his eyes. He blinked, then he rubbed glass eyelashes, peering around for the slightest hint of movement. While dabbing liquid out of the corner of his eye, he noticed a familiar shape, half buried, abandoned. A shopping cart. He blinked hard, bringing his eyes back into focus. Snow had accentuated the shape of the cart, balancing on the thinnest of steel edges and packing the inside with a weekly shop, fit for a snowman. It was not Ata's cart. He knew that. No smell, no knots. But in spite of the cold he hesitated and poked a finger into the wire mesh, wiping away a sluggish tear as it slipped off his eyelid. Then he kicked the cart, hard. It tipped over, the snow cover sloughing off as one, leaving the cold metal exposed and the snowman's shopping lying smashed on the ground.

Then he walked on without looking back.

CHAPTER
58

"My armpits smell of strawberries," said Buster.

Poppy looked at the little boy, suspended for a second between laughter and incomprehension. The blend of perspiring cavity and luscious fruit into one sentence was almost too much for her tired mind to grasp. She sighed. Sophisticated thoughts were beyond her now. She had trouble remembering what had happened in the previous minute, let alone understanding the meaning of anything. Had Marcie just asked her a question? She was not sure. Had she answered it yet? Maybe. And what about strawberries? Did Buster say he had some? If so, why had he not given her one?

Seeing him rubbing his hand under his arm, she recalled the comment and an automated response kicked in. She laughed; so did the others. Then she managed to remember a question she meant to ask.

"Did he go at ten o'clock?"

"Ten sixteen," replied Marcie.

"That's over three hours."

"Yes."

"What time does it get dark?"

"Around four."

"I wonder what he'll bring back?" said Ryan.

"Sausages with fried onions," said Marcie.

"Bacon," said Buster.

A shifting in the hard-backed chair caught their attention. They all turned to Rennie.

"What if he eats it all himself before he gets back?"

"He won't do that, Mom," said Marcie. "Hey, Poppy, are you feeling all right?"

She was certain Marcie had asked her a question that time, but she was not sure what the answer would be. Then it came to her.

"Yes."

It was all she could manage.

CHAPTER
59

A single image crowded Fred's view: squares of ice forced through webbing as his shoes lifted up and down. Swamped by sadness and worry, he focused continually downward, his neck bent into a curve. Driving snow had closed down the periphery of his vision, and he was forced to swipe the air in front of his face to open up sight of the route ahead. Just as another swipe shot up, he became aware of a large shape ahead of him. He stopped. He stared. He achieved a feat not previously known to man. He jumped in snowshoes. He had arrived.

The community centre was shaped like a box, had no discernible entrance, and the windows were black as liquorice. He felt his energy levels beginning to slump as he scanned the facade, his life force draining out of him like acid from a fractured battery. But he managed to summon a final morsel of strength and set off, staggering around the side, scrambling along in an odd way, bent forward with his hands stretched out in front of him. The first door was locked. Unable to accept this fact, he circled the building again until he found himself back at the original corner. Momentarily thrilled by the sight of footprints, he slumped inwardly as he recognized his own distinct pattern embossed on the snow. Then something he had been pushing to the back of his mind came to the front.

There was no shelter.

He had heard that tears could freeze on your face but had never imagined it could hurt so much. They started small but grew, filling up the bottom of his eyelids, spilling warm lines onto his cheeks. Still unfrozen, they reached the side of his nose then stopped, forming a crunchy crust along the rim of his balaclava.

But this was not to be the end of his journey. A mechanism was at work. Deep in his subconscious, well protected from the air greying his skin, a primal instinct was warming up. So while he stood on a freezing street, enduring what felt like the most intense level of despair he had ever known, his body was planning for survival, assessing, plotting, weighing the options and tipping new ideas in the direction of his conscious mind.

He looked towards the museum. Abandoning any pretence at fitting into the streetscape, it reared its shoulders into a model of solidity rarely seen in a city so young, with snow piled high on the roof and resembling a gothic castle that had stumbled into suburbia. A corner of the boundary fence had collapsed under the weight of snow and he clambered through the gap with ease. This time the absence of footprints was reassuring, calming him as he went up the steps, turning sideways and struggling to bring up the snowshoes. As he approached the entrance he could see a rectangular black shadow ahead, and an obscene glow of happiness tore through his body. The door was open.

CHAPTER
60

"Poppy, are you all right?"

"What?"

"Are you feeling all right? You said something ... weird."

"I did?"

"Yes."

"I think I dozed off."

"That's all right."

"Marcie?"

"Yes?"

"What time is it?"

"Nearly three."

"Marcie?"

"Yes?"

"What time is ... oh."

She picked up her sketchbook and thumbed through it. "Who's torn a page out of my book?"

"Not me," said Marcie.

"I didn't," added Ryan.

A small silence followed.

"Fred'll be back soon, won't he, Poppy?" said Ryan.

"Of course he will!" said Marcie.

"What will we do if he doesn't come back?"

"Of course he'll come back. He's got the snowshoes, hasn't he?"

"He'll be back soon though, won't he, Poppy?"

"Ryan, what's got into you?"

"I'm hungry and I'm cold and ... I don't want to be the leader."

CHAPTER

61

Hunger was projecting a panorama on his mind as Fred entered the museum. Chocolate bars, salted chips, raisin cookies. He leaned against the wall, waiting for his eyes to adjust to the dark, and a lonely reception desk came into view. Sighing, he undid his boots then groaned as his socks failed to circumvent the trail of slush following in his wake.

He had been inside this building before. "Let's go and find out what happened to all those bison," his father had said, two weeks after they arrived in the city. He shuddered at the memory of the snake pits on the second floor. Some clever herpetologist had constructed a tableau of the local celebrity — garter snakes, their rubber bodies spilling out from a toyshop basket. He and Charlie had gasped in delight at the sight of them, but there had been something about the mean-tailed reptiles mangled up in knots that acted as the setting for more than one nightmare in the following days. As he approached the reception desk now, he could think only of shedding skins and snake flesh roasting on a spit.

The vending machine was where he expected it to be, next to the pay desk. His rumbling belly cajoled his walk into a run as he spotted it, then he was beside it, pulling open the door, poking in his head, and breathing in its air like a famished pig sniffing out truffles. The machine was empty; his cynical side knew it would be. He sniffed again. The chocolate scent had gone, leaving behind nothing but the smell of a never-opened cupboard.

Stomach howling, he turned back towards the corridor. He started to run, deciding that even a discarded sandwich would make it worth exploring. He followed the yellow arrows painted on the floor and a button of happiness popped into his body as he hopped from one to another in damp socks. After days of indecision, there was a sweet certainty about the markings. Their precision soothed him, and he turned and doubled back at their every command. Then the arrows stopped. He stopped too, and peered into the windowless space ahead. Narrowing his eyes squeezed shapes out of the darkness, and soon the outlines of objects began to emerge — on the floor, on the wall, beside his feet. Stepping forward, his foot sunk down and a sound squeaked out from beneath his heel. He bent down to touch the floor but stopped as he heard the sound of human voices. His heart fired up, pumping vigorously in his chest. He rubbed his breastbone. Who was there? Were they following the arrows towards him? He rubbed harder. Were they as obedient as he? Remembering the blood on the snow, he ducked down and, balancing half a buttock on the unknown lump in the dark, sat still. Two people were close by, perhaps a silent third, listening or thinking, or too tired to speak.

"I'm hungry," whined a male voice.

"There's nothing here, let's just go."

"But I'm hungry."

"Shut up! I'm sick of listening to you."

"I'm sick of listening to *you*."

As Fred hunkered down, his arm brushed something unknown. It was massive and lumpy and smelled of the inside of his grandmother's leather handbag. It felt furry, too. Not living furry, but dead, dusty, dried up furry, with hair that had long since stopped growing. With sandy granules at the roots.

He stroked its huge bulk, his hand coming to rest on a glassy eye — a teddy bear's dead eye, but bigger and cold. Exploring further, he discovered the second eye, minus the glass ball, and his finger poked into an empty socket, enclosed by ragged leather membranes. He stroked rhythmically, caressing the crusty folds of an oversized ear before delving into the skin of a dried-up nostril. Feather-light granules met his touch as he fingered the floor. They stuck to his cuffs, forming a dusty tilth beneath his nails as he went, swirling and spreading. Pushing his hand in deeper, he came upon a small, spiky object. Solidified mats of substrate lifted up as he pulled on it, then they broke into morsels. Tentative touching revealed the prickly seams of a mitten and he slid his hand inside, feeling the crumbs that lined the tip of the thumb. It fit.

A loud crash interrupted the moment. He dropped the mitten and stared in the direction of the sound.

"Here's my coat for the winter. Hey, it's got a fucking tail."

"What about matching slippers?" came a reply. "Ugh, is that a duck foot?"

"Stockings anyone?"

The third man launched into a joke, blundering through jibes about his grandmother's underwear, when he was drowned out by snorts of derision mixed into the tinkle of shattering glass. Fred's breathing doubled in speed. He did not like the sound of them, but sound was all he had. Feet shuffled closer, a cough hacked its way from the back of an unfamiliar throat, and loud blood pumped in his ears. Then he heard the sound he most wanted. Silence.

He sat still for a long time. Fear had eclipsed all other emotions during the past few minutes but, as he sat in the dark, hunger and cold crept back, badgering and tormenting his body into action. But he needed a second to think, just a moment to process the sounds that had filtered out of the cold darkness.

Leaning against the giant teddy creature, hugging it by its legs, he started to relax. His breathing slowed to normal, and he pulled the flashlight out of his pocket and switched it on.

The details of the murky shapes were instantly revealed. Great stuffed animals, no longer mere upholstery but magnificent beasts with antlers, surrounded him. But they were damaged. One was missing an ear and the second had rough slashes cut down both flanks. A third lay on its side like a side of old meat, its body angled ungraciously on the ground, stiff feet pointing sideways. Swivelling the light around in a half circle, he saw hundreds of human footprints in the fake snow. "Bite me" was written in the flattened flakes, the last E partly scuffed out.

He heaved himself up and panned his flashlight slowly around. Fragments lurched out of the dark and he swung around faster, feeling a sudden rush of euphoria as the light swept the walls, revealing a huge painting of ice and sky and thin wisps of cloud. He jumped up. He felt delirious. His thoughts swirled and swirled as an arctic scene of extraordinary beauty wrapped around him. He paused, and waited, waited for his heart to stop pounding and his chest to stop wheezing.

He realized then where he was — inside the diorama. Charlie had told him all about them. Uncanny places, they harboured snapshot scenes of real life, with stuffed animals, dried plants, and expertly painted backdrops melded together to create an everlasting moment that deceived the senses and wrong-footed all expectations. "It's all about the relationship of the pieces," his father had said. "Move one piece or change the angle slightly and it's all wrong."

As his flashlight jumped towards a far corner of the room, a scene of shocking humiliation met his eyes. Three plastic humanoid figures lay on the ground: a man, woman, and child, perfect representations of their type. All naked, except for a single shoe remaining on the foot of the child. The woman's hair had been wrenched off and scattered on the floor. One leg of the man figure had been bent back into a shape no living human could ever achieve, and the mouth of his child had been stuffed with artificial snow. Behind them was a sign, the writing just visible:

"INUIT FAMILY GROUP — ARCTIC PEOPLE USING TRADITIONAL METHODS AND ENGAGING IN CARIBOU HUNT TO OBTAIN MATERIALS FOR CLOTHES, SHELTER, AND FOOD."

As he stepped off the fabricated snow onto the wooden floorboards of the corridor, he cried.

CHAPTER
62

Removal companies take everything. It's their job. Not just furniture, or books, or clothes, but the small minutiae of life that their customers do not have time to pack. Limp cloths, still damp from wiping, are folded inside sheets of paper, half-eaten jars of peanut butter are pressed into boxes, and coins gathered from the gap in the back of the sofa are poured into envelopes.

Poppy remembered their last day in London as she looked into Fred's freezing room, leaning on the door handle to offset the weakness in her legs. Empty shelves, empty drawers, empty bed. Shaking off a shiver, she pulled the duvet around her shoulders, then up over her ears, chilled by a new thought. This is what his room would look like the day he left home.

She bent down and picked up a paperclip off the floor, sending a breeze up the back of her legs. Then she heard a voice.

"Auntie Poppy."

"Oh, Buster."

"I'm cold."

"You should have stayed by the fire."

"Will you come down?"

"Buster, I want to be on my own for a moment. You go down and I'll come in a minute."

"I want to stay with you."

"Buster, go down now. I said I'm coming."

"You come."

"Buster. Go downstairs."

"Please come."

"Look. Just go." She took hold of his shoulders and manoeuvred him around to face the door. "Go!"

His shoulders felt bony, almost weightless and, as she shoved him out of the room, they gave way, slipping out of her hands. He stumbled forward then crashed to the floor, rolling onto his side and folding inwards like a distressed beetle.

"Oh ... Buster, come here. I'm so sorry."

A flick of wet caught the back of her hand as she bent to pull him up. She saw tears on his cheeks. He gripped her leg, digging his fingers into her shin. The duvet fell to the ground.

"Buster, let's go down."

She untwisted his hand and picked him up. He curled his arms around her neck and she sighed as an undeserved surge of warmth crept onto her chest.

She had no words. No apology was big enough for the boy in her arms. She sat down on the bedframe and arranged his body onto her lap, lining up his knees before pulling his fleece down over his hips. He sniffed, wiped his nose on her shoulder, then laid his head on the smudge of shining mucus. She sniffed too, and he giggled as she wiped her nose on his fleece. After tucking a stray hair behind his ear, she began stroking the back of his neck, up and down, round and round. Fred had loved that when he was a baby, up and down, round and round.

CHAPTER

63

Fred was on his way home. He followed the arrows in reverse order. The usual visual markers had disappeared, revealing nothing but the backs of information signs and the hidden mechanisms of interactive display. He had to stop twice to recover his bearings as the edges of the corridor worked against him, sending him stumbling against the cold wall. On a normal day he would be going against the human flow, dodging strollers and side-stepping art students, but today there was no one, no one to tell him he was going the wrong way. That was how he came to find the room. Set back from the main wall, it was visible only to those looking for it — a black door with a silver keyhole. He stopped, he turned the handle, he went in.

Inside was a small room dominated by a single desk, centrally placed. Where one might expect to find a computer screen, there lay a rectangular ink blotter. A fountain pen lay beside a bottle of frozen ink. The lid was off. He turned to leave, thinking it to be a mock-up of a nineteenth-century fur trader's office, of no interest to a ravenous boy, when he noticed a coat slung over the back of the chair. A winter parka with a zipper and Velcro cuffs. Then he spotted a coffee cup resting atop a wooden dresser. Picking it up, he found it contained the solidified remains of an abandoned refreshment, providing a further clue to contemporary living. He sniffed inside then licked it with a stretched tongue, savouring the bitter aftertaste. Spurred on by the signs of human occupancy, he started searching the drawers, hoping and praying that the previous occupant was a "stuffer."

It was a term coined by his father. Charlie had spent his entire life working in offices and prided himself on his analyses of workplace behaviour. When it came to eating habits, he had identified two main types: aesthetes and stuffers. Aesthetes had the interesting jobs and were too busy to eat. They skipped breakfast, were too wrapped up in something fabulously interesting to eat lunch, and only had a meal when they got home. Stuffers, on the other hand, had boring jobs and, to ease the tedium, developed elaborate rituals that revolved around food. They constantly nibbled biscuits from a secret drawer and had regularly topped-up supplies in a discreet corner cupboard. You were either one or the other, his father had decreed and, as Fred opened the third drawer down to reveal a textbook example of a stuffer, he could have given his father a hug that stretched right across the Atlantic.

The drawer was full. He crammed a piece of frozen chocolate straight into his mouth, followed by another, cutting his lip as he bit. Feeling nauseous, he stopped eating to examine what he had. This person was clearly an aficionado of office snacking — chocolate, cookies, and chips covered a secondary layer of raisins, apricots, and nuts. He opened his rucksack and packed his treasures neatly, solids at the bottom, delicates at the top. Then he grabbed two bottles of orange juice and pushed them down the inside of his coat, pausing only to lick a wedge of frozen froth from the top of the larger one. Next he pulled a small bottle of gin from the pencil drawer and stuffed it inside his jacket. This was a final category that his father had failed as yet to name, but he could outline their behaviour with confidence: secret drinking, obviously, inexplicable rudeness on occasion, and, most damning, falling asleep at their desks. Body buzzing with chocolate, he pulled his pencil out of his pocket and scribbled a note on the inkpad.

"Had to borrow food. Thanks." It was almost illegible.

He heaved the loaded rucksack onto his back and, pausing only to screw the lid back onto the bottle of ink, left the room.

CHAPTER 64

Poppy sat at the top of the stairs holding a shoe — a boy's shoe, prematurely aged by grit and browned by the salt of the city. She pushed her fingers down inside, feeling the shape of her son's toes embossed in the leather at the tip. It felt stiff. And cold. The front door was visible from where she sat and, as she turned the shoe over in her hand, she stared at the snow rushing past the glass, settling in tiny piles on the window lip.

She would see his face at any moment. His hood would be covered in snow, maybe his eyelids would be crusted with ice, but he would be there any moment, she knew he would. She pulled hard at the leather tongue; it ripped at its root, and black threads stuck up in defiance. She wanted him back. She wanted him back now. But he was coming. He was. She would see his face any moment. She definitely would.

She stared at the glass. Snow rushed past, and tiny piles settled on the waiting lip.

CHAPTER 65

The distinctive red lips of an inflatable snowman were what saved him. What a joke. Sagging mournfully in the corner of a garden, it was the only landmark of any distinction for what seemed like miles. But it instantly quelled the panic rising in his chest as he blundered around the edge of his neighbourhood. The small intake of food had energized him, but one of the shoes had seized up as he reached the last part of the journey home and the final steps hurt. With one boot trapped in a downward position, his knee was forced into a permanent bend, sending a stabbing pain through his thigh every time he shifted his weight. By the time the house came into view, he was ready to give up, ready to lay his head in the snow pillows and pull a blanket of defeat over himself. But somehow, after a brief stop, waiting to catch his breath, he managed to haul himself up to the front door.

They virtually dragged him in — several pairs of hands grabbing and hugging, brushing frost from his eyebrows. They laid him out on the sofa like an accident victim, Marcie pushing a pillow behind his head and Buster holding his hand as he longingly eyed the rucksack. Ryan untied the snowshoes, struggling and cursing over the frozen knots, while his mother rubbed his chest, undoing his coat between rubs. Rennie sat utterly still. In the flourish of activity, he was aware of her expression, her longing to ask, but not following through.

"I didn't find him," said Fred.

She stared at the floor, then back at him. "What about at the shelter? Had nobody heard of him at the shelter?"

"There was no shelter."

They all stopped moving.

"No shelter?" said Poppy.

"No, the building was locked. Deserted. I couldn't find anyone."

"No one?"

"No. There is no one out there. I don't understand it. No footprints."

"No footprints?" repeated his mother.

"No, but I did get a little food. At the museum." He nodded towards the rucksack that now had a small boy's arm around it.

"We can have some now but we must be careful, it has got to last."

"How long has it got to last?" said Marcie.

"I don't know. The shelter wasn't where they said. There's nothing happening out there. Nothing."

There were too many questions. He had to eat. Pushing the clutter off the table and tipping out the food, he marvelled at the restraint they all showed. Even Buster managed to hold back, bending forward to sniff a bar of chocolate, but not actually touching it. He put the sweet things to one side, not wanting them to experience the low after a sugar high, and divided up the nuts and raisins into six piles. No one moved. They just followed his hand moving from bag to table, then back to the bag again.

"Let's eat," he said.

Ryan stuffed a handful of nuts into his mouth, chewing fast, his jaws grinding and lips smacking over each other like a starving bear. "I will love you forever," he said between mouthfuls. "I'll give you my skateboard and my bike and ..."

"Just eat," said Fred.

He ate more slowly than the others, picking up the nuts, one by one. Conversation interfered with eating so for a while there was silence. That was probably why they all heard the knock. Not loud, more of a quiet tap; it could have almost been the wind.

"Did you hear that?" said Poppy.

"There's someone at the door," said Buster, matter of factly.

An image of Grabowski loomed large. Had he heard about

the chocolate? Had he come to take it from them? Fred began stuffing food into the rucksack, then stopped. He glanced at Poppy, imagining she could read his thoughts, but she was already out of her chair, following the others to the hall. They were crowded around the front door by the time Fred joined them. He squeezed through with a mumbled "excuse me" then, standing on his toes, he peered through the window. Blowing snow obscured the view, but suddenly the top of a head appeared, as if someone had sat down then stood up.

"Open the door!" said two voices in unison. There was no hesitation this time. They pulled on the handle, just avoiding the collapsing wedges of snow that had been clinging to the frame. A tiny old lady sat on the doorstep, her head resting on her chest. Beside her stood an elderly man, one hand leaning on her shoulder, the other groping the air to find a hold.

Fred was ashamed of the thought he had at that moment. He tried to blot it out the second it appeared, but it stuck fast. Forget the desperate faces, forget the trembling hands held up for support, forget the grey hair shaped by nets of frost. All he could think of were the heaps of nuts waiting on the coffee table: six piles, divided equally.

Poppy shepherded the couple inside the house. They were in bad shape. The woman could hardly stand unaided. She flopped over like a puppet without strings as she was helped to the sofa. The man was stronger, padding obediently along the hall, sitting down on the sofa and wiping his steamed-up spectacles on his sleeve. His face lit up when Buster picked up a raisin and handed it to the old lady; he folded over her fingers to keep it from dropping on the carpet. Fred glanced at his own pile. Was it any smaller? He could not tell.

At first the newcomers seemed unable to speak, but if little else, the group of listeners had time on their hands, so they waited. The man was transfixed by the fire, only remembering the woman by his side when she gave a slight moan. He picked up her hand and rubbed it between his.

"Are you feeling a wee bit better, Morag?" he said.

The voice sang in Fred's ears. Something started churning inside his belly as he listened to the soft Scottish tones. Johno had started life in Scotland. He had never lost his accent and for a moment, sitting in that freezing room, thousands of miles from his best friend, the longing to be back in his old home was stronger than the fear of the moment.

"Yes, thank you, Angus." The woman's voice was faint; Fred leaned forward in his chair to catch the words.

Not seeing any need to introduce themselves, the strangers talked only to each other, their heads touching. Only the odd phrase escaped the intimacy. Fred caught "slippers," then "lovely bed," but the drizzle of second-hand reassurances acted on his mood as he sat slumped back in his chair, almost sending him to sleep. Through half-closed eyes, he saw his mother break off two squares of chocolate and hand them to the couple. The man known as Angus half sucked, half breathed the sweet into his mouth, then turned to face them, an explanation clearly forthcoming.

"We were watching the tele when the lights went out. That quiz was on — you know, the one with that daft bloke in it. Morag was just bringing in the tea when it all went dark. Fell right over, she did. Tipped my tea in my lap. She's never done that before, have you, hen?"

He paused and wiped his glasses before continuing.

"We lost all the biscuits under the couch. Morag wanted to get the kettle straight back on but I told her, there's no electricity, lass. We've got no electricity ..."

They all listened intently to the tale of biscuit crumbs and boiling kettles, which started in a cheerful fashion but took a more desperate turn. Morag, cheery on the first day of the blackout, was the one who had pulled extra blankets from the bottom of the closet and produced emergency batteries from a secret hiding place. She was soon replaced by the woman who sat around the fire with them, silent and too cold to warm up. The sentences became increasingly muddled, stalling frequently and, two minutes later, the old man stopped and gazed at the wall again, the wealth of details replaced by a void.

"How did you get here?" asked Poppy.

"We walked." He turned to his wife. "Morag, did we walk?"

The old lady did not reply, just stared at the fire.

"Don't worry about that," said Poppy. "Where do you live?"

Both faces were blank now. Then the man beamed. "Someone came to the house."

Fred sat bolt upright. "Someone came to the house?"

"Someone came," continued Angus, trying to rub a frown out of his eyebrows. "But Morag didn't want to go. She likes to have her own bed." His voice trailed off as he glanced at the tent. "But they're coming back for us."

Fred felt his lungs compressing in his chest. "Angus, you're not there anymore, are you?" He was too tired to disguise the weariness in his voice.

"Are you sure you can't remember where you live?" said Poppy gently.

"We have a double garage, don't we, Morag? But I can't remember if we shut the doors. The house is beige." He looked hopefully around the circle. The circle was silent.

Fred was picking some grit out from behind his ear when he noticed Morag was shaking. It started with her hands but quickly spread to her shoulder, then her head.

"She's got too cold," said Angus.

"Bring her closer to the fire and put this blanket over her knees," said Poppy.

Morag continued to look dazed as they manoeuvred her closer to the stove, wrapping a blanket around her shoulders. With a rapid and inculpable switch of loyalty, Buster was at her feet, undoing her boots and pushing her feet into Poppy's slippers. They were too big and hung loosely off her toes.

"Thank you, thank you," Angus kept repeating.

Meanwhile, Fred was calculating — calculating and assuaging. Their situation was changing; adjustments had to be made. Six people had become eight. Six piles of nuts would become eight. The piles would be smaller.

CHAPTER
66

Poppy watched her son sort. It was hard to imagine more attention being lavished on a small heap of food. Was he sorting by type? she wondered. Biscuits, chocolate, raisins, and nuts. She began to suspect there might be an alphabetical aspect to the classification, but noticing that raisins preceded nuts, she looked for evidence of some subtle taxonomy that was not immediately obvious. Cataloguing in order of calorific value, maybe, or intensity of flavour. But all flavours were intense these days. That first raisin she devoured seemed at the peak of its deliciousness. It felt wrong to eat it, like drinking a vintage wine that had not yet aged to perfection. Her allotted square of chocolate held an intensity she had never experienced before with food, the sugar dissolving straight into her veins and leaving her desperate for more. Now Fred was rationing it, noting down the contents in his notebook, adding neat rows of ticks with an orange felt tip.

He looked different. Something had changed since he returned from outside. Was there something he was not telling her?

He looked up and smiled at her. She smiled back.

⌒

Poppy turned her attention to their newest arrivals. Morag sat silent almost all of the time, but Angus spoke for the two of them, filling the room with almost uninterrupted commentary. As if reading a long and ancient Scottish poem, he weaved fragments of memory from the last few days with observations on Morag's frail condition, with the occasional anecdote from his boyhood thrown in. His glasses were white and too big for his face, habitually removed when he looked at something closely. Blue veins circled his wrists and his eyelids hung loose at the bottom, unable to catch the liquid that constantly leaked out of his eyes. Much attention was spent on this area of his face, with constant dabbing with a large handkerchief that also doubled as a polisher for his glasses.

She had felt fond of the old couple almost immediately. No real process of acquaintance seemed necessary — they just slotted in. It was as if they had arrived with the others and taken their places by the fire, Angus nodding at comments about past incidents as if he had actually been there. They displayed a ritualistic self-sufficiency, Angus seeing to Morag's needs while she nodded in thanks or squeezed his hand, displaying all the qualities of a couple who have been together for a lifetime. They had clearly been laid low by the experience of the last few days, particularly Morag, who found it hard to walk and had an odd swelling on one side of her face. They allotted the old lady prime position in the tent that night, second from the end, where the risk of being hit on the head by a collapsing broom handle was the lowest.

The inside of the tent had become increasingly squalid.

Compressed bedding held pockets of human smell that wafted upwards whenever the duvets were disturbed. The pillows were shiny with grease, and debris that no one had the energy or motivation to clear lurked in the folds of the duvets. Flattened tissues, abandoned socks, reeking, according to Buster, of actual cheese, and three silver compact discs that no one could account for, were among the items. Angus and Morag, oblivious to the squalor, let out identical sighs and lay back on the mattresses, ready for sleep.

CHAPTER 67

"There you are!" Marcie's voice cracked into a whisper.

Fred jumped as a penny of light fell onto the floor.

"Can I come in?" she said.

"Of course," he replied. "It's bloody cold, though."

He could hear Marcie joining him in the storage space under the stairs; something cracked beneath her heel.

"And bloody dark," she said.

He laughed at the unfamiliar accent. A pocket of warmth fell across his feet.

"Is that a blanket you've got there?" he said.

"Yeah. Want to share it?"

"Yes."

"Fred, you're shivering." Warm breath closed over his ear.

"I'm okay."

"What are you doing in here?"

"Just thinking."

The blanket skimmed his knees.

"Hey, Fred, what's that smell?"

"What smell?"

"Apples or something ..."

"I can't smell anything."

The blanket shifted an inch.

"They're sweet, aren't they?"

"Who?"

"The old folks."

"Yeah ... lovely."

"It makes things more difficult, though, doesn't it? More mouths to feed."

"Mmm."

"Fred?"

"Yes?"

"I'm scared." Something brushed against his shoulder. "I wasn't before, well, not so much. It's odd, now that Grabowski's gone, we should be able to relax a bit, but now that he's gone, I ..."

"What?"

"I can really see what we're facing. Do you feel that, too?"

"I try not to think about it."

"I try not to think about my dad, but I do, all the time."

"Someone will have taken him in."

She sighed. "Sure."

"Is your mum all right?" he said, instantly regretting the change of subject.

She sighed again. "She'll be fine."

He began to shiver. "We'll have to go back to the tent in a second."

"Yes."

He tucked his chin into his chest then felt the touch of cold fingers on his hand, the smallest of holds. He squeezed his fist together but not before a single finger had eked its way into his palm.

"Fred! Is that a raisin in your hand?"

"Oh, I ..." He paused.

Silence thumped in his ears; the darkness absorbed his shame like blotting paper. Then he heard his name again, wrapped in a delicious coat of concern. "Oh, Fred."

He felt like he was being undressed as she folded back his fingers and picked up the raisin. Electricity switched on. It started in toes, shot up his legs, and ended in his lips as a single raisin was slipped into his mouth.

CHAPTER
68

Poppy found a tiny corner of empty space on the page. But not too tiny. Enough room for a final drawing. She picked up a stub of pencil and, tucking her feet beneath a cushion, settled down to draw. The remaining pages of her sketchbook were full. Dog-eared. Smudged. She sharpened her pencil and a tiny sofa began to fill the tiny corner. A warm, comfortable place for the children to sit. Fred, Marcie, Ryan, and Buster. She wanted to squeeze every single child onto the tiny sofa. The lead snapped. She was too tired to sharpen it. Rope hair replaced threads. They coiled into knots on the shoulder of each grey child. So tired. Fat eyebrows, fat smiles, giant dot nostrils. She wanted to squeeze every child onto the tiny sofa.

Fred, Marcie, Ryan, and Buster.

CHAPTER
69

The sound of crying broke Fred's doze early the next morning. He sat up on the sofa, instinctively gripped the poker, and pushed it onto the fire, nursing a sliver of wood.

"Sweetheart, it doesn't matter."

He perked up at the sound of Rennie's voice drifting through the canvas.

"Is he all right?" Poppy's voice was softer.

"Yes, just a little accident."

The teeth of the tent zipper separated, and Poppy's head poked out followed by an acrid whiff of urine.

"Ugh," she said, "I feel like I've been dragged through a hedge backwards."

Fred said nothing.

"Long night, Fred?"

"Yeah, I'm shattered."

"My turn tonight."

"No need, Mum." His heard his voice flattening. "There's nothing left to burn."

"What, nothing at all?"

"Nothing."

She crawled out of the tent and sat on the arm of his chair. "What are we going to do?"

He felt oddly devoid of feeling as he watched her place her hands over her face, muffling the end of her sentence. "Oh, God."

"Mum, the whole thing's too big," he said. "We just have to make the best of things and hope this is the last day."

She frowned. "The last day?"

"Of the blackout."

He noticed her hands folded in her lap, the fingers still.

She looked up at him. "Fred, I have something to burn."

He knew she would say that. Not the precise words maybe, but he knew she would say it. But before he could consider his reply, time began to speed up. Poppy picked up her fleece and forced her hands into the sleeves, swearing as the folds trapped her fingers, then swearing some more as her fists popped out through the cuffs. Time ran faster. Dull, stagnant time that had languished so heavily over the past few days accelerated as he watched her start to run across the room, tearing up the stairs and slicing through the cold, faster and faster, colder and colder. He rushed after her, chasing her along the landing, lunging and snatching at the back of her fleece, only stopping at the door to the study.

"Mum, no!"

She spun around to face him. "We have to."

"Mum, you can't."

"I have to."

"Mum, think! How long are they going to last? Half an hour at most. Please don't. Please, Mum."

She ignored him, picked up an armful of sketchbooks, and lunged towards the door.

"Hold these!"

He had to catch his balance as she shoved the pile of books into his arms. Then she was back at the shelves wrenching at covers and breaking off spines. Paper slipped from between pages at random then flew up, diving sideways in the breeze from her body.

"Mum!"

"Look, Fred." She faced him, breathing fast. "What use are these books anyway? Paper and ink and rubbish, just rubbish!"

"Auntie Poppy, why are you shouting?" An anxious face had appeared at the door, low down.

"Buster, get back to bed. Now!" The face disappeared.

She turned back to face him. "Fred, take these."

The sketchbooks were heavier than he expected and, as she stacked them up into his arms, he felt a soggy weakness oozing through his muscles.

"That's it," she said, clutching an armful of books. "Let's go."

Forcing the flashlight between her chin and the top book, she fled the room.

⌣

Running with a pile of books balanced beneath your chin is hard. Finding stairs in the dark is even harder. Fred gripped the handrail tightly as he felt his way downwards with only toes to guide him. The sound of a commotion raced up to meet him.

They were all out of bed. Shouting. For a moment he thought a fight had broken out as he entered the room. Arms, books, and crumpled hair broke in and out of the thin beam of light shining across the room.

"Poppy, you can't." Marcie's voice was squealing, high and painful.

"Auntie!"

"You can't." He caught a glimpse of Ryan's mouth as the flashlight slipped off the sofa.

He rushed forward. "Mum. Please stop."

"Get away from me!"

He did not know his mother could roar. The sound penetrated his ears as he stood beside her, clutching the books. Up close, tears were visible, teeming out of her eyes, wetting her neck. He dropped the sketchbooks on the floor. He grabbed her elbow. "Mum, stop!"

"Get! Off! Me!"

She wrenched her arm out of his grip and threw a sketchbook on top of the embers. Yellow flames jumped up, devouring the pages, swallowing up everything: trains and dogs and oranges and pies and children and sofas, and searing brown holes into the huge prairie sky.

CHAPTER 70

"What are we going to do?"

Her son chugged out a heavy sigh but made no attempt to answer her question. The last three books were burning fast. Fred had been right about that. He had actually helped her place the final ones on the fire, passing them to her one by one. She had been surprised at the sense of calm that took over her body after the first book vanished into the flames. It was almost a relief, to do the thing that she had been dreading for so many hours. But seeing the distress on her son's face had been more painful than burning her sketchbooks, and now she felt wisps of relief as she watched him sitting still at last, holding his hands towards the fire.

"All I can think is that we bring everything into the tent," he said. "Water, food, and every piece of clothing we can lay our hands on. Insulate as much as we can. Then close the tent and wait."

"Wait for what?" she said.

"The lights to go on."

Their eyes met, but neither spoke.

"But the cold, Fred. How will we bear it?"

"I don't want to go out there again, Mum. I can't."

"You don't have to. Let's bring the clothes down." She half smiled. It hurt the corners of her mouth.

As they trailed upstairs to collect the clothing, Poppy was alarmed to see the state of the unheated bedrooms. A layer of ice coated the walls, lining every fold and indent like the inside of a neglected fridge. Traces of absentee belongings lay everywhere — memorials to heavy chairs embossed into the carpet, a rectangle of dust bearing testimony to Charlie's long-since incinerated pile of car magazines, and a trail of tiny paper circles that formed a path to the gaping belly of the hole punch lying beneath the window. The clothes felt stiff and she felt a deep longing as she fingered one of Charlie's shirts, pushing a cold button through a cold hole.

"Do we need Uncle Charlie's pants?" asked Buster.

Her young charge had recently extended his newly created web of familial ties to her husband, now "Uncle," whose absence he felt with touching pathos.

"Yes, they'll keep your bottom warm."

As they piled the last of the clothes inside the tent, she could hear Fred explaining the situation to the others. Morag lay on her mattress, but the rest had gathered around him, forming a loose circle in the centre of the tent.

"The fire will go out very soon. We have some heat in the tent now, but we need to save what we have for as long as possible. Ours bodies make heat so we must think of ourselves as human radiators."

He had an authority in his voice that she had never noticed before, his thoughts ordered by invisible bullet points and articulated with a precision that seemed to soothe the group of listeners.

"This means we need to wear as many layers as possible. It's important to share. Share duvets and blankets." He flicked a glance at Marcie. "We must keep the zip closed and only go out when we absolutely have to."

They nodded in unison but each person displayed a different emotion. Marcie's anxious face scanned the circle while Ryan's expression was obscured as he bit his nails aggressively, a stark contrast to his mother's stare of indifference. Buster looked plain wretched. Angus was more animated than usual, bobbing up and down on the mattress, muttering that Morag needed more blankets and asking if they had any hot water bottles.

They lay down on the mattresses and watched the fire go out. The embers cooled and the colours changed, throbbing red replaced by a tired, granulated grey. A trail of smoke jumped up from the charcoal at the last moment, twirling joyfully, before thinning as it drifted upwards.

Fred zipped up the tent.

CHAPTER

71

"We can't just lie here," said Marcie.

No one had spoken since the fire went out.

"Are we waiting to die?" said Rennie from the edge of the tent.

"We are not waiting to die!" said Fred, his voice cracking with annoyance. "We can't start thinking like that. We have each other. We're not alone like Mrs. Sullivan."

"Mrs. who?"

"You know, Mum. The old lady on the corner. The one who ..."

"Fred, don't!"

The circle went quiet. Poppy ached with cold, hardly daring to move in case a gap opened up in the parcel of clothes that wrapped her body. Only her mind was active, sifting through the layers of their predicament. Why were they so resigned? They were trapped, of course. But why were they trapped? Why had no one come to help them? She thought of the freezing air waiting to pounce the second they opened the door, the millions of snowflakes seeking a landing. What if no one came? Ever? She buried her head beneath the duvet and felt her shoulders relaxing as her breath warmed a small cave around her face. She thought of Charlie, his fingers running through her hair ...

Suddenly someone was shouting. "Morag! Hen! Wake up!"

Someone else clicked on the flashlight. The shouts grew louder. "Wake up, hen!" With every entreat, the old man's voice grew louder and coarser. The rounded edges of his Scottish accent sharpened; the pitch went up. A new voice filled the tent. Splitting the air.

"She won't wake up!" roared the old man, knocking off his glasses. He stopped, then turned to them, lowering his voice. "Morag won't wake up."

Marcie seemed to be the only one capable of a reaction. Shuffling over the duvets to the other side of the tent, she kneeled down beside Angus and took Morag's hand, placing it under the front of her fleece. Her hair fell over her face as she leaned forward, placing her ear close to the old lady's nose. Finally, she stroked her forehead, just once, then sat back, removing the limp hand from her stomach and placing it on top of the duvet.

"Angus, she's completely cold."

The old man stared at her as if she were speaking another language.

"Angus, I think Morag is dead."

The young girl had managed to step forward. She had managed to touch the old lady and she had managed to tell Angus what had to be told, but she seemed unable to manage the grief that swooped down on the old man. There was no physical reaction. He did not cry, or collapse, or even move at all, but an intense aura of despair seemed to emanate from him. Poppy could feel it, like a scent with no smell. Marcie seemed to feel it, too. She moved back as she finished speaking, edging onto her own mattress and fixing her gaze on her pillow.

No previous experience in life had prepared Poppy for a moment such as this. With her resilience worn thin by hunger, cold, and incessant worry, she did not have the stamina to cope. They sat in silence. With all the thousands of words in the English language, all the clauses, all the fragments, all the old sayings, all the slang, there was nothing of any use at that moment. The silence continued. Even Buster was shocked into silence. It was Angus who spoke first.

"Would you like a hot water bottle, hen?"

"Angus, we can't make a hot water bottle," said Fred. "We don't have any electricity."

"I think we should just make her comfortable," said Poppy, easing herself forward and smoothing her hand across Morag's pillow.

"I'll straighten out her duvet," said Marcie, snapping her stare off her pillows and tidying an imaginary mess.

Angus sat back on the mattress, not speaking. His head seemed to have sunk into his shoulders. He was smaller. Poppy noticed Fred rubbing his chin where Grabowski had hit him. Then he laid a hand on the old man's shoulder.

"Angus, you know Morag would be much happier on the sofa. She could stretch out her legs and wouldn't have to put up with all of us snoring."

The old man did not look at him.

"So Ryan and I are going to take her to the sofa."

"You mean touch her? Do we have to touch her?" Sitting on the periphery of the scene, Ryan's demeanour up until now had passed unobserved, but Poppy now saw a quiet boy suddenly animated, splurting out hurried, unplanned sentences.

"It's all right," said Fred, "we'll keep her in the blanket and lie her on the sofa. It will be all right."

The calm utterances previously extended to Angus were

now aimed at Ryan, and Poppy heard a stream of encouragement as they tightened Morag's blanket around her body, lifted her up, and hauled her through the tent flap. Angus followed behind. He hovered at the entrance, then stepped out. Moments later the sounds of an argument cut through the tent flaps.

"Angus, you need to come back in. We all need to go back in the tent now. It's our only chance."

Poppy heard a sob in her son's voice as he reached the last word. Both she and Marcie reacted, untangling their knees from the bedding and moving to the opening at the same moment. Morag was the only peaceful member of the group visible through the cloth doors. She lay on the sofa with a blanket pulled up to her chin, her face pinched white. Beside her sat Angus, perched on the arm of the sofa, holding his side as if it hurt. He was flanked by Fred and Ryan, who each clasped the old man's arms. Fred looked more distressed than she had ever seen him. His face was flushed, and she was frightened by the way he pulled roughly at the man's arm. Ryan stood bewildered.

"Mum, we have to get him back inside the tent."

With the onus thrown back at her so suddenly, Poppy was surprised she could react with such speed. She climbed through the entrance and picked up a hairbrush that had been lying untouched on the coffee table for several days. Bending down, she started to brush across Morag's head, the static-charged hairs springing upwards with every stroke. Angus seemed mesmerized. He relaxed his arms and tipped his head forward onto his chin. Ten strokes later, she stopped.

"Morag is ready. We can go in now."

Persuaded by the roughly assembled logic of the hair brushing ritual, Angus allowed himself to be steered back into the tent, ready to join the others in their blanketed world.

CHAPTER

72

Seven people slept in one bed that night. Fred had no idea how much time had passed. All he knew was that they were inside the tent, Angus and he pressed against the canvas, the others slotted between them. Heat seeped out of the covers and, in spite of his warnings to the others, he got up and left the tent. It only took a moment to strip the pink blanket from the body lying on the sofa, then he was back inside the bed, shivering and covering his ears, trying his best to block out the ugly moans of anguish coming from the old man four feet away.

They lay still, three families moulded into one. The weight of the bedding limited movement but, as Fred lay crushed, he made an effort to keep busy. He flicked the flashlight at the brown stain above his head, he estimated the thickness of the mean layer of ice forming on the water bottle beside his pillow, and he scratched the itch that was tickling his nostrils.

His mother's voice came into his left ear, watered down.

"Freddie, what is going to happen?"

"I don't know."

"But, Fred, what is going to happen?"

She was repeating herself. They were all repeating themselves. Sentences were coming out backwards, sticking to furred up tongues.

"I need a drink."

"Fred."

"I need a drink."

"Mom."

"Charlie?"

"I'm so cold."

"Mum?"

"Mom."

"I need a drink."

"Freddie."

"I ..."

Pushing a hand beneath his pillow, he dragged out the raincoat. The skin felt brittle, crackling like a freshly fried papadum and, as he yanked it towards him, the shoulder ripped. He lay back and sighed. The coat was breaking down, drying up like a fish out of water, and he did not know how to stop it. He tried forcing a glob of saliva to the front of his tongue, but none came. Too exhausted to do anything else, he fingered the feathery rip then pushed the coat back beneath his pillow and turned to look at Marcie, her face just visible.

She was in distress; her eyes told him that.

"Don't close your eyes. Please don't," he said. She gazed towards him. "Don't close your eyes."

She did not answer. He moved forward, dragging his hand from under the covers, and touched her lips — dry as paper. "Don't close your eyes, please."

She closed her eyes. There were freckles on the lids.

～

The intense longing that Fred had felt for his old home was replaced by a desire for his future. It was not as if he saw his life slipping away, he simply could not visualize it — it was blank. He could not imagine time beyond that particular moment. What had been and what might have been were merging, and all thoughts returned to the inside of the tent. He looked at the brown stain. He looked at the broom handle, perilously close to collapse. He tried to think, grasping at transparent thoughts. Then he pictured Charlie forcing down the zipper, snapping back the blankets and wiping ice from their frozen faces, one by one. He did not want to die in this city, so far from home, its ground too hard to dig a grave.

A sign flashed across his mind: "Immediate cremation, eight hundred dollars."

CHAPTER
73

When it happened, Fred did not understand what it was. Nothing really changed. The brown stain remained. The rattle coming from the inside of Angus' chest kept its regular rhythm. But a subtle change was activating one of his senses; it was a smell, a smell of burning dust.

As he heaved himself into an upright position, the aroma changed, burning dust transforming into burning wings. The acrid smell of a dead moth, singeing inside a light fitting, was unmistakable.

Only just tolerating the pain in his joints, he dragged himself out of bed, prising up the bedding and heaving himself onto his knees. He shook like a terrified hamster. Although several pounds lighter, his body felt like lead as he crawled towards the tent flaps and struggled with the zipper. Paying no attention to the stiff little body laid out on the sofa, he headed for the heaters lining the walls. The metal casing was wet, dotted with water. He touched the top, basking in the heat coming through the grill. Next he bent forward and licked the dusty water, running his tongue down the sides to catch the drips, not caring that the tip was burning. With the edge taken off his thirst, he picked up the cable of the reading lamp and plugged it in.

The light went on.

No more circles of torchlight, no more mysterious corners

too cold to explore. The lamp threw an instant air of normality over the room and everyday items were displayed in an everyday light — a hairbrush packed with hair, a coffee cup, a pencil chewed at the end, a sofa, a dead woman. The sight of Morag gave him a jolt and, remembering his family, he shuffle-rushed back to the tent and pulled back the canvas. No one had moved since he left; anxiety spiked his body as he surveyed the motionless heaps.

"Mum." He could not raise his voice much above a whisper; his throat hurt. "Mum, the heaters are on." He had spoken the sentence they most wanted to hear, but no one was listening.

"Mum!"

Ryan's face appeared from beneath a pile of coats. "Fred?" His voice croaked.

"Ryan, the heating is working. The lights are on."

The boy sat up, turning his shoulders in circles. Then he rubbed the back of his neck. "You sure?"

"Look."

As he pulled back the flap, a beam of light fell onto the end of Poppy's duvet. A tiny spot in the cotton moved.

"Mum." He was ready to cry. "Mum, the power's back."

A face emerged at the end of the bed. Trampled, one eyelid glued shut and hair bunched up inside a collar. A blue swelling decorated her chin.

"What ... are we?"

"Mum, the heat's back, the heat's back," he said, unsure if he had said the same thing twice. Keeping his eyes on his mother's face, he forced his hand under Marcie's duvet, taking her toes in his hand. They were stone cold.

"Marcie. Marcie, wake up."

She did not move.

"Marcie!"

He did not say her name again. With his slowly thawing

brain running at reduced capacity, he could only recall one little piece of first aid. He kneeled beside her and, summoning his last scraps of strength, shoved back the bedding and pulled her up by her shoulders. She was a rag doll, her head flopping onto her chest then rolling sideways as he moved behind her. Before anything else could happen, he put his hands under her armpits and clasped them together beneath her breasts. Then he pulled back abruptly, forcing a loud grunt, part human, part cow, out of her mouth.

"What the hell?" said Ryan.

But before he could reply, Marcie coughed, shook her head, then looked up at him, blinking fast. Her face was puffy and her eyes slightly crossed, but she managed to speak. "I'm thirsty," she said.

Fred said nothing. He could not. During the few moments it took for Marcie to come to her senses, he kneeled back on his haunches, he flicked a hair off his eye, he sat perfectly still. But inside, very deep down, a tidal wave of happiness rolled through him.

⌒

A moment later he uncovered Rennie and Buster. They were squashed up together like the contents of a shopping bag flattened in the back seat of a car. The mother held her son in a tight embrace.

"Rennie, Buster. The lights are on," he said.

"Fred?" said Rennie. He leaned in closer. "Is Buster all right?"

"I think he's asleep."

He watched her rub the little boy's face, stroking back and forth across his cheeks until he spoke at last. "Mom."

"What time ... day ... how long?" said Rennie.

"It's nearly morning," he replied calmly. "Of the ninth day."

Angus was extracting a long thread of hair from his mouth when Fred reached his side of the tent.

"Angus, the power is back."

The old man looked at him and nodded, just once.

⌒

Leaving his family to wake up, Fred busied himself with the water supply, lining up bottles on the heater, which clicked and cracked like an octogenarian limbering up for a long-overdue work out. Feeling a similar lack of lubrication in his own limbs, he goose-stepped back to the tent, noticing a coffee cup on the legless table as he passed. A button of ice swirled along the bottom. He shook it, and took it over to Marcie, who was lying on her pillow, gazing up at the brown stain.

"Drink this, there's more coming."

"Tha ..." she said, taking the cup with trembling hands.

"Mum, I'm going to see what's working."

Poppy raised a fistful of skinny fingers but said nothing.

He shambled up the stairs, procrastinating on every step. All the lights were working and he flicked each switch as he went, finally reaching his bedroom. He plugged in his computer and turned it on. As if nothing had ever happened, it hummed to life. He scrolled to his inbox. Three hundred and four unread emails sat waiting. Charlie Forester, repeated line after line, page after page. A lengthy list of George Foresters followed and a smaller column from John MacDonald, all filed in alphabetical order.

He opened the first email, dated December 8. Eight days earlier.

Fred,
I know there's no electricity but I am sending this anyway. Are you both okay? Please contact me any way you can. Of course the damn phones aren't working. I'm still stuck here in London, and there's

no information coming out. You know, there's a huge storm blowing your way and the blackout is affecting a big chunk of the prairies. Half the country's gone down. Please let me know you are okay. Take care of Mum for me (and yourself).

Love, Dad

PS *Grandma and Grandad send love (lots of it).*

Scrolling down the list he opened another, at random. December 12:

Fred,

I know it's pointless to keep writing but it's all I can think to do right now. Please let this be the day you answer me. Please. We're spending the whole day by the TV. We take turns to pee in case we miss something. There's nothing else on the news. Half the country's paralyzed, even the military has run out of petrol, but they keep saying help is on its way. It's got to be, hasn't it? Mum told me not to get on the flight. I should have listened to her. I know you'll be taking care of her. You are, aren't you, mate? She couldn't be on her own, you know that. She'll be relying on you. I love you, Freddie, and please, if you get this, tell Mum the same. I know I've said this in every mail so far but here it is again. You have remembered the extra wood supply in the crawl space, haven't you? I'm sure you have.

Love, Dad xx

Heart pounding, he opened the last one in the list, sent earlier that day, December 15.

Hi Freddie,

You know I never believed in God but I've invented one of my own and I keep praying to him. I don't suppose you'd approve. I wonder what you and Mum are doing now? I expect you're tucked up by the fire, aren't you? Don't scare Mum too much with your stories. We

have been by the TV *as usual. We shout whenever the ads come
on and interrupt things, but it doesn't stop them. Grandad's going
to get you and Johno tickets for the cup final for when you come over.
He knows a bloke in the pub. Fred, I know you must be okay.
You're clever. You'll be hearing from me in an hour or so. Give
Mum a hug for me.*

    Love, Dad xxx
PS *Remember the wood in the crawl space.*

He felt dizzy as he clicked on the reply box. Three words were
all he could manage.

    Dad,
    Okay.
    Fred

But before he could press the send button, the lights went out
again.

PART THREE

Four weeks later

CHAPTER
74

Fred was making a fire. It was his responsibility now and he had perfected the art. Precision airflow, plus large quantities of paper and dry wood were the main ingredients. His mother had always made the evening fire before the blackout, but he quickly discovered that she was incompetent at it, on every level. He could not believe how stingy she was with the newspaper and had lost count of the number of times he had reminded her to add more logs at the start. Now it was his job. He felt a quiet satisfaction while watching the first shy flames catch the corners, followed by a roar as everything took hold. This was the part that scared his mother. She would run over in a jumpy panic, rushing to close down the steel window that controlled the airflow, extinguishing the fire completely.

They had an enormous supply of wood now. The crawl space was packed solid. That was where they had found the logs that saved them in those terrible hours after the second blackout hit. He had dragged Ryan out of the tent, and neither of them could remember how they made it down the narrow stairs to the storage space beneath the house. The ceiling was less than four feet high down there, and his back was struck by excruciating cramps on the bottom step. It was as dark as a pothole in the middle of a mountain, and they had to navigate with their hands. He had never been right inside before, preferring to watch from the hatch in the floor whenever his father went to check on the metre. As he methodically patted the ground, he feared the unknown in a way he had never experienced before. Plunging his hands into the threads of a frozen spider's web had only increased his sense of foreboding,

rosie chard   237
SEAL
INTESTINE
RAINCOAT

and he felt terrified as he groped the bare insides of the boxes that littered the floor. When his fingers did finally brush up against something warm and firm, it took several moments of hysterical giggling before he could accept it was only the back of Ryan's head. After that, they whispered to each other until a terrific shout from Ryan told him the log pile had been found.

Extracting the wood took a long time. Only later did they learn that they were succumbing to hypothermia, a deadly mixture of shredded thoughts and deluded happiness conspiring against them. The matches were lost, and it is conceivable that the god he refused to believe in might have stepped in at that point and made him trip over the corner of the rug, just in time to spot the small box lying on the floor. The power cut only lasted one more day, but those final twelve hours were marked by an outbreak of near hysteria as they warmed themselves up and gulped down melted snow, their joy at having a fire again tempered only by the quiet figure lying motionless on the sofa. The storm lasted one more day before ending quite suddenly, leaving behind a city in shock.

He dwelled on those past moments a tad longer, before returning to his current task, scrunching up the paper and forcing it to the back of the stove with the poker. An old headline caught his attention.

"WE MAY DROWN OR COOK BEFORE THE OIL RUNS OUT."

He snorted, screwed up the paper, and threw it on the fire. Further ripping revealed a small black-and-white photo on the inside page of the previous day's edition, and the fire-making ceased for a second time. Whoever had captured the image had zoomed in close on a human leg, lying on ice. The shoe curled upwards, black and speckled with purple paint.

He read the article running beneath a simple headline.

WHEN WILL IT END? ANOTHER MAN FOUND FROZEN
TO DEATH IN CITY STREET.

Last night police officers were alerted to the presence of another
body lying under a bench in outer Winnipeg. A homeless man
appears to have frozen to death whilst spending several nights
in a parking lot near the perimeter highway during the blackout.
Enquiries at downtown hostels resulted in the man being identified as 71-year-old Ataninnuaq Innukshuk, a native Inut man who
originated from Nunavut. Police are hoping that this will be the
last body to be found following the blackout. A full list of victims
will be published in tomorrow's edition.

People talk of a heart breaking. But that was not where it hurt.
The feeling lurked deep in his stomach, next to where he felt
hunger. It came instantly, filling his belly with a lumbering sadness. Ata would not be telling him stories in the mall anymore.
He would not be scrunching up his nose or sharing dregs of
cold tea with him ever again. The bench would be wiped clean,
all trace removed. That is what had happened when Hamish
had died. Fred's ginger hamster had suddenly grown old, reaching his last day faster than they expected. He had stroked the
tiny animal on his lap as usual the night before, but the next
morning he lay still inside his bedding and would not wake
up. The belly pain was there that time, too. It stayed for a long
time and he did not want to eat. Poppy and he had cleaned
out the cage for the last time, her voice quiet, and instead of
chucking the old straw straight into the bin, she put it into a
clean plastic bag that sat outside by the shed for ages. They
washed the cage afterwards, his mother patting it dry with a
paper towel. Hamish would have hated all that cleanliness;
he had liked things smelly and old.

Ata had been his friend before the blackout. In his previous life, as Fred liked to think of it, Ata had been his first real friend in his new city. The old man had grown up learning all the skills of survival but he had not survived. He had told Fred the story. He had given him the raincoat.

CHAPTER 75

The moment had arrived. They could not postpone it a second longer. Junk was cleared from the new table and a damp cloth run across it. Charlie insisted on smoothing down the corners of the newspaper prior to running a finger down the list of contents. Poppy watched him. She had become aware of new aspects of her husband's personality since his return from London. From the moment he had run down the airport escalator on that first day back in the city, he had been different. A previously unobserved quality was felt in that initial crushing hug and had continued every moment since his homecoming. He treasured her; she could feel it.

"Page four," Charlie announced.

Fred saw a need to help with page turning and the whole process slowed as father and son knocked knuckles before the double page was found and smoothed flat. Poppy sighed.

"ONE HUNDRED AND THIRTY SEVEN DIE IN CITY BLACKOUT DURING KILLER STORM."

She stared at the headline, postponing the moment. She displaced a particular brand of sadness reserved only for great tragedy as her eyes began to move down the page. It was alphabetical. Her eyes scanned the letters, hovering on "A — Abbott

James, Anderson Thomas ..." before skipping unwillingly to "K — King Brian, Kress Dwayne."

Only by touching the newsprint could she accept what she already knew. Dwayne Kress, the ordinary man whose myth had increased exponentially during the days by the fire, had died on the morning he left them, freezing on the edge of a sports field just three miles from the house. All the times they had spoken about him, dialled his number on the phone, wished him back, thought of him and, yes, prayed for him, he was already dead, his life snatched away by an insignificant fall, quickly amplified by cold, that left him stranded out of earshot.

Rennie had told them on the phone, her voice squeaking out a brief explanation before the line went dead. Now it was official. Dwayne Kress was part of the final death toll, part of the list, his name earmarked for a lifetime of remembrance — ink on paper, words from sad lips, scratches into stone. Her thoughts moved to his wife, enduring years of sofabound solitude, receiving small parcels of happiness from her children and dwelling on the last moments on the doorstep with her husband.

Fighting back tears, her finger slid further down the list. Never had an alphabet been so cruel. The words "McVittie Morag" looked blacker than the surrounding print and abruptly conjured up an unwanted image: skeins of white hair stuck to the arm of the sofa. She cried then. She cried so much she hardly noticed that her son was holding his finger beneath another name higher up the column. She wiped her face with the back of her sleeve and leaned forward to focus on the unfamiliar name. "Innukshuk Ataninnuaq."

"Freddie, did you know him?" she said.

Fred glanced at her. He looked sad in a way that she had never seen before. Then he started to talk, and as she felt

Charlie take her hand beneath the table, she listened to her son's story of Ata. She heard about the bench in the mall, she heard about the man whose spirit had joined them in the circle around the fire, and she heard about the seal intestine raincoat.

CHAPTER 76

Fred noticed new hinges on the museum door. His fingers were sweaty as he handed over a ten-dollar bill, leaving damp thumbprints on the Queen's cheeks.

"Two tickets, please."

He had not been back since the blackout, and changes had been made. The vending machine remained by the pay desk but rows of chocolate bars were visible, setting off a huge surge of emotion. The arrows remained on the floor, but were inexplicably red. He allowed his feet to follow them.

The Inuit gallery was deserted when they arrived, but the scene displayed to no one was magnificent. Three enormous caribou dominated the foreground — antlers held erect above polished eyeballs, buffed to a gleam. Standing behind the animals was the family of humans: a mother, father, and child.

Fred ducked beneath the rope and stepped onto the artificial snow, his feet sinking down a fraction. He walked forward, feeling guilt at the footprints following his every move, and he attempted to walk cleanly, shaking fragments off his soles as he approached the father mannequin. Upon close inspection, the figure was extremely handsome, benefiting from a look of hopeful optimism that someone had sculpted on his face. He was smiling at something in the distance. Fred placed his bag down and reached for the collar of the mannequin's caribou parka. He imagined it felt warm as he peeled back the fur collar. He scooped it up, acutely aware of the softness of the belly fur lining the inside.

"Hurry up, Fred, someone might come," whispered his companion loudly.

But he did not want to hurry. He started folding the parka, but the parka would not fold. No amount of tucking in sleeves and smoothing down hairs induced it to lie flat, and finally he laid it on the ground, its back sticking up like abandoned road kill.

Naked plastic skin diminished the grandeur of the father figure. Black tape ran down one leg, and there were scratches on the arm that looked as though they had been sanded. The number 17050 was visible on one thigh, blurring into the skin like a worn out tattoo. Fred picked up his bag and pulled out the coat. He shook it out gently and held it up to the light. Only a slight crackle, shooting out from beneath one of the transparent armpits, broke the silence in the room. With the hands of a father dressing his newborn baby, he lifted up the coat and pulled it over the mannequin's head. It fell soundlessly to the knees, coming to rest against the fur trim of the man's sealskin boots. He smoothed down the black wig, arranging the ponytail into the centre of the back. The mannequin continued to look at something in the distance, smiling.

There was nothing left to do so they walked across the dry snow, onto the wooden floorboards. Then they strode down the corridor, against the direction of the arrows, pushed open the heavy entrance doors, and jogged down the steps. Fred picked a red hair off the sleeve of his jacket as they walked down the street and disappeared around the corner.

The Inuit diorama was deserted. A new coat on the back of a father looking into the distance. He was smiling. An elderly man entered the room. Walking backwards, he dragged his rake across the snowflakes, removing the last trace of footprints as he stepped onto the wooden floorboards of the corridor.

EPILOGUE

The *Bear Man* boarded a plane to Thompson after he left the restroom at the Winnipeg airport. When the blackout struck two weeks later, he spent nine days alone on his farm eating through his store of smoked goose and frozen pickerel cheeks.

The *Tired Man* knew he was going to have a wonderful holiday as his plane descended towards Miami. But he burned both shoulders sunbathing and when he stood on the bathroom scale three weeks later, he had gained eleven pounds.

Johnny saw the sea for the first time when his plane landed in Florida. Exhausted by the intense heat, he could only dream of his home in Winnipeg.

The *Elderly Gent Drinking Coffee in his Car* scalded his knee at the first junction after crossing the railway. It still hurt when he went to St. Boniface hospital to have the dressing changed. He spent the blackout in a crowded waiting room where he mastered the art of sleeping in a chair.

The *Woman Putting on Mascara at the Crossing* was eating dinner in the canteen at the University of Manitoba when everything went black. She could not start her car and walked eight miles in gale-force winds to her home in St. Adolphe, only to find her house had burned down.

The *Lost Truck Driver with a Dog* never found Alberto's market. He was lying on his bed in a motel on Bannatyne when the television screen turned black. His dog Chipper did not like the cold and, while jogging up and down the icy corridors, they befriended two truckers from his hometown in Delaware, Ohio. They plan to meet up in Minneapolis next fall.

The *Boy Squashing his Face on the Car Window* moved down to his basement on the first day of the blackout. He had eaten thirty-six tins of hot dogs with eight bottles of ketchup and drank seventeen litres of coke by the time it was over. He adored curling up in a sleeping bag and playing cards with his mother and father half the night. It was the best holiday he had ever had.

The *Man in the Red Coat* strode to the next crossing on McPhilips and Ellis after jumping off the train. He climbed onto the last carriage of a train to Vancouver and arrived in San Francisco four days later with nothing but a handful of pine needles in his pocket.

The *Traffic Patrol Girl* became trapped in an elevator between the second and third floors of Portage Place Mall when the blackout began. She scorched her throat shouting and could not utter a single word when her father prised the doors open with a jemmy and carried her home on his shoulders.

The *School Counsellor* found the spare key to Riverton High School in an old envelope at the back of his cupboard. A thrilling sense of purpose filled his body as he set up a shelter for one hundred and fifty-seven people in the school gym, and he'll never forget the sight of so many grateful faces lining the bleachers.

Kyle was walking home from his guitar lesson on the day the power went off. After slipping on ice and twisting his ankle, a passing stranger carried him to a house on Dominion Avenue and wrapped a crepe bandage around his foot. He and "Uncle Bob" burned three handmade kayaks on the stove over the next few days, drank twelve bottles of undiluted blackcurrant cordial, and learned to play *Smoke on the Water* to perfection.

The *Angry Trucker at the Gas Station* spent four days at his house in North Kildonan trying to remember who his friends were. Police carried him from his home on December 11 suffering from hypothermia. The thought of nurses with icy fingers slipping him into bed will forever be burned into his memory.

The *Pedestrian at the Gas Station* was glad he had faith. He helped the vicar at St. Boniface church drag the emergency generator up beside the altar and spent nine days sleeping on pews with seventy-five other people. They sang several hundred hymns during their incarceration and he can now recite the full text of the "Last Supper" from the Gospel according to Mark, in French.

The *Young Man in the Trilby Hat* visited every apartment in his building during the first minutes of the blackout. Twenty-seven people spent nine happy days in his room, eating dried chicken noodles soaked in beer.

The *Gas Station Clerk* was applying online for a new job when the lights went out. He walked to his mother's house four blocks away and they had their first proper conversation in eighteen years.

The *Sales Clerk in the Mall* packed a small suitcase after her roof collapsed and trudged one block to a Chinese restaurant on Princess Street. Here she joined a small circle of aunts and uncles around a wood-burning stove and learned how to make a dragon out of a single piece of paper.

The *First Boy in the Mall* met his neighbours for the first time when they moved into his house on Wellington Crescent. It was his first chance to try out his goose-down sleeping bag, thermal underwear, and felt slippers. He was pleased with their performance.

The *Second Boy in the Mall* became angry when his parents would not help him look for his dog, Shep. He could not find a single pawprint in the snow when he ran down his street to look for him. It was only after a random stranger invited him into a house eighteen blocks away that he survived the storm.

The *Third Boy in the Mall* had always been scared of the dark. His father hit him with the back of his hand when he said he couldn't find the flashlight. There was no water to clean off the blood.

The *Woman with the Cloth in the Mall* knew no one in the city. When she spotted a rescue party at the end of her block, she hid beneath her bed until they were gone. She was shouting out stories of her childhood home when she was helped from the house by a police officer on December 10.

The *Owners of the Antique Warehouse* opened up an ancient hearth in the basement of their warehouse on the first day of the blackout. Eight people they called in from the street joined them around the smoky fire, and they proceeded to burn an entire wardrobe, thirteen chairs, four coffee tables and seventy-six pieces of timber that they had been saving for repairs.

The *First Woman at the Checkout* started up her generator for the first time in three years and spent the nine days without electricity holed up in her farmhouse with eleven neighbours, one granddaughter, thirteen chickens, and four one-year-old calves.

The *Second Woman at the Checkout* drove her parents to Winnipeg airport on the first day of the blackout, using up her last few drops of gas. They sat in three adjacent chairs in the departure lounge, watching snowflakes fly past the windows, wondering if they were ever going to get away.

Tracy was drinking her second bottle of vodka in a basement in River Heights when the room was plunged into darkness. She lay on her back, closed her eyes, fell asleep, and didn't wake up.

The *First Police Officer at the Gas Station* broke his leg on the fifth day of the blackout when he drove his snowmobile into a ditch. After crawling to a nearby sawmill in St. Norbert's, he spent the final four days with a ninety-three-year-old man who was more than happy to resume his medical skills learned so thoroughly in the final days of the World War II.

The *Second Police Officer at the Gas Station* rescued one hundred and twenty people from their homes in east St. Paul. He has been unable to play the piano so well since losing the tip of his finger to frostbite.

The *Man Who Slipped in a Puddle* found his hands were shaking when he delivered his baby daughter onto the sofa in his frigid living room. In a state of confusion, they named her Sooty.

The *Woman in the Print Dress* lost sight of her husband in the crowd at the store. She climbed into the back of a pickup truck in the parking lot, pulled up the collars of her four children, and waited for the driver to appear.

The *First Security Guard at the Store* was unable to persuade a woman and four children to leave the back of his truck when he decided to attempt the drive home. He felt trepidation as they walked towards his front door, then relief as the woman searched through his kitchen, opened some cans, and produced the most delicious meal he had ever tasted. On December 20 he drove her back to her home in Southern Manitoba and never saw her or the children again.

The *Second Security Guard at the Store* felt happy frying eggs on an old barbecue that he found in the basement of his house in the north end. His neighbour carried him out of the building on December 8, quiet and still from the carbon monoxide poisoning his blood.

The *Woman Crying at the Store* discovered she did not need the medication she had been taking for the past eleven years. She spent nine days in bed with her husband, after which she decided she no longer cared for him.

The *Husband of the Woman Crying at the Store* learned to tolerate his wife's freezing feet for the first time in his life during nine days in bed, and he fell in love with her all over again.

The *Twins in the Neighbouring House* were shocked when an English teenager knocked on their door three hours after the second blackout. They pulled on matching parkas, followed his back through the snow, and joined a circle of people huddled around a stove.

The *Man Running in the Snow* ventured from his condominium on the morning of December 14. He did not hear a young man calling to him two blocks away and, after twisting his ankle, died of hypothermia in a snowbank at eleven o'clock that same day.

The *Man Waiting for his Brother* was unable to find the shelter he had heard about on the radio. On his way home he spotted a large pile of wood hidden beneath a tarpaulin and, with the help of his brother, dragged it back to his house, lit a bonfire, and felt warm for the first time in days.

Police caught the *First Man in the Museum* breaking into a house on Ballantyne and Ellis on December 15. He couldn't believe his luck when he was led to a warm cell and given a large bowl of hot soup. He is now serving three years for armed robbery.

The *Second Man in the Museum* kicked in the door of a house on Stradbrook because he ran out of wood. He carried all the furniture into the backyard and made a fire visible from half a mile away.

The *Third Man in the Museum* chewed on a piece of frozen raw meat when he couldn't find anything else to eat. He endured stomach cramps for two long days and when the lights came on had no idea where he was.

Charlie Forester sent three hundred and twenty-one emails to an inbox in Winnipeg during the blackout. He made eighty-six phone calls, visited the Canadian embassy in London eighteen times, and shouted at his father. He lost four pounds in weight.

There is no record of the whereabouts of *Rusty Grabowski.*

ACKNOWLEDGEMENTS

I would like to thank the staff at NeWest Press for all their encouragement and hard work, especially Tiffany Foster and Lou Morin. I would also like to thank my editor, Doug Barbour, for his constructive comments. Natalie Olsen's elegant design is much appreciated.

I am indebted to Dave and Mary Elliott for their suggestions during the formative stages of the novel, their subsequent flow of comments, and for such generosity with their time. I am grateful to Wayne Tefs and Chandra Mayor for their thoughts on the first draft of the manuscript. Thank you to friends in Winnipeg and London for their interest and all the helpful feedback, especially Kim Olynyk, Anna Robertson, Mark O'Neill, Tara Mawhinney, Hedy Heppenstall, Sandy Gravette, Allan Ramsay, Chloe Chard, and Liz Jensen.

Special thanks to my family — Nat, Phoebe, and Ollie — for their continuing enthusiasm and support.

SOURCES

Research sources for *Seal Intestine Raincoat* include the arctic collections at the Manitoba Museum in Winnipeg and the Pitt Rivers Museum of Anthropology and World Archaeology in Oxford, England.

Two films also provided invaluable research footage:
Nanook of the North, Directed by Robert J. Flaherty (1922)
The Journals of Knud Rasmussen, Directed by Norman Cohn and Zacharias Kunuk (2006)

Rosie Chard grew up on the edge of the North Downs, a range of low hills south of London, England. She received her first degree in Anthropology and Environmental Biology from Oxford Brookes University, and later qualified as a landscape architect at the University of Greenwich. Chard practised in London and Copenhagen, Denmark, until she and her family emigrated to Canada in 2005. She now lives in Winnipeg, where she divides her time between writing and garden design. *Seal Intestine Raincoat* is her first novel.